EVELYN'S HUSBAND

EVELYN'S HUSBAND

Charles W. Chesnutt

EDITED BY MATTHEW WILSON AND MARJAN A. VAN SCHAIK
INTRODUCTION BY MATTHEW WILSON

UNIVERSITY PRESS OF MISSISSIPPI   JACKSON

www.upress.state.ms.us

The University Press of Mississippi is a member of the
Association of American University Presses.

Copyright © 2005 by University Press of Mississippi
All rights reserved
Manufactured in the United States of America

First edition 2005

∞

Library of Congress Cataloging-in-Publication Data

Chesnutt, Charles Waddell, 1858–1932.

Evelyn's husband / Charles W. Chesnutt ; edited by Matthew Wilson and
Marjan A. van Schaik ; introduction by Matthew Wilson. — 1st ed.

p. cm.

Includes bibliographical references.

ISBN 1-57806-760-X (cloth : alk. paper)

1. Triangles (Interpersonal relations)—Fiction. 2. Rejection (Psychology)—
Fiction. 3. Caribbean Area—Fiction. 4. Married people—Fiction. 5. Boston
(Mass.)—Fiction. 6. Older men—Fiction. 7. Islands— Fiction. I. Wilson,
Matthew, 1949– II. Van Schaik, Marjan A. III. Title.

PS1292.C6E94   2005

813'.4—dc22   2004027263

British Library Cataloging-in-Publication Data available

INTRODUCTION

The publication of Charles W. Chesnutt's novel, *Evelyn's Husband*, along with its companion volume, *A Business Career*, sees the completion, with one exception, of the publication of the novels that Chesnutt left in manuscript.[1] In these fictions, Chesnutt is writing in the genre of the white-life novel, in which African Americans write exclusively about white experience. When Chesnutt completed these novels, this was a relatively new genre. In the late 1890s, Chesnutt and Paul Laurence Dunbar began, concurrently, to write white-life novels, and while Dunbar's were published, Chesnutt's have remained in manuscript for over a hundred years. A review of Dunbar's first white-life novel, *The Uncalled* (1898),[2] is revealing, for it helps contextualize the position of an African American who attempted to write white-life fictions in this period. "*The Bookman* for December 1898 objected to the characters in *The Uncalled*. Claiming that Dunbar should 'write about Negroes,' the reviewer lamented that 'the charming tender sympathy of *Folks from Dixie* is missing' and asserted that Dunbar was 'an outsider' who viewed his action 'as a stage manager'" (Williams 174). At the turn of the century, neither critics nor publishers nor white audiences were willing to listen to the voice of an African American who had stepped outside what they assumed to be his "proper" role—as a writer who represented his own folk's experience, narrowly construed as rural and Southern, and as a race spokesman. The expectations that African American writers were to be representative remained much the same for the better part of a hundred years, and while there is no general consensus among the few critics who have written about the genre of the white-life novel, almost all assume that African American writers must serve as race spokesmen, a position diametrically opposed to what Chesnutt himself believed. He wrote, as he said in 1928, accepting the Spingarn Medal from the NAACP, "not as a Negro writing about Negroes, but as a human being writing about other human beings" (*Essays and Speeches* 514). From that subject position, his conviction was that he could write not only about African American experience, but also (and exclusively) about white experience.

Chesnutt's universalist subject position and his hope that his work could be received outside the matrix of race has been contradicted by the reception of and lack of attention to white-life novels. David Roediger has recently written that the "serious 'white life novel' has left very little impact on American literary criticism. Even its most spectacular successes, such as James Baldwin's *Giovanni's Room* or Zora Neale Hurston's *Seraph on the Suwanee*, are little read. Less artistically successful works, such as Richard Wright's pulpy and revealing account of loss and violence in the white middle class in *Savage Holiday*, vanish with hardly a trace" (8).

The neglect of the genre of white-life fiction is due to the persistence of the color line in literature. In 1928, James Weldon Johnson claimed that "white America has a strong feeling that Negro artists should refrain from making use of white subject matter. I mean by that, subject matter which it feels belongs to the white world. In plain words, white America does not welcome seeing the Negro competing with the white man on what it considers the white man's own ground" (479). The neglect of the genre has to do not only with the competition Johnson identified, but with a sense of imaginative trespass, as if, in the view of white readers, African American writers have had no right to represent white-life exclusively because to grant that right would be to acknowledge the permeability of the color line. Chesnutt himself commented on the presence of that heavily demarcated literary line when he wrote that Howells "has remarked several times that there is no color line in literature. On that point I take issue with him. I am pretty fairly convinced that the color line runs everywhere so far as the United States is concerned, and I am even now wondering whether the reputation I have made would help or hinder a novel that I might publish along an entirely different line" (Chesnutt, *Letters* 171). Of course, the novels "along an entirely different line" are his white-life novels, and until this day, the answer is that such works, at the very best, do nothing to help the reputation of an African American writer.

That is not to say, however, that Chesnutt's ambitions in the white-life novels are the same as in his race fictions.

In the white-life novels, he is clearly trying to write fictions that he hoped would become popular successes with a white audience. William L. Andrews, the only critic of Chesnutt to have mentioned them at any length, is not sympathetic to Chesnutt's ambitions in these novels. "Each of these undistinguished narratives," he writes, "had sprung from a similar motive—to write especially for the popular market—and each was concocted only after novel-length color line stories had failed to make headway either in the publishers' offices or in the bookstores" (*Literary Career* 131). Clearly, as Andrews argues, Chesnutt was trying, in these novels, to gauge the taste of his potential white audience and "to tailor a long work of fiction to the tastes of genteel readers" (122). In these works, Andrews claims, Chesnutt failed "to find . . . that spark of conviction and serious purpose which appears" in his race fiction (122).

But as we have begun to realize in recent years, the use of popular forms—the adventure, the romance, and melodrama—does not preclude serious cultural work. A popular genre, Hans Robert Jauss has written, fulfills "the expectations prescribed by ruling standards of taste, in that it satisfies the desire for the reproduction of the familiarly beautiful; confirms familiar sentiments; sanctions wishful notions . . . or even raises moral problems, but only to 'solve' them in an edifying manner as predecided questions" (25). While Chesnutt was trying to fulfill expectations completely enough to have a popular success in *Eveyln's Husband*, he was subtly subverting the genre he was working in, much as he did in *The Marrow of Tradition* and *The Colonel's Dream*, and as a result, he created another of his fictions of eccentric design.

Nothing is known of the composition of *Evelyn's Husband*: Helen Chesnutt does not mention the novel, but on the basis of a 1903 rejection letter from McClure Phillips, Andrews dates its composition to before 1903 (131). In turning down the novel for the publisher, Witter Bynner wrote:

> I doubt that "Evelyn's Husband" will do your reputation much good. It might be published to fair advantage, perhaps; but we are convinced that in leaving your earlier work . . . you have made a literary misstep. This sounds rather harsh, I am afraid. I don't want you to think for a minute that we are not appreciative of the many excellent and charmingly written passages . . . particularly your narrative and running comment, which is so vastly better than your dialogue. Though we are returning this, I shall be decidedly interested to hear of the progress of the novel you sketched to me, centering about an Octroon" (Bynner).

Setting aside, for a moment, the question of any merit of the novel, we can see in this rejection the same pattern that was at work with Walter Hines Page's earlier rejection of *A Business Career*. In the same letter he rejected the novel, Page suggested to Chesnutt that he assemble the volume that would eventually become *The Conjure Woman*. Editors, publishers, and audiences preferred (and continue to prefer) that African Americans write exclusively about African American experience, thus they help to preserve the color line in literature.

Writing specifically about *Evelyn's Husband*, William L. Andrews says that this "unquestionably" is "the worst of his seven unpublished novels," and he calls it "diffuse and improbable" (130). Rather than rating the novel and conceiving of it in these negative terms, I prefer to read the novel as wonderfully and self-consciously baroque. The novel, which begins as a domestic comedy, morphs into a wildly implausible adventure story in which conceptions of white manhood are at stake. As evidence of Chesnutt's self-consciousness about the forms with which he is working, I would point to the way in which one of the characters defines his experience in the novel. He calls it, at various points, an experiment and a "rare comedy" (197) and a "tragic farce" (275). That last term in particular points to Chesnutt's use of an eccentric design in the novel; he creates a hybrid form which begins as a novel of manners and ends as a hyperbolic adventure story.

There is an analogue to *Evelyn's Husband*, Frank Norris's *Moran of the Lady Letty* (1898), a novel that Norris, like Chesnutt, wrote in an attempt to produce a bestseller. Its initial setting is also the upper class, and the novel begins: "This is to be a story of battle, at least one murder, and several sudden deaths. For that reason it begins with a pink tea among the mingled odors of many delicate perfumes and the hale, frank smell of Caroline Testout roses" (1). The central character, Ross Wilbur, goes to a tea party where he tells a girl who has just come out that a group of young girls, "'girl in the aggregate like this . . . unmans me'" (5). After he leaves the party he is inveigled down to the San Francisco docks where he is shanghaied onto a fishing boat, crewed by Chinese, bound for Baja, California. Like in Kipling's *Captains Courageous* (1897) Wilbur is toughened by his experience and begins to be transformed from a social dilettante into a "real man." Once they arrive, they encounter Moran Sternersen, "a half masculine girl" (98), formed by her experience of being at sea. Together Ross Wilbur and Moran seize the ship from the Chinese, and after a series of complicated developments, Ross discovers, in a hand-to-hand fight with another group of Chinese, his own atavistic self, "the primitive man, the half brute of the stone age" (214). In the same fight, he encounters Moran, who is filled with "bersirker [sic] rage" (219), and the two of them fight quite brutally until Ross throws her on her back and grinds one knee into her chest. "'You've beaten me, mate—'" Moran says, "'. . . you've conquered me, and . . . mate . . . I love you for it'" (221). The fight restores proper gender roles: Ross has gotten back into contact with his own "primitive man." His masculinity has been restored in the process of subjugating her, and she is transformed from a wonderfully independent masculinized woman into an implausibly cringing female who makes no effort, later in the novel, to defend herself when attacked by one of the Chinese, and she dies whimpering for Ross to come to her rescue.

In their equally hyperbolic fashions, *Moran of the Lady Letty* and Chesnutt's *Evelyn's Husband* participate in the discourse of beleaguered masculinity around the turn of the century. In broadly cultural terms, anxiety about masculinity, as Gail Bederman has demonstrated, could be seen in the concern about women's education and the falling white birth rate, in concerns about immigrants, in the rise of organized athletics, in Theodore Roosevelt's displays of masculinity as hunter and Rough Rider, and, as Amy Kaplan has pointed out, in the celebrations of the recovery of American masculinity in the Spanish American War and in its immediate imperial aftermath. Kaplan quotes Senator Albert Beveridge asking in a debate over the annexation of the Phillippines: "'What does all this mean for every one of us? . . . It means opportunity for all the glorious young manhood of the republic—the most virile, ambitious, impatient, militant manhood the world has ever seen'" (660). Kaplan argues that the popular historical romance of the day, novels like Richard Harding Davis's *Soldiers of Fortune* (1897), function as "fictional equivalents of the Phillippines . . . as a site where a man can reassert this 'militant manhood' . . . " (660). Obviously, the adventure novel itself can function as another such site, and in Norris's *Moran of the Lady Letty*, Ross returns transformed by his experience of violence; he now has a proper masculine desire to accomplish something in the world, a proper manly contempt for the life he lived before. Back in San Francisco, he says to his former society friends, "'That sort of life, if it don't do anything else, knocks a big bit of seriousness into you. You fellows make me sick . . . As though there wasn't anything else to do but lead cotillions and get up new figures!'" (258).

Of course, we need to notice the unmarked marker: in this period, there is a crisis of *white* masculinity, a crisis that also manifested itself in events like the Wilmington, North Carolina coup d'état/pogrom (which was the basis for *The Marrow of Tradition*) and in the explosion of lynchings of African American men throughout the United States. Gail Bederman has written that white Americans in this period were "obsessed with the connection between manhood and racial dominance" (4), a discourse which constructed African American men as brutish and primitive and white men as the epitome of civilized restraint. However, there also seems to have been a countervailing idea—that white men must demonstrate their manliness by their momentary recovery of what Bederman terms "the natural man," a term which was the binary for "white man." "Where 'the white man' embodied civilized manliness, 'the natural man' embodied primitive masculinity. Lacking civilized self-restraint, the natural man acted upon his 'natural' impulses." Those "natural" impulses were seen in the coverage in the national press about lynching; reporters "continued to assert that 'masculine' impulses toward sex and violence, although savage and illicit, were 'natural.'" Modern men had, for the most part, successfully repressed the "natural man," "but when they joined lynch mobs, they allowed the savage within themselves free reign." As a contemporary journalist noted, within every man, a "'savage is waiting to assert himself if only encouraged'" (Bederman 72). What made the white man better than the natural man was his ability to suppress and repress, but that very ability then threatened his racial dominance.

As Theodore Roosevelt argued, a total repression of "the natural man" would make America into an effete nation, and the further consequences of that suppression would be the continuance of the falling white birth rate—in a term that Roosevelt gave wide currency at the time, the consequence would be "race suicide." For cultural spokesmen like Roosevelt there was a terrible danger in losing contact with "the natural man," but then too much indulgence of "the natural man" would mean that there was little to distinguish between the superior and inferior races.

Chesnutt interrogates these ideas of white manhood in the fantasy/adventure portion of the novel when the two main male characters are cast away on a desert island in the Carribean. It is almost as if he were attempting, by using the seemingly nonconfrontational genre of the adventure, to represent the problem of white manhood which he explored in another genre, that of race fiction, in *The Marrow of Tradition*. When the two main male characters, Cushing and Manson, are marooned, they immediately become white. When the narrator reintroduces Cushing as a castaway on the desert island, he is immediately characterized as a "white man" (157). Up to this point in the novel, Cushing's race has been unmarked, his "whiteness" taken for granted. Once transposed into the realm of adventure, Cushing's race needs to be marked, as is Manson's when he is also shipwrecked. The first words out of Manson's mouth, once Cushing has said hello, are: " 'Thank God! . . . a man, a white man, and an American . . .'" (179). Before becoming white on this desert island, Cushing had considered himself "a fair type of the cultivated man" (172). He had had no great passionate experience: "He had looked upon passionate love, with its offspring of jealousy, hatred and revenge, as something for the vulgar, who did not possess the resources of culture or the consolations of philosophy. His sudden passion for Evelyn had been his first awakening . . ." (173). His second awakening had been his desire for revenge on Manson, after he eloped with Evelyn on Cushing's wedding day : he ". . . had rankled under a fierce and gnawing jealousy; he had felt the poison of hatred, the animal longing for revenge" (174). Now, stranded, alone with a man who conceives of himself as his mortal enemy, Cushing has to confront his own elemental man, and he becomes more than the effete dilettante he was at the beginning of the novel. In order to recover his own white masculinity, Cushing has to be immersed in the primitive desire for revenge that he has repressed in himself, but the arena of this confrontation is not social. Chesnutt does not use realistic markers in the novel in the way that he does in his other fiction, and in doing so, he is pointing to how the novel is concerned, almost in the abstract, with the idea of white manhood, and to how he is entering the national debate over white manhood from an ostensibly nonracial point of view.[3]

For these reasons the publication of *Evelyn's Husband* demonstrates how Chesnutt carried over into popular fiction one of the major preoccupations of his racial fiction. The exploration of whiteness he developed in his race fiction continues in this novel, but in the nonconfrontational guise of a popular fiction. In addition, in generic terms *Evelyn's Husband* is one of Chesnutt's most radical experiments in crafting fictions of eccentric design. The bifurcated narrative—high society social novel and adventure story with a denouement in Brazil—can be seen as an experiment he learned from and carried over into the writing of *The Colonel's Dream*, the novel that Chesnutt wrote after *Evelyn's Husband*. The publication of this novel allows us to understand more clearly Chesnutt's development as a writer; it provides the intermediate step between *The Marrow of Tradition* and *The Colonel's Dream*, and allows us to see how he became the writer who manipulated genre in ways he did in *The Colonel's Dream*. Finally, the publication of *Evelyn's Husband* greatly expands our sense of Chesnutt the writer: in this novel, free of the responsibility of confronting the race question in the United States, we see Chesnutt at serious play, a note found early in his work in the sketches published in *Puck* such as "A Roman Antique," a note missing from his work since at least the publication of "The Passing of Grandison."

The publication of this novel of Charles W. Chesnutt would not have been possible without the support I received from the Pennsylvania State University. I received two grants from the Capital College Research Council and one from the Institute for Arts and Humanistic Studies of Pennsylvania State University. These grants allowed me to pay for the copying of Chesnutt's manuscript novels and to travel to Fisk University Library several times to work with Chesnutt's original manuscripts. I would like to thank the special collections librarian at Fisk, Beth Howse, for her help with my numerous requests, and John Slade for giving permission to publish this novel. Finally, a letter from Witter Bynner to Chesnutt is quoted by permission of the Witter Bynner Foundation for Poetry.

Note on the Text

The copy text for this edition is a typescript with hand-written revisions by Chesnutt in the Charles W. Chesnutt Collection, Special Collections, Fisk University Library, Nashville, Tennessee. The manuscript can be found in Box 7, folders 16–21.

Evelyn's Husband is only lightly revised both in pen and in pencil. There are also some comments and queries that seem to be in a hand other than Chesnutt's (possibly these comments were written by Walter Bynner who rejected the book for McClure Philips). For instance, in Chapter XVI, when the blind Manson is talking to Cushing (whom he knows as Singleton), Manson says about Cushing that "I would n't know his voice if I heard it." The word "obvious" is in the margin in another hand, and Chesnutt has subsequently canceled that sentence. The editor, I assume, has also marked a number of sentences with question marks. In the absence of any indication of Chesnutt's intention in those instances, I have made no editorial changes, since Chesnutt clearly responded to the editor's comment that the sentence above was "obvious." However in one instance, I have made a change even though Chesnutt did not respond to a query in the other hand. This writer noted the inconsistencies in the name of the warship that nearly rescues Manson and Cushing. At one point it is called the *Illinois*, while later it is named the *Oklahoma*, and since it is given the latter name more often I have changed the name *Illinois* to *Oklahoma*, and I have also changed an earlier reference to this ship flying the "Union Jack" to flying the American flag.

The majority of changes in *Evelyn's Husband* involve typographical errors probably attributable to his typist (and since Chesnutt never finalized the manuscript, those errors were never corrected.) Throughout the manuscript Chesnutt has revised to tighten his prose, and this in most noticeable in the first twenty-five pages of the manuscript. Throughout his use of contractions is clearly inconsistent, and I have retained those inconsistencies. I have also retained Chesnutt's nonstandard, but correct spellings: e.g. "skilfull," "gravelled," "dishevelled."

Matthew Wilson

Notes

1. One more novel, "The Rainbow Chasers," remains in manuscript. Chesnutt abandoned this novel before he fully worked out a revision of the plot, and were it to be published, it would need to be in a critical edition, where readers would be able to compare the two versions of the plot. A play, "Mrs. Darcy's Daughter," also remains in manuscript.

2. Chesnutt owned a copy of Dunbar's *Uncalled* (McElrath, "Chesnutt's Library" 108).

3. See my book *Whiteness in the Novels of Charles Chesnutt* for a fully developed argument about the presence of whiteness in this novel.

Works Cited

Andrews, William L. *The Literary Career of Charles W. Chesnutt.* Baton Rouge: Louisiana State UP, 1980.

Bederman, Gail. *Manliness & Civilization: A Cultural History of Gender and Race in the United States, 1880–1917.* Chicago: U of Chicago P, 1995.

Bynner, Witter. Letter to Charles W. Chesnutt. 6 Sept. 1903. Charles W. Chesnutt Papers, Special Collections, Fisk University Library.

Chesnutt, Charles W. *Charles W. Chesnutt: Essays and Speeches.* Eds. Joseph R. McElrath, Robert C. Leitz, III, and Jesse S. Crisler. Stanford: Stanford UP, 1999.

———. *To Be an Author: Letters of Charles W. Chesnutt, 1898–1905.* Eds. Joseph R. McElrath, Jr. and Robert C. Leitz III. Princeton: Princeton UP, 1997.

Jauss, Hans Robert. *Toward an Aesthetic of Reception.* Trans. Timothy Bahti. Minneapolis: U of Minnesota P, 1982.

Johnson, James Weldon. "The Dilemma of the Negro Author." *American Mercury* 15 (1928): 477–81.

Kaplan, Amy. "Romancing the Empire: The Embodiment of American Masculinity in the Popular Historical Romance Novel of the 1890s." *American Literary History* 2 (1990): 659–90.

McElrath Jr., Joseph R. "Charles W. Chesnutt's Library." *Analytical and Enumerative Bibliography* 8 (1994): 102–19.

Norris, Frank. *Moran of the Lady Letty: A Story of Adventure Off The California Coast*. 1898. New York: AMS, 1971.

Roediger, David. Introduction. *Black on White: Black Writers on What It Means to Be White*. Ed. David Roediger. New York: Schocken, 1998: 3–26.

Williams, Kenny J. "The Masking of the Novelist." *A Singer in the Dawn: Reinterpretations of Paul Laurence Dunbar*. Ed. Jay Martin. New York: Dodd, Mead, 1975: 152–207.

EVELYN'S HUSBAND

I.

SHALL INDIAN SUMMER MATE WITH SPRING?

Mr. Cushing was waiting for the ladies. The occasion of his attendance was a symphony concert, to which he was to accompany Mrs. Thayer and her daughter—or, to place them in the order of their relative importance in Mr. Cushing's consciousness at this moment—Miss Thayer and her mother; a shifting of values according to the law of life, by which the young come forward as their elders retire, but which may mean more in some cases than in others. In this instance it had meant a great deal to all of the parties concerned, though no one of the three understood quite what it meant to either of the others. For years Cushing had come to the house to see Mrs. Thayer; at present her daughter Evelyn was the compelling attraction. His pathway thither, once lighted by the lamp of friendship, was now illuminated with the torch of love.

The place where Mr. Cushing sat waiting, was the comfortable parlor of a small but handsome flat on one of the upper floors of a modern apartment house in the Back Bay section of Boston, within a stone's throw of Beacon Street and but little farther from the classic precincts of the Public Garden. Mr. Cushing had come in his own perfectly

3

appointed carriage, which was waiting below, in charge of Mr. Cushing's English coachman, Simpson, while a footman in livery stood at the heads of Mr. Cushing's magnificent bay horses. Leonie, Mrs. Thayer's dark-haired, black-eyed maid, had answered the ring at the doorbell, and with a respectfully familiar, not to say expansive smile of welcome, had taken Mr. Cushing's hat and coat. The ladies, she had said, were dressing, and would soon be ready. He had needed no one to usher him into the parlor, which he had entered with the air of one thoroughly at home.

The room was a marvel of taste. A bay window at the front, flanked by two smaller openings, looked out upon a broad street, along which, east and west, stretched the handsome residences of the wealthy. To the southward, across the wide street and over the tops of the houses beyond, were visible in the middle distance the tiled roof of the Public Library, the façade of the Art Museum, and a little to the left, the graceful spires of Trinity Church. The walls of the room, harmoniously decorated in pale green, gave place to a few oil paintings— some of them gifts of Cushing—and to many choice photographs. The furniture was luxurious, not so much in the way of fine wood and soft upholstering, though it was both fine and comfortable, as in its perfect harmony of form, color and combination. Edward Cushing was a man of taste, of culture, and of wide experience. He occupied a beautiful old home on a historic street, in the same spot where his ancestors, solid men of Boston, had dwelt, in successive houses, for two hundred years. Yet not even in his own library, which reflected his tastes and fitted him as the shell the nut, was he quite so comfortable as in Mrs. Thayer's little parlor.

To what extent use was responsible for this feeling would be difficult to say. Leonie had admitted Mr. Cushing, in much the same way, for ten years past,—ever since, a child of twelve, she had been taken by Mrs. Thayer to be trained in her service, from the Home for Friendless Girls where philanthropy had provided her with a refuge from the neglect and bad example of a drunken father and a dissolute mother. If she had not profited in every way by the training, it was certainly not the fault of her mistress; heredity has a way of intruding its claims, now and then, against the influences of environment. Leonie had wondered more than once—her mind was given to imaginative excursions—how many years more she would continue to admit Mr. Cushing in the same way. Of late she had learned enough, by diligent eavesdropping, to lead her to the belief that he would not continue much longer to come upon quite the same footing.

It had never occurred to Cushing that his own taste, carefully studied, had been the guide to the decorations of the room. Despite a wide experience of life, he had a man's obtuseness in matters feminine, and had never until recently, and then only in part, realized the extent to which the element of sex entered into the subtle sense of completeness which pervaded this little interior.

Mr. Cushing sank into a low arm-chair beside a mahogany table upon which stood a lighted lamp. His hand, resting mechanically upon the edge of the table, touched a leather case, which, upon his opening it casually, proved to contain several photographs. He smiled pleasantly at the first of them. Dear Alice! In her clear eyes could be read loyalty to the memory of her husband, Cushing's friend; patience with her children, one of whom had tried her sorely; cheerfulness under burdens which would have crushed a less steadfast spirit;—the clear-eyed, smiling friend by whose hearth he had always been welcome. The portrait, which was several years old, was that of a woman of thirty-six, in the slow-ripening maturity of the New England type. A more astute physiognomist than Cushing might have read there still other qualities—a fine pride, a delicate reserve, and a firm-ness of character—which to him had been swallowed up for the most part in the refulgence of her more obvious virtues.

The second portrait, evidently taken much earlier than the first, showed a vigorous man of thirty-three or -four, with curly hair—a sign of energy; a square jaw, which would denote pugnacity, endurance; evidently a man of affairs, and a man of power, though a close scrutiny revealed certain lines of weak-ness; the portrait of Henry Thayer, Cushing's friend, Alice's husband, Evelyn's father, who had died in the prime of life, leaving his young wife and two children to face an uncertain future. Cushing and he had been classmates at Harvard, at a time when classes there were small enough for their members to become acquainted with one another during the four years of their undergraduate life. Entering the college with an ath-letic record from some small Western institution, Thayer had been warmly welcomed to the student body, in which Cushing was conspicuous. The scholarly but dilettante Bostonian, and the energetic, athletic Westerner, had been from their first meeting sworn friends; Thayer's strong will and heady spirit had proved irresistibly attractive to the thinner-blooded aristocrat, who, in fact, never made any pretensions to superiority because of either family or wealth;—having been born to both, he enjoyed their advantages with an easy unconsciousness which endeared him to his friends. During their college life Thayer had perhaps profited most by the friendship; it had opened to him social and other opportunities which helped to form his manner and extend his acquaintance among those who in after life might further his ambitions.

Their friendship had not ended with Commencement Day. Upon leaving the University, Thayer, who was poor and ambitious, burning to conquer the world and eager to grasp the most effective weapon for that purpose, which, according to the spirit of his age, was wealth, had secured a clerkship in a bank and set out to make a fortune. Having a comfortable patrimony, and a less definite ambition, Cushing had been in no haste to select a career. He had thought for a while that he would like medicine, his father's profession, and had matriculated at the Harvard Medical School; but a certain fastidiousness revolted at the dissecting room, and the prospect of daily contact with disease and deformity became less pleasing as it drew nearer in the perspective. He finished his course, however, for the honor of his name, wrote a brilliant thesis upon the origin of zymotic diseases, graduated *cum laude*, and then went abroad.

Before leaving, he was able to congratulate his friend upon a promotion, and upon his marriage to Alice Starr, a charming young woman of good family. Cushing had a large income, derived in part from certain old houses down on the wharves, and in part from conservatively invested securities. He spent a delightful year or two of wandering, and returned home in time to stand as godfather to the infant daughter of his friend, an animated little bundle of lace and linen, which was christened at Trinity Church as Evelyn Cushing Thayer.

Finding the thought of medicine more and more distasteful, and impelled neither by necessity nor any urgent ambition, he entered the Harvard Law School, hoping to develop a taste for the profession, or at any rate to prepare himself for a career in politics or the diplomatic service, should he feel inclined to enter either;—some of his ancestors had won distinction in both, and the family name carried a certain prestige which might be counted upon to help him with either the electorate or the appointing power.

Meanwhile Henry Thayer had gone into business on his own account. The reclamation of the Back Bay district was in progress. Thayer was enabled, through connections formed while in the bank, to get in on the ground floor. He proposed to take Cushing with him into certain schemes. His zeal and enthusiasm overcame Cushing's conservatism, induced him to invest a large part of his capital in the venture, which enriched them both, Cushing the more since he had ventured most. But Thayer had done extremely well, and upon the foundation thus laid might have built up by safe methods a solid fortune.

At this point, however, he developed a weakness fatal to his hopes—a too eager desire for great possessions sapped his judgment, which is the vital factor in finance. A second opportunity for speculation occurred, promising larger profits, but less securely founded. Thayer, acting promptly, went in; Cushing hesitated, and lost his opportunity—much to his profit, for the bottom of the scheme dropped out, and Thayer was ruined. He might have recovered from the blow had there been nothing else but failure to contend with; but an attack of typhoid-pneumonia supervened, and in a week he died. Cushing was by his deathbed. His last thoughts and his last words were for the welfare of his wife and children, now widowed and orphaned and impoverished. One of his hands was held by his sobbing wife, who clutched it despairingly; the other lay in the firm grasp of Cushing, who steadied his friend's passage over the dark river.

"I would n't so much mind going, Ned," whispered the dying man, "if it was n't for her and the children. You'll look after them—a little—won't you, Ned?"

"I will—as though they were my own," his friend had declared. Comforted by this assurance, Thayer had breathed out his life with a smile of gratitude.

Deathbed promises, made under stress of emotion, are often disregarded. Cushing remained faithful to his. He was his friend's executor, and saved a surprising amount from the wreck. The widow knew nothing of business, and only after some years and considerable reflection did she understand how so much could have come from so little. To have known of this disguised beneficence earlier would have added keenness to a secret sorrow. Divining it so late brought a chastened gratitude which found expression not in words, but in subtle ways which gave her a sense of satisfaction. Reserving her thanks for the occasion, long hoped for, when she could in expressing them, offer him some other return, she had found it grow increasingly difficult, as the slow years rolled on without bringing the occasion, to speak upon the subject. Cushing had carefully guarded her self-respect. Without the fruits of his benevolence she would not have known how to live or to provide for her children. But should he learn that she knew the real source of her income, she felt that it would be impossible for her any longer to accept it— all the more impossible because she loved him.

He never divined her knowledge, nor her love. With a singular obtuseness, he accepted his own knowledge of something of which he believed her ignorant, as the basis of a devotion which any other man would have been justified in ascribing to a tender interest. A scheming woman in her place might easily have entangled him. There were things said, things that he never heard, which their world would have held to justify all the arts which honest women may employ to spur the reluctant male. But Alice was proud; she would be the sought and not the seeker, and her burden of secret obligation disarmed her. For years she had hoped; for a short time hope had deceived her into expectation. No longer hoping for his love or expecting it, she still cherished his friendship, conceiving in time another method of paying off her debt.

Mr. Cushing turned to the third photograph, that of a handsome boy, resembling Henry Thayer in every feature, but with a curious and sinister inversion—wherever there had been strength in the father's face, there was weakness in the son's. It was not by any means a hopeless face, but merely that of a weak and unformed youth who might turn out good or bad, with the chances somewhat in favor of the worse alternative. Cushing gave the photograph but a brief glance and turned it over with a sigh, to encounter the face of a radiantly beautiful girl who had just crossed the threshold of womanhood.

"Ah! Evelyn!"

Mr. Cushing's face softened into a tender smile, which faded a moment later, when, moved by a sudden misgiving, he turned his shoulder and looked at his own reflection in a small mirror, in a hand-carved wooden frame, which stood near him on the table. The light from the lamp fell squarely upon his face as he sat there in the low chair—he had slightly lifted the shade with one hand so that there might be no illusion. The mirror reflected, without flattery, the face of a man past forty, with a high broad forehead, thin nostrils, a clean-cut and slender nose, slightly curved, a delicate chin, clean shaven, not too salient; hair not yet gray but growing thin upon the temples; grey, reflective short-sighted eyes, requiring glasses. To leave the mirror, Cushing was tall, slender, erect and well preserved, with manners which reflected a life of ease and intellectual freedom—a fine gentleman, in the very best sense of the term.

His scrutiny of himself was interrupted by the maid.

"Miss Evelyn will be down in a moment, sir," she announced.

Cushing's eyes went back to her portrait. From infancy for much of the time her growth had been the slow unfolding of the bud; but there had been breaks in their intercourse to emphasize from time to time her wonderful development. For Cushing had been more or less of a wanderer on the face of the earth. He had been admitted to the bar, but the mass of detail through which it is necessary to cut one's way in the practice of the law, in order to reach its fine underlying philosophy, had seemed to him to demand too great an expenditure of time:—the game was scarcely worth the candle. Nor had he, so far, gone into public life. A very cursory study of the conditions which dictate political advancement had disgusted him with politics; it had seemed to him necessary, in order to attain the heights, first to explore the depths; and Cushing was fastidious. Republics, too, were ungrateful, and popular favor uncertain. He had therefore deferred for a while longer the selection of a definite career; and, with entire good humor, and with no pessimistic scorn of the world, had spent a year or two in travel. He was known in the clubs of every great capital, and his name was upon the rolls of many.

Upon his return from a winter on the Mediterranean he had found Evelyn, whom he had dandled on his knee, a year before, grown into a long-limbed school-girl, whose dark clustering curls framed an oval face with lustrous long-lashed, heavy-lidded eyes. She had become shy, demure, self-conscious, and Cushing had assumed a serio-comic sort of reverence in addressing her. Later on, a tour of the South American republics, (in preparation for a contemplated book upon these undeveloped lands, with their curious experiments in ethnology and government), had occupied him away from home for several years. When he returned Evelyn's skirts had lengthened, and her childish angularities were rounding into delicate curves. When he came home after another Winter's absence, spent at a hotel in Italy, where he had worked upon his book, discovering that authorship also had its drudgery, Evelyn had become a beautiful woman.

A judge of beauty—a man of his taste and leisure could scarcely have been otherwise—Cushing determined that Evelyn should bear his name and share his fortune. After a few words with Alice had convinced him that her daughter's heart was entirely free, it seemed to him that his wooing ought not to be difficult. He had much to offer a woman. Possessing Evelyn's confidence and respect, it ought not to be difficult to win her love.

He spoke to Alice of his hopes. She heard him with conflicting emotions.

"I'm glad you've thought of her, Edward. Few things could make me happier. I've tried to make her worthy of some one as good as you. Another woman might come between us;—this marriage would strengthen our friendship."

She did not tell him that she had guarded Evelyn's heart for this very end. She had not wished to lose him. If she could not give him herself, she would give him her daughter.

At Cushing's request, she broached the subject to Evelyn, who after the first shock of surprise, raised no objection. The prospect was not unpleasing; many women would have thought it alluring. Mr. Cushing was rich, and a young woman reared in the full tide of contemporary American life would scarcely despise its deity. Mr. Cushing was cultured and kind; she had been trained to regard him as the ideal man. From infancy her childish tricks and graces had been rehearsed with a view to their effect upon him. At school the hope of his approval had been an incentive to industry. To marry him would raise her from a position of genteel poverty to one of opulence and large outlook and leave to her mother what had been spent upon her maintenance and education. She accepted his offer with becoming gratitude. The date for the wedding had not yet been set.

Nevertheless Evelyn, thus upon the point of yielding her independence, shrank for a moment from the sacrifice of her individuality. Mr. Cushing had been none too soon. Evelyn was nineteen, and conscious of her beauty. She had looked forward to marriage, at some time in the future, as a matter of course, but had dreamed of love as something very different from her feeling for Mr. Cushing, and of marriage as something more than a conventional union with an elderly admirer. Mrs. Thayer too, though she had prayed and hoped and schemed for this marriage, hesitated for her own personal reasons—hesitated like the martyr who for principle's sake goes bravely to the stake yet shrinks to see the torch applied. At her suggestion that Evelyn should have time to become accustomed to the idea, Cushing had been content to wait a few months before bespeaking a definite date for the consummation of his happiness. And since Evelyn was still in school, it was deemed best to defer the announcement of their engagement until the close of the term, which had been reached this very day.

Looking back from his own reflection in the mirror to the youthful face of the portrait, Cushing felt a sudden and fierce impulse to foreclose his claim upon Evelyn. He was growing distinctly older; though his hair had not begun to silver perceptibly, he would soon be old. Many men at his age were grandfathers. He had wasted much time; whatever else he might expect from life must be gathered quickly. Evelyn was young—very young. He could not bring her youthful ardor, but he could give her everything else necessary to make a woman happy. But he must lose no time, he must take no chances. He would ask her this very night to name their wedding-day, and to fix it as soon as possible.

There was a light step in the hall, the rustle of silken skirts, and the original of the photograph stood before him. Evelyn wore a gown of clinging white which set off her dark beauty wonderfully. Her cheeks were aglow with excitement, her eyes sparkling with anticipation. With a lively greeting she advanced to the middle of the floor, where she paused and turned slowly around in order that he might see her from every side.

"How do you like my new gown?" she demanded anxiously.

"It is perfectly lovely," he declared,—"only less beautiful than the wearer. It is the robe of sea-foam worn by Venus when she sprang from the sea."

"That's a delightful compliment. *Merci, monsieur,*" replied Evelyn, sweeping him a low curtsey. "But I had always thought of Venus as fair."

"Because her statues are all of white marble? But they were all colored to the life, you must remember;—Greek art was faithful to nature. The Greeks were southern, and dark. The great painters, too, were mostly southern. Titian's Venus—"

"Was a red-haired Italian, like his model, I suppose. But my hair is dark."

"And Leonie has dressed it beautifully. I shall be proud to be seen with you to-night."

"It's awfully good of you to take us. Mama'll be ready very soon. We won't be late, will we?"

"No, there is plenty of time. It is n't eight yet."

While Evelyn stood before him, vibrating with youth and energy and pleasurable anticipation, a wave of strong feeling swept over Cushing—love, desire, a vague jealousy, directed at no one in particular, and a more distinct pang of misgiving. Cushing had lived too long, traveled too much, seen too many women in too many lands not to know the meaning of those slumbrous, heavy-lidded eyes, those pencilled brows, those full red lips, the firm, full contour of that perfectly moulded chin. Such eyes, clear and limpid now, were unsounded wells of feeling; such lips were made to give as well as to receive passionate kisses. Women of Evelyn's type were common in Italy and Spain, lands of love and languor. To what extent could culture modify temperament? In the serene atmosphere of her mother's home these fires had never been kindled. Would wealth and ease smother them, or fan them into flame? and if the latter, to what extent could he satisfy the needs of such a soul, in such an envelope?

"There comes mama," exclaimed Evelyn.

If Mrs. Thayer had changed since her latest photograph,— it dated back three years,—the difference was not apparent. Her gown was of white satin, the corsage was worked in an elaborate design. Whatever lines the searching quality of the sunlight might have revealed in her face were certainly not visible in the tempered light of the parlor. Of the virginal type, a widow at twenty-two, and having led a sheltered life, Alice Thayer had retained much of her beauty;—had Evelyn not been present, her mother would have seemed almost young. Though the secret wish of many years had never been granted her, the canker of disappointment had neither soured her temper nor marred the gracious serenity of her countenance. Her social obligations, her church activities, the care of her children—which of course came first in importance—and a deep interest in certain obscure charities which brought no glory but wrought much good, had so filled out her life as to leave little time for vain regrets. Until Evelyn was ten Alice had been spoken of as "that young Mrs. Thayer." The word had changed, in time, from "young" to "young-looking," but even now, in spite of the nineteen years between them, no one seeing them together and ignorant of the relationship would have placed them in different generations.

Cushing gave her his hand with the smile of protecting tenderness he had always had for his dead friend's widow. He had smiled at Evelyn with a different kind of tenderness;—the one had been that of love, the other was that of friendship.

"You too are beautiful, tonight, Alice. You are the lily, Evelyn the rose; both beautiful, each the perfect counterpart of the other. I shall be envied tonight."

"I have forgotten my handkerchief," exclaimed Evelyn with a happy laugh. "I'll go and get it while you pay mamma compliments. She's ever so much more beautiful than I am."

Mrs. Thayer was blushing with pleasure in spite of herself.

"Hurry, Evelyn. Thank you, Edward. You know how much I value your praise. It makes me very happy to have such a daughter to give you. I fear my other child will bring me only sorrow. Wentworth is in trouble again—my poor boy!"

"I am sorry. When did you learn?" The gravity of his tone marked the depth of his interest. Wentworth was the son of his friend Henry, and of his friend Alice Thayer—the weak-faced young man whose photograph he had looked at.

"His roommate telephoned in from Cambridge this afternoon. It started a day or two ago, and culminated last night. He had been talking about New York, and about the—girl. There is an address—"

"Give it to me," demanded Cushing, taking out his notebook. "I'll find him tomorrow. There's nothing to prevent my leaving on the early train."

He made a careful memorandum of the address.

"*She* does not know," murmured Mrs. Thayer, lowering her voice as Evelyn was heard returning. "I did n't wish to mar her pleasure."

"It was like your kind heart," said Cushing. "Do n't tell her at all. I'll bring him back before she learns of his absence."

They went downstairs to the carriage.

Evelyn leaned luxuriously back upon the cushions. In a few months the carriage would be her own. She would be able to command whatever wealth could purchase, taste demand, or industry supply. Mr. Cushing was generous and very much in love. It would be nice to marry a rich man; but there need be no hurry about it. He would probably speak about their wedding, when he had a favorable opportunity; but she would put him off a while longer. She would like to enjoy her independence a little while, and see what being engaged was like. Of course, if he and mama should urge her, she might have to make the date earlier.

II.

THE SYMPHONY CONCERT

The carriage drew up at the curb. Cushing dismounted, helped the ladies out, and passed with them beneath the canvas canopy leading to the doorway of the hall. Upon entering the lobby Evelyn caught sight of a young man of their acquaintance.

"There's Willie Rice, mama," she whispered as they moved slowly forward with the throng. "He's looking at us."

Upon catching Evelyn's eye, the young man referred to lifted his hat and bowed to the ladies. Evelyn's glance, as she acknowledged the salutation, rested only a moment upon Rice's cheerful though somewhat vacuous countenance, and then wandered toward the young man beside him, who had mechanically lifted his hat with that nice adjustment which marked him as merely the companion of Mr. Rice and not an acquaintance of the ladies themselves. The absence of expression which accompanied this formal act lasted only an instance, however, for scarcely had his eyes fallen upon Evelyn before they lit up with a very palpable gleam of interest and fastened themselves unswervingly upon the girl's face. He did not even remove them while he turned slightly toward Rice, and put some question to him, which Evelyn rightly surmised to be concerning their party, for Rice continued looking at them while his lips moved in reply. So pointed was the stranger's look, so frankly admiring that Evelyn was conscious of it, and after she had turned her eyes away felt herself blushing furiously.

There was some congestion in the lobby, and before they reached the auditorium Evelyn involuntarily threw a second glance toward her unknown admirer, by which she was able to take in swiftly several details of his personal appearance. He was a stalwart young man, of about twenty-eight, she guessed—he was really thirty-two—broadshouldered, erect, with a clear open countenance, and boldly chiseled but not unhandsome features. Evelyn felt an unaccustomed thrill as she again met his eyes, still fastened upon her face, and for a moment was unable to turn her own away; while Cushing's voice, which was murmuring something in her ear, sounded far away.

"Look to your skirt, Evelyn," said her mother sharply, noticing her preoccupation though not perceiving its object; "someone will step upon it."

Evelyn recovered herself with a start, clutched her gown with her hand, and made an irrelevant reply to Cushing's remark. In a few minutes they had taken their seats in Cushing's box, and while the orchestra was playing an over-ture, looked around the audience in search of friends or acquaintances.

The concert was of unusual excellence. Evelyn who was fond of music and herself possessed no mean skill at the piano, drank in the swelling harmonies with clean delight. Tonight, for some reason grounded in the mysteries of life, whose forces at times seize us and bend us, consciously or unconsciously, and not concerning themselves at all with our first wishes in the matter, to their purposes, she was attuned even more keenly than usual to emotional impressions. The music touched the finest fibers of her being, lifted her to great heights, filled her with vague ambitions, vast confi-dences in herself,—intoxicated her, in other words, with something like the exhilaration of opium or some kindred drug. She was scarcely conscious of her mother and Cushing, both of whom were absorbed, Mrs. Thayer in an intelligent and therefore more discriminating appreciation of the music than her daughter's; Cushing in the study of Evelyn's dark beauty, and the thrill of his own late-blossoming passion.

The concert was in two parts, and the curtain fell at the end of the first, for a quarter of an hour's intermission. The beautiful auditorium was flooded with light, and murmurous with fluttering fans, comments upon the performance, and the movement of part of the audience toward the foyer. As Evelyn's eyes ran over the house, they fell on Mr. Rice and his companion of the lobby, who were occupying the box directly opposite their own, upon the other side of the stage. Instinctively her hand flew to her opera-glass. At the same instance the unknown, who had been scanning the boxes, directed his lorgnon toward her. After a moment of scrutiny Evelyn handed the glass to her mother, and turned her face away. When her eyes, after a brief glance around the room, involuntarily moved back, the tall young man was talking eagerly to Mr. Rice, still, however, without turning his face away from Evelyn, who became conscious at this moment that Cushing was saying something. She paid no attention to him, however, until her mother spoke.

"Evelyn, do come out of that trance! Edward is speaking to you."

"The music has entranced her," said Cushing. "I merely remarked that I must telephone my house, if I may be excused. I shall return immediately."

"Certainly," said Evelyn, with an abstracted smile, as Cushing bowed himself out to seek the telephone in the box office.

He was nearing the exit when he met Rice and his companion, who had left their own box and were moving around the rear aisle toward the boxes on the other side. Cushing was acquainted with Rice, who belonged to a well-known family, and to whom he nodded, noting the appearance of his companion, a strikingly handsome fellow, he thought, in a bold free way, who walked with a springy step, and held his head high—he had seen his picture somewhere, an artist or engineer or something of the sort—he had forgotten his name—supposed to be a rising man, and in the public eye.

The two gentlemen found their way to Mrs. Thayer and Evelyn. Mr. Rice shook hands, and begged to introduce his friend.

"Mr. Manson," he said, "Hugh Manson, the famous architect."

"I'm delighted to meet the ladies," said Manson, when Mrs. Thayer had shaken hands with him, "but I repudiate the fame; not that I don't desire it, but simply that I have n't achieved it. I have not yet arrived, though I hope to do so."

He had preempted the seat by Evelyn with an unconscious ease which made the act seem perfectly natural; and though his words were addressed to both the ladies, his eyes were for Evelyn alone. Evelyn thought them bold; but it was an admiring and withal a respectful boldness to which she felt hardly inclined to take exception.

"You're too modest, Manson, quite too modest. The man who built the Standish, and St. Swithin's Church, has arrived already; the rest is merely a matter of finding time to earn your commissions. He is more than an architect, Mrs. Thayer— he's an artist. He has the old Greek instinct for form. Had he been a writer, he would have been an epic poet. But instead, he builds us sonnets in homes, epics in churches and swelling blank verse in apartment houses."

"And prose," added Manson, "in the shape of ware-houses and freight depots."

"It is the prose that pays, my boy," said Rice, laying his hand upon Manson's shoulder familiarly. "Fame is all well enough, and you are going in for it. But your clerks can do the prose while you pocket the shekels—and it's money that talks."

It was money that talked in Rice's case, there could be no question; for while he was an amiable young gentleman, of good habits, it was a common saying that he had more money than brains. This comment was not really so harsh as it seemed, since he had a great deal of money, and would have required a great deal of brains to be wise in proportion to his wealth. He knew enough, moreover, to take care of his money, and also to admire talent in others and cultivate the friendship of people wiser than himself. He had for some time intended to marry, and had considered a number of young ladies from that point of view. They had been, however, among the most talented and beautiful, and therefore the most in demand; and in no instance had Mr. Rice, with whom decision was not a strong point, been able to make up his mind before some one else had carried off the object of his amorous calculations. He was at present fancy free, and quite impressed by Evelyn's beauty.

"Manson is building me a house," continued Rice. "I should like to have you ladies look at the plans. You have such exquisite taste, Mrs. Thayer, that I'm sure you or Miss Evelyn might give me some new ideas."

"They are at my office," said Manson. "If the ladies should happen to be in the Bronson Building any time soon, I should be pleased to show them the drawings."

Mr. Rice kept on talking about his house. Manson had picked up Evelyn's fan from where it lay upon the ledge of the box; a delicate piece of carved ivory—a gift from Cushing on his return from some foreign journey. While seeming to listen to Rice, his eyes were fixed upon Evelyn. Openly or covertly they never left her, but drank in every detail of her young beauty—her glossy brown hair, her slumberous eyes, her rich southern coloring,—the belated inheritance of some distant ancestor; her rounded arm, her tapering fingers, the long supple limbs outlined beneath her clinging skirt, and terminating in little feet daintily slippered. He saw no more than Cushing had seen, but he saw it with an artist's eye, and what he did not see he divined with an artist's imagination. Evelyn basked in this silent worship with a sense of exhilaration even more pronounced than that which the music had evoked. Cushing's approval had pleased her; this man's admiration sent the blood galloping through her veins.

Mrs. Thayer became curiously watchful of this little drama, and was growing a trifle restless and wishing that Cushing might return, when the lights were turned down.

"There goes the curtain," said Rice, "and we must go back to our seats. By the way, have you ladies seen Carpenter's paintings—there's an exhibition of them, you know, at Knapp's, this week."

"Yes, I know," returned Mrs. Thayer, "we are going tomorrow afternoon."

"And don't forget to step in, and look at my plans, Mrs. Thayer—and Miss Thayer. I shall depend upon you. I really want your advice, upon several important points."

"That young man is good-looking enough," said Mrs. Thayer when they were gone. "He would really look quite distinguished, if his manners were better formed. His attentions are too pronounced, upon so short an acquaintance. Remember, Evelyn, you are engaged."

The gentleman to whom she was engaged entered the box at this moment, having met the other two men leaving it.

"I had to wait quite a while to get the 'phone," he explained by way of apology. "A lady, whose sick dog had been left in charge of a trained nurse, was receiving a report of the dear sufferer's symptoms. It was quite touching."

"How was the dog?" asked Evelyn, with flippant anxiety.

"Better, it seemed. But you have had company."

"Yes," said Mrs. Thayer, "Willie Rice and a friend."

"Mr. Manson, the rising architect," said Evelyn, giving her attention to the stage, from which however it wandered involuntarily now and then, to a box across the room, in which those who were seated were plainly visible in the light from the stage, and from which she caught ever and anon a flash from a pair of keen gray eyes.

III.
MR. CUSHING IS URGENT

When the concert was over, the young men were waiting in the lobby, and bowed with marked empressement as the ladies passed. To Evelyn, as the carriage whirled them swiftly through the streets, they seemed to be leaving light and life behind, and she leaned back in silence while Mrs. Thayer and Cushing discussed the merits of the opera and the singers. How old they seemed to her, her mother and Mr. Cushing, when they spoke of the soprano's voice nineteen or twenty years before! They belonged to another generation; nineteen years before, Evelyn had been an infant in long skirts; twenty years ago she was not born.

"Won't you come in, Edward?" asked Mrs. Thayer, as they reached home.

It was late, and before his engagement to Evelyn, Cushing would scarcely have gone in at such an hour; but he was still strong in his purpose of the early evening. Moreover, he wished to speak privately to Mrs. Thayer, which Evelyn's presence had so far prevented.

"I think I will, for a little while," he replied, giving his coachman instructions to wait.

Leonie opened the door. She was glad to see the ladies return, for in the novel she had just been reading, there had been a gruesome prophecy, which had attained fulfilment in a murder, a ghost, remorse and suicide. Not even the romantic marriage of the heroine, a surpassingly beautiful young variety actress, to the son of a multimillionaire brewer of Hackensack, had quite dispelled the influence of these horrors, which had fascinated even while they repelled. And although the checkered career of the beautiful Madge Mullen had appealed to her undisciplined imagination—Leonie yearned in secret for a dramatic career and the romance of love—she was beginning to find solitude irksome and to wish that the ladies would come home.

Evelyn, followed by Leonie, went to her room to lay off her things. Obeying a sign from Cushing, Mrs. Thayer left her cloak in the hall and led the way to the parlor.

"I've made inquiries over the long distance," he said, in a low voice. "I fear Wentworth is in a bad way. I shall leave for New York in the morning, and stay until I can bring him back."

"Thank you, Edward. You are good to us—always good to us—too good to us."

"Wentworth is more than my ward now, he is my brother, and so I shall regard him. And now, Alice, dear Alice, may I see Evelyn a little while alone? I must ask her to name our wedding day.—I—am growing old, Alice and cannot wait. You may trust your treasure with me; I will guard her safely."

"I would trust my life with you, Edward," she said without a tremor, as she hurried away.

Evelyn came in, and Cushing went forward to meet her.

"Sit here by me, child," he said, drawing her toward the sofa.

The word was unfortunate. To call her child was to emphasize his own years. Evelyn obeyed gracefully, but with conscious reluctance.

"I am going to ask you a question, Evelyn—dear Evelyn!"

She foresaw it and shrank from it. She had promised to marry him, and had looked forward calmly to the many advantages of such a position. She had thought she loved him; she did love him, but her love, she felt to-night, more than ever before, was in no whit different from the love she had felt for him since infancy.

"Evelyn," he said, with a passionate vehemence that alarmed instead of thrilling her, "Evelyn, my darling, I can wait no longer. Tell me when you will be mine."

It had come, the question she had dreaded for a month. All her life she had been in leading-strings. Her mother had guarded her thoughts, had curbed her speech, had supervised all her actions. At school she had been under the restraint of masters and mistresses, and to Evelyn, though always docile, the hand of authority, even if gloved in velvet, was often irksome. To-night, while the music crashed around her, she had dreamed of liberty and of love. A pair of glowing eyes had looked into her own with an unmistakable message. Now had come her guardian, her good, but elderly guardian, to demand of her a definite date on which she should give up, not liberty, which she had never enjoyed, but the hope, even the possibility of freedom. She could not do it, at least not tonight, of all nights.

"Oh, please," she gasped, "please do not ask me tonight, Mr. Cushing. Let me get used to the idea. I am so young!"

"You must get used to my name," he replied. "Call me Edward; see how easy it is!"

"Edward."

It was not easy. He did not know how hard it was for her to pronounce his name. All her life she had called him Mr. Cushing. To change one's form of address from the formal to the familiar without a corresponding change of feeling, struck Evelyn as strange to say the least. It was more than merely wanting in deference; it savored of positive disrespect.

"There," he said, pressing her hand gently, "you can just as easily say 'the first of next month.' "

"Oh, no, no," she said with a tremulous vehemence, which he ascribed to mere maidenly modesty, and which only heightened his ardor.

"Or, if it please you better," he conceded, regretfully, "the first of the following month. I don't wish to hurry you, dear; but consider my loneliness, and how much I want you!"

Evelyn thought that he could not be so very lonely, or he would have married long ago. And surely he had not suffered from loneliness while in Boston, for at such times, ever since she could remember, he had been at their house nearly every day.

Evelyn's silence gave Cushing an opportunity to realize for himself a little of the absurdity of a bachelor's plea of loneliness—a bachelor of forty-five. He was lonely, had been lonely every moment that he was away from her, since the dawn of his passion, he went on to explain, lest she might be skeptical.

"Before I thought of you as a wife, Evelyn, my solitary life did not disturb me. But now, dear, as your loveliness grows upon me, I tremble at the fear of losing you. Tonight you are more beautiful and more desirable than ever. Tell, me, Evelyn, when shall it be?"

Evelyn's thoughts strayed involuntarily back toward the theater. Her lover wooed beautifully. With a suddenly upstirring cynicism, Evelyn wondered to how many women he had made love. He was old enough for her father. She had regarded him, nearly all her life, in a light not very difference from that of a parent. Why should a woman marry a man whom she did not love with a great, fierce, passionate love, which would sweep her off her feet and compel her to do and dare all things for her beloved?

"O Mr. Cushing, give me a little more time," she faltered.

"How long, my dear?" he persisted. "Do not make it long. I love you so. I wish to make you happy. I need you in my home, in my heart. May I ask you again—next week?"

"Oh, not to-night anyway!" she pleaded in her turn. "I—I must talk to mamma. Another time! Do not think me ungrateful; I know how good you are. Thank you so much for the concert. It was beautiful, it was grand!"

He drew her gently toward him. She submitted passively to his embrace. He went away disappointed, but not discouraged; determined to press the point until he received an answer. He could easily imagine that she might wish to see something more of the world before tying herself down. But he was selfish—he acknowledged it to himself—he could not afford to let her see too much. So far her fancy was free, her affections disengaged. To marry her now would break no ties, shatter no illusions, cause no regrets. That she was not wildly in love with him he saw very clearly, but he did not despair of awakening in her a stronger feeling than she now possessed. He would make her life so large, so full, so free, he would surround her with such luxury and comfort and love, that gratitude alone would compel her affection. Never before in his life had Edward Cushing felt more completely and thoroughly selfish than during this solitary drive homeward; and never, since the time, three months ago, when he had first spoken to Alice of her daughter's marriage, had he experienced the feeling which now oppressed him in the shape of a conviction—that a man held no woman safe until they were united in the bonds of matrimony. After that, he would have a sure vantage ground, he could look out for himself; but if any one should rob him of her now, this ewe-lamb whom he had brought up by his own hand; whose very clothes, jewels, education, the culture which had softened and polished and refined her natural gifts into the charm of perfect womanhood, his bounty had provided, though she knew it not—if any man should seek to rob him of her now, it would be an evil day for the thief. He could murder such a man, could crush him as a reptile beneath his feet. He was surprised at his own vehemence; he had not thought himself capable of such primitive passion.

Evelyn felt no disappointment when her mother informed her next day that Cushing had been called suddenly to New York, and would not be able to accompany them to the picture exhibition. Mrs. Thayer would have deferred the visit until another day, but Evelyn wished to go, and seemed so restless and ill at ease during the morning that her mother was anxious to divert her. Evelyn had volunteered nothing concerning the interview with Cushing; but Mrs. Thayer had known its purpose and was anxious to learn the outcome.

"Edward did not stay long last night," she remarked tentatively.

"No, mamma," replied Evelyn.

They were at breakfast alone, and Evelyn as soon as she had answered, became deeply absorbed in the bottom of her coffee-cup.

"I thought—indeed he told me—that he would ask you to fix a date for your wedding."

Evelyn did not reply for a moment.

"The subject did come up," she said, with well-simulated unconcern, "but we decided to wait a little while longer."

Mrs. Thayer was not deceived, but she had always maintained a certain reserve with her daughter. This had required no great effort—was indeed rather a matter of temperament. Several centuries of ancestry reared upon the hills of Vermont, had endowed her with some reflection of their granite rocks and winter snows. Education, and twenty years of life had left her, not cold, nor yet too cool, but entirely calm and self-contained, a rarely balanced nature, which never in its deepest grief or joy quite forgot itself. Evelyn's disposition was more in accord with her warmth of coloring. Most young women of their acquaintance led their mothers by the nose, so to speak; but Mrs. Thayer, while devoting her life to her children, and having scarcely any thought but for their happiness, had guarded her authority as a parent, feeling this course doubly needful since her children had no father with whom she might share it, and because experience had long ago shown the need of a strong hand in her son's case; and she had always looked forward with a certain apprehension to the time when Evelyn should begin to assert herself. It was her theory, too, that young people, in order that they might learn to respect others, should have their own individuality respected. There had never been a serious difference between her and Evelyn, and hence she had never found it necessary, since her daughter had grown up, to make any forcible assertion of her authority. She had always preferred, where there was room for difference of opinions, to bring Evelyn to her point of view by advice and suggestion, which had so far rarely been ignored.

"You should not forget, Evelyn," she said pleasantly, "that Edward is offering you a splendid position. We have been hanging on to the edges of society all your life—you little realize how slender the hold has sometimes seemed—and now you have the opportunity to play a leading role where you have heretofore been only in the back row of the chorus. It is a chance at which any girl would jump."

"Yes, mamma, but I *am* rather young to be laid on the shelf. If I were ten years older, or even five—"

"That is a very absurd notion, Evelyn. Marriage is woman's sphere. You are as old as I was when I was married; and I married a poor man, whose future was uncertain, while Edward can give you all that a woman could want to make her happy. I would not have you mercenary, but when every other condition of happiness is present, wealth is a blessing for which one cannot be too thankful. It is a sacred trust, which will give you great power for usefulness. As to being laid upon the shelf, that would not be possible with the wife of Edward Cushing. For you, a poor girl, unbound by any promise to another, to hesitate before the opportunity to marry a good man, and such a man! is scarcely less than wicked."

"But I—I have n't refused to marry him. I promised as soon as I was asked. We are engaged; is n't that enough for a while? He has waited so long to marry, that he can surely wait a little while longer."

"You should not trifle with so serious a matter, Evelyn, nor let any childish nonsense stand in the way of your future. *I* think the wedding day should be fixed, and the engagement announced. Edward is the soul of honor, but a man should be married while he is in the notion—especially one who, as you say, has waited so long. Should his mind change, habit would render it easy for him to remain single. Be guided by experience, Evelyn, and do not put him off too long. Few women have such an opportunity, and of those few reject it."

Mrs. Thayer was entirely convinced that a marriage with Cushing would bring perfect happiness to her daughter, or she would never have urged. To Alice, Edward Cushing was easily the wisest and best of men.

The force of her mother's arguments was perfectly apparent, but Evelyn was haunted by a perverse spirit this morning, which had all the time been seeking some selfish reason for her mother's desire to hurry forward the marriage. Evelyn had known for some time that the family income was absorbed to the last penny in the effort to keep up appearances, and that any serious misfortune, such as erratic conduct of her brother rendered always possible, might spell ruin to their precarious though perfectly respectable footing. That her mother should desire to escape from so unsatisfactory a situation was natural enough, even if it were necessary (which Evelyn felt at this moment was being done) to sacrifice her daughter to that end. For Mr. Cushing in marrying her would doubtless marry the whole family, as the phrase went. How much better, how much simpler, how much more appropriate it would have been for her mother to have married Mr. Cushing! They were nearly of an age; her mother was the younger of the two. The result to the family would have been the same, and Evelyn would have been left free to choose her own career, and, if needs be that she marry, her own husband. Evelyn had never heretofore viewed her marriage to Cushing in the light of a vicarious sacrifice for the family advantage; and even now, as these rebellious thoughts surged through her brain, her well-trained conscience reproached her for them. There was no earthly reason except her own new-born disinclination, why she should not marry Mr. Cushing. Both duty and interest impelled her to do so. So she offered no dissenting arguments, and permitted her mother to believe that she had brought her around to her own point of view.

IV.
THE SECOND MEETING

Evelyn and her mother took the street-car to Knapp's, which was on Tremont Street opposite the Common. Carpenter's exhibit was the result of a year of work upon the Mediterranean. The paintings were cleverly done in the artist's characteristic style, or lack of style, to quote certain invidious critics who maintained that Carpenter, who wrote novels and built railroads, as well as painted pictures, had invented a style of his own, whereby he avoided the detail demanded of a conscientious artist and left to the spectator's imagination the labor which more properly devolved upon the painter.

They had scarcely entered the room, when Mr. Manson, their new acquaintance, came forward with outstretched hand and beaming countenance. He wore a loosely-cut suit of white flannel, which exaggerated his bigness somewhat, and he carried a Panama hat in his left hand. Mrs. Thayer noticed that his hands were hairy, his fingers spatulate, and his nails irregularly cut. A large solitaire diamond ring upon one of his fingers rather emphasized these defects;—his hands were scarcely those of a gentlemen, though the young man was not bad-looking, and there was something undeniably fresh and virile about him. Into his extended hand, such as it was, she placed her own slender gloved extremity, with a smile, the coldness of which would have been apparent to one more sensitive or less pre-occupied than Manson. All day long he had waited for this hour; since two o'clock he had run into Knapp's every fifteen minutes, to see if Evelyn and her mother had arrived. He gave the girl's hand a frank pressure, and perceived at once, though she simulated polite indifference, that her breath came quicker and her eyes glowed. In reality Evelyn was delighted. She saw no defects in this young demigod who had dawned like the sun upon her horizon. The pressure of his hand sent the blood bounding through her pulses; his presence seemed to wrap her in a very cloak of happiness.

Manson walked along with the ladies, at first keeping Mrs. Thayer's left, while Evelyn was on her right. He soon managed, however, by stepping forward to point out some feature of a painting, and falling back at a convenient moment, to place himself next to Evelyn, where he kept his place until the ladies left. He was fluently critical of the paintings, and displayed, Mrs. Thayer thought, a very discriminating taste, with a freshness of viewpoint and a frankness of expression that were novel and entertaining, if somewhat unconventional.

But after half an hour, she began to notice his absorption in Evelyn, and that the girl was hanging upon his words in altogether too entranced a fashion.

"I think, Evelyn," she said, "that we had better be going."

"Just a little while longer, mamma," pleaded Evelyn. "We have n't nearly seen all the pictures, or looked at them enough."

"Oh, don't go yet, ladies. Now, that view of the Acropolis, while fine, is not true. Art is permitted to idealize, but should not juggle with facts. If I were painting Mrs. Thayer, for instance, as "Summer," or Miss Thayer as "Spring," I should feel privileged to idealize, if I could find anything to improve upon;—my subject would give me license. But if I were painting a "Portrait of Miss Thayer," I should be compelled to paint a picture which would faithfully reflect her features. That picture does not correctly represent the Parthenon. I have at my office, which is only a couple of doors away, some photograph of that immortal ruin, and some sketches of my own, which I flatter myself are technically correct, to say the least. And then there are Rice's plans that he is so anxious for you to look at. It is only a step from here. I'd be so glad to have you come!"

Evelyn was prompt to speak before her mother had time to object.

"Oh, yes, mamma, we are going to Thornton's, to see about the proofs of my photographs; and Mr. Manson's studio—is it a studio or an office?"

"It will be a salon—a palace—while it is honored by your presence, and afterwards. Heretofore it has been merely a plain office."

"I fear we hardly have time," demurred Mrs. Thayer.

"Oh, mamma, but we promised Mr. Rice! It will take only a moment."

The young man was fluent, too fluent, Mrs. Thayer thought, and his compliments too extravagant for good taste. Evelyn, moreover, was too impressible and too much interested. But the virile compulsion of Manson's smiling face and clear eyes was not without its influence upon even Mrs. Thayer, and a few minutes later, against her own impulse, they were lifted swiftly skyward to the top floor of a neighboring sky-scraper.

Manson's office consisted of several rooms, in one of which, through an open door, they could see, bending over drawing tables, a number of draughtsmen, several of whom looked up from their work to fix their eyes, as long as good manners would permit, upon the two beautiful women who had invaded their workshop. The walls of the reception room, where Manson asked the ladies to be seated, were hung with large drawings of the elevations of buildings, some of which, Manson explained were rejected designs, while others had met a better fate. There were samples of brick and building stone upon the mantel, and in one corner a cabinet of sections of polished wood. There was a handsome rug upon the floor, and several comfortable armchairs, two of which the architect placed for the ladies near a carved table in black oak.

Manson brought out the plans for Rice's house and explained them at considerable length. There was a ground plan, floor plans for the several stories, elevations—front, side and rear—and many details of interior finishing.

Mrs. Thayer was struck by the perfect harmony of taste which pervaded the whole. She was compelled to admit, whether Mr. Manson was quite a gentleman or not, that he was an architect of unusual skill and taste.

When he had put away Rice's plans, after the ladies had expressed their enthusiastic approval, Manson produced an album of photographs of the masterpieces of ancient and modern architecture, on which he descanted with easy knowledge. Evelyn had heard her guardian talk pleasantly of foreign lands, but this man spoke with a confident air of authority which carried conviction, and with what seemed to Evelyn inspired genius. She had heard many a lecture on European architecture; indeed a considerable portion of Evelyn's life had been devoted to the hearing of lectures. She was familiar, by description, by pictures and by magic lantern views, with the cathedrals, shrines and palaces, ancient and modern, of the old world. But Manson's description lent them a new meaning, and threw a romantic glow of light and life around what had before been but the dry bones of scholarship.

Evelyn did not pause, as her mother might have done in like case, to analyze her emotions, to consider how far a cultured interest in history and art accounted for her feelings, or to what extent they were affected by the magic of Manson's voice, the magnetism of his handsome face and stalwart form. For Evelyn was in that stage of life when the emotions are supreme; restrained, of course, by culture, convention, and conscience, but not yet subdued by reflection and experience. She spent in Manson's office the most delightful half hour of her life, and it seemed, at its close, to have lasted only a few minutes, a few crowded, glorious minutes, into which had been condensed more pleasure, it had seemed to her, than in all her life before.

When Mrs. Thayer rose to go, Manson was speaking of the characteristics of Greek art, which was indissolubly connected with Greek architecture, of which it was, in the main, an adjunct, and of his hope that he might bring about, so far as it was applicable to different conditions of climate and modes of living, a renaissance of those principles of beauty and form, which in surviving so many centuries, had proved themselves possessed of an enduring charm—a charm which should not be buried in museum and art schools, but reëmbodied in brick and stone and marble for the delight and informing of the men and women of their own generation.

"I should like to go over with you," he said, "sometime when we happen to meet there, the Greek casts in the museum. I am sure I could point out things that few of the visitors comprehend. They see the lines, the contours, but after all, they are to them but lifeless models—beautiful indeed, but the mere dead symbols of a vanished past. But to the truly enlightened, who can reconstruct in imagination that wonderful era, they are parts of an immortal whole. The dear, bad old gods are dead, but the things which they personified will live on forever! Were they to die, then beauty would be dead, and who would care to live in a world without beauty?"

This was all very fine; in spite of her prejudice, Mrs. Thayer was impressed by it; though, had she not seen how fine his own work was, she might have considered it a frankly amusing sort of egotism for this underbred young man to suggest that he might point out to her, who had grown up in an atmosphere of culture, any new beauties in the Elgin marbles. But to Evelyn it was all delicious, enthralling. Were Phidias alive, he would doubtless have bowed respectfully to the criticism of this modern master. Was it not likely, possessing so high an order of genius, and having the labors of the ancient Athenians as a foundation upon which to build, that he should achieve still greater things than they?

When they left his office, Manson accompanied them to the door of the photograph gallery a little distance down the hall. When they had finished their visit and were on their way to the elevator a few minutes later, he happened also to be going out. When they reached the sidewalk, he wondered whether they would not have an ice at a neighboring confectioner's. Evelyn would have assented, but her mother forestalled her.

"Indeed, Mr. Manson, we are very much obliged, but we really must be moving on. Thank you for a delightful half-hour. I shall tell Mr. Rice what I think of his plans—your plans."

While they were shaking hands, their group was augmented by a fashionably dressed lady, in middle life, who had alighted from a carriage at the curb. The cut of her gown, elaborately plain, the gold-rimmed eyeglasses, the rippling bands of grayish hair; the perfectly appointed equipage, all marked the lady of position and wealth.

"How do you do?" she asked, giving Mrs. Thayer her hand, "I hope you and your beautiful daughter will be at my reception Thursday evening."

"Thank you, Mrs. Archer, we shall be on hand, unless something unexpected happens to prevent us."

Mr. Manson came forward. "Good afternoon, Mrs. Archer. I'm afraid you don't remember me—Mr. Manson."

Mrs. Archer gave him a little stare, but unbent again immediately.

"Oh, yes,—Mr. Manson—I remember you quite well— Willie Rice's friend. Did you receive the invitation to my reception? No? I'm sure I ordered it sent; there must have been an oversight. I'll see that you have another card before tonight. You'll be sure to come? We need dancing men. Of course you dance?"

"Oh, certainly," said Manson, "and I shall be glad to come." In fact Manson danced only indifferently well, but he would have lied cheerfully, had he not danced at all, rather than to have forgone the acceptance of this eleventh hour invitation.

"We'll find you plenty of partners," continued Mrs. Archer, "and Evelyn—Miss Thayer—will probably be the belle of the ball. I shall expect you all. *Au revoir.*"

She swept into the building. Manson finished his adieux and stood hat in hand as the ladies moved off down the street.

"Evelyn," said her mother, when Manson was out of hearing, "that young man's attentions are too pronounced. We must n't encourage him."

"Mr. Manson?" returned Evelyn, disingenuously. "Did he seem so? He was very nice to us both, I thought. Don't be alarmed, mamma; I'm engaged, you know."

"Yes," said her mother, "but he doesn't know it."

In spite of her prompt disclaimer, Evelyn was silent and self-absorbed all the way home, and filled with a very pleasant elation, of which the novelty was its chiefest charm. Young men—callow young men—had fluttered around her ever since she was fifteen; and older men had unbent to pay her little compliments on her beauty. But to-night, for the first time, she had felt the impact of a strong will, to which her own nature had responded with alacrity and pleasure.

V.

A KENTUCKY MOUNTAINEER

In the next morning mail came two letters from Cushing, written the night before at New York, upon the letterhead of an uptown hotel. One was for Evelyn. It was couched in a style of mingled familiarity and fervor,—that of one who, having occupied for a long time a certain relation toward another, suddenly grafts upon it a new and different feeling—that of a schoolmaster for instance in love with a pupil who has grown up in his school. To Evelyn, still under the influence of yesterday's novel emotion, the letter was inharmonious, jarring: behind the fervent lover she could read the fatherly guardian. From another, expressions of love might have given her unalloyed pleasure; from Cushing they merely spoiled a friendly letter from an amiable gentleman to whom, no doubt, she owed a debt of gratitude and affection.

Mrs. Thayer's letter gave her greater satisfaction; but in it, too, the bitter was mingled with the sweet. Her son had plunged into a wild debauch. Cushing had spent the whole afternoon in search of him, and had found him late at night, in company with the person whose influence had drawn him to New York. He had proved to be in an ugly mood, and scarcely manageable without force, which Cushing, though legally his guardian, had no disposition to use unnecessarily. He was hopeful, however, that a night's sleep would bring the boy to reason, so that they might return the next day. But for the fact that it might keep him too long away, he had thought of setting the forces of the law in motion against the woman, so that she might be for a time, at least, put beyond the power of mischief. He would at any rate see that she was kept under survey, and as far from Boston as possible.

"If I am not at home by tomorrow evening to accompany you to Mrs. Archer's, I shall write to Simpson to bring the carriage around for you. Telephone him the hour at which you want it. I would not have you and Evelyn miss the ball for anything. It is the event of the season, and Mrs. Archer is our very good friend. I had meant to present Evelyn to her in the character of my promised bride."

In the afternoon Evelyn was seized with a desire to visit the Art Museum. Manson's eloquent panegyric on Greek art and architecture had lifted her spirit, she thought, to a height where it might commune with the soul of this ancient and immortal people as shadowed forth in these poor, mutilated fragments of a once glorious embodiment. She said nothing to her mother of her intention, but merely remarking that she was going to the library to return a book, left home about three o'clock. Her errand at the library was completed in a few minutes. It was but a step across Copley Square to the Art Museum.

Whether the soul of Greek art had exerted its influence to draw Manson to the Museum on this particular afternoon, or whether the subtle intuition of love had warned him that Evelyn would be there—whatever the motive that called a busy man of affairs from his office at such an hour, Evelyn had scarcely had time to make up her mind that she would first go up and look at a recently acquired canvas, a present to the Museum, and to ascend to the turn of the stairway under Veretschagin's vast canvas, when she heard a quick footstep, and Manson was beside her.

Evelyn's heart beat tumultuously. She made no effort to pretend surprise. While she had had no reason to expect him, it seemed the most natural thing in the world that he should be there.

"Oh, it is you," she said, with a quick smile. "I came to see the casts; but first I am going to look at the new Claude Lorraine."

"I had a presentiment," he said, "that I might find you here. You know my grandmother was a witch, and claimed the gift of second sight. She was tried once in court, for casting the evil eye, and barely escaped conviction. I may have inherited some of her supernatural powers."

For the moment Evelyn hardly noticed what he said. The sound of his voice, low, deep, resonant was like the music of Italian opera, which elevated, thrilled and satisfied. What he said was but little more important than the book of the opera. It was enough that he was speaking, and to her. She felt all a maiden's pride of conquest. She was not free, but her shackles fitted her lightly, and, as yet, had not been riveted on; she was indeed scarcely conscious of them, except in Cushing's presence, and she glowed with triumph at having brought to her feet this glorious young man. Whatever might happen thereafter, this hour should be hers, with no watchful mother and no jealous fiancé to mar its happiness.

They wandered from canvas to canvas. Manson's views, Evelyn noticed, when she had recovered her poise somewhat, were not quite so positive on painting as on architecture, nor his instinct as nice on coloring as on form.

They were passing before the large canvas of "A Scene in the Cumberland Mountains" by a well-known American painter. The artist, with the insight of genius, had caught and with a superb skill had fixed upon the canvas, the high, thin air, through which, with distant nearness, the mountain peaks marched in stately procession until lost in a dim perspective.

"Ah, wait a moment," exclaimed Manson, laying his hand upon Evelyn's arm. "Upon just such a mountain-side I first saw the light of day. That thin blue ether was my natal air. That cabin perched upon the mountain-side, might have been—one like it was—the home of my own childhood."

"How interesting!" exclaimed Evelyn. Her demigod, if he had not descended from Olympus, had breathed the free mountain air, had not grown up in too close contact with the sordid earth. Surely so great an upward stride as he had made must involve a romantic history.

"Tell me," she said impulsively, "tell me something of your life!"

Her request was as spontaneous and as unconventional as his touch upon her arm a moment before. Yet, caught in the full tide of elemental impulses, neither of them was conscious of anything out of the ordinary.

"Would you really care to know?" he asked simply. "Then let us sit here before the picture."

The room was vacant, except for the occasional passage of an attendant, so that Manson could talk undisturbed. They sat down upon the seat fronting the canvas. He took Evelyn's opera-glass from her hand and twirled it upon his fingers as he spoke.

"I was born," he said, falling easily into the narrative vein; he was a fluent speaker and liked to hear himself talk—"I was born in eastern Kentucky, thirty years ago. My people were not the descendants of cavaliers, proud of the deeds of their ancestors—not all of them noble—nor slave-holders drawing their wealth from the toil of other men. They were poor-whites—how poor you could hardly understand!— and their ancestry was a sealed book, which no one knew and few would care to open. They had no pride of race, for they knew nothing of history; the specimens of white men around them were nothing to be proud of; there were no negroes among them, by comparison with whose estate to magnify their own. They were ignorant,—so ignorant that my father could not write his name, nor my mother even read. My grandmother, rest her shrewd old soul! did not know her letters, and was tried by an intelligent mountain court fifty years ago for witchcraft! Such was my ancestry. Think of it, flower of culture, flower of womanhood—there are thousands in these mountains today—white people at that—to whom art, science, history, culture—even comfort—are a sealed book, for want of the key of knowledge to unlock them, and we call ourselves civilized!"

"How shameful!" exclaimed Evelyn, involuntarily, her voice breathing pity and indignation, her mood responding to his touch like a sensitive instrument.

"Shameful indeed!" But they don't realize their degradation, and so they are not unhappy. We, who are more fortunate, think of ignorance in terms of knowledge, as the living think of death in terms of life. My old professor, in arguing the doctrine of immortality, used to remark how dreadful was the thought of annihilation, of no life beyond the grave, of the cold clammy clay, the darkness, the desolation of eternal night! His reasoning had one flaw: it pictured death in terms of life; it assumed that we would be conscious of our state, the very essence of which was the loss of consciousness. My mountain relatives knew no other life. They raised their scanty crops and their scraggy cattle on the hill-side, and killed their razor-backed hogs in due season. If they could turn the corn God had given them into the whiskey for which they could find a market—as they believed they had a right to do—without the intervention of the tax-gatherer, the men might have money enough to buy coffee and gun-powder and tobacco and the women a calico gown now and then.

"But though they had no pride, they had a sturdy self-respect. Having no inferiors to make them haughty, so they had no lordly class to place them at a disadvantage, for in the mountains all were poor and therefore all were equal. They resented patronage and revenged injury. We had in our family a feud which had lasted for many years. My grandfather, my two uncles, a cousin, had all bitten the dust. Fortunately for me, there was a lull in hostilities when I came along: all the grown men on the other side were dead. The young ones were not old enough to shoot, and my father did not make war upon women and children. He was at least that much better than some of his neighbors."

"What a shocking custom!" shuddered Evelyn.

"Shocking? Ah, well, it all depends again upon the point of view. Your father was a soldier, was he not?"

He thought he had learned all about her. He had a way of seeking to find out things that he wished to know.

"He was too young. My grandfather was colonel of the 21st Massachusetts," said Evelyn proudly, "and was breveted for gallantry in action. He left an arm upon the field of Gettysburg."

"And you are proud of him! Yet war is barbarous—shocking! You go out and stand up and shoot at men who have done you no harm, better men perhaps than you. My mountain ancestors in their neighborhood feuds, shot only those who had injured them."

"But patriotism," said Evelyn, "humanity, zeal for a noble cause—for such things men go to war."

"And if they are right, their antagonists go to war for exactly the opposite. I could never be made to see that both sides of a moral question were right. And, after all, is patriotism any more than self-preservation, love of family, love of home? They are all stems from the same root. The way we feel about them depends upon the way we look at them—as when we look at men and women. As I look, for instance, at you, I feel—"

"Pardon me," said Evelyn quickly, "we were speaking of yourself. You did not remain on the barren mountain-side. Tell me how you came down into the valley?"

"It was simple enough. My people were emancipated by the Civil War—though they did not know it—no more than they had known that they were slaves to ignorance and to a false social system. They fought for the Union by instinct, while the poor-whites of the valley fought, under a mistaken leadership, to perpetuate their own degradation. After the war, you good people of the North went South to teach the negroes, who needed it badly enough, God knows; and after a while you discovered that there were neglected white people who might perchance be as well worth the saving."

"One day a New England Yankee wandered to our mountain. He talked to us of books, of schools, of cities; he fired my childish imagination. From that time I walked back and forth every day, five miles each way, to the mission school which he taught in the valley. He gave me the key; I unlocked the door; that is all."

"Ah, no," said Evelyn, "that cannot be all; you did not open the door so quickly. There must be more that is worth the telling."

"Again the point of view! Those intervening years of struggle are worth much to me; they made me—but they might weary you. When I had learned what good old John Waring could teach me—"

"John Waring!" exclaimed Evelyn, "He was my mother's cousin."

"Then there is another tie between us," declared Manson promptly. Evelyn, grasping with eager instinctiveness the point of affinity, inwardly assented without pausing to wonder what was their first bond of union. "When I had learned what he could teach me, I went to a mountain college—a mission college. Your cousin found help for me; I accepted it as a loan, which I have long since repaid; what I owe him otherwise I can never repay. At my mountain college I learned to draw; I developed the instinct of form, and felt the stirrings of creative power. After leaving there I taught school for a few years, saved my money, and went to Columbia College. There I studied hard, and in order to support myself, worked at whatever my hands found to do. I was too poor to belong to a fraternity, or to shine in social circles. Well-to-do men with their own way to make had little time to spare for the shabby student who worked for his board, and pored over his books until midnight. I might have done well in athletics, for I am big and very strong, but I had n't the time. I made a few friends; I accomplished my purpose; I secured a good education, and graduated with honors."

"How grand, how noble!" exclaimed Evelyn enthusiastically. Her eyes shone with sympathy for this frank egotism, which appealed to her own awakened self-assertion. She had discovered one of nature's noblemen, a self-made man, beside whom the gilded youth of cities were unworthy of mention.

"Thank you. I found employment as an architectural draughtsman. A year or two later I was sent abroad by a technical journal, to make drawings of the cathedrals and other public buildings of Europe. When I came back the way was clear for me to try my fate. I opened an office. I am my own master. I shall succeed."

"Indeed you will!" exclaimed Evelyn with conviction. He leaned slightly forward and bending toward her, looked straight into her eager eyes with his own glowing orbs.

"I have left out the greatest thing that ever happened to me. I met you. I want you for my own."

Evelyn started, and returned, with a cold shiver, to the realities of life. The purring of her captured lion had fascinated her; but now he was beginning to show his claws, and this sudden challenge broke the spell. It was necessary to terminate this dangerous interview, and to do so at once, and leave no room for misconception. But it need not be done too harshly.

"You are somewhat precipitate," she said, rising to her feet. "We hardly know each other. And even if we were better acquainted, how do you know that I am free, or have the right to listen to such things?"

He had risen and kept beside her while they moved slowly toward the door; for after the first few yards Evelyn's rate of progress was scarcely more than a snail's pace. In the statuary room which they passed on their way out, a young Greek of the degenerate modern type which seeks our shores, to black our shoes, stood in rapt devotion before a cast of the Discobolus. Somewhere in that insignificant head with its commonplace contour lurked some far-drawn ancestral love of beauty. The race had lost the imagination to conceive, the power to execute, but still retained, in this bootblack of the street, enough of the divine spark dimly to appreciate the work of its ancient forbears.

Evelyn glanced from the worshiper to the statue. Certainly none of the beauty of the old Grecians had come down to those who bear their name and mutilate their ancient speech. But Manson might have been the artist's model. There was the same shapeliness of form, which conventional morning-dress did not conceal, the same free movement of the limbs, gracefully unconscious, breathing strength and suppleness; the same rounded head, with short brown curls. It seemed to Evelyn, as though an ancient Greek of the Golden Age had been reincarnated in this Kentucky mountain poor-white.

His next words strengthened the impression. Evelyn had expected her announcement to plunge him into gloom; but his confident expression showed no change.

"You are not married," he said after an almost smiling pause, "and I shall not believe you are engaged until you say so. But if you were, I should not give you up until you reached the altar."

"But if I were bound in honor?"

"I should not be bound; and I recognize no other man's rights until the law has fixed it."

"But you surely would not tempt me to break my plighted word. Would that be honorable?"

"It would not be honorable for you to marry one man while you loved another, and even if you were promised, I should make you love me before your wedding day arrived, and then I should be the bridegroom."

It was a pagan speech. Thus might Paris have wooed Helen. He was the man, she the woman. The race to the swift, and the battle to the strong, and love the prize and spoil.

"You are too bold," she said reprovingly. "I must go home. Please leave me here."

"My road lies in the same direction," he asserted.

"No," she said, "it does not. I shall take the car."

"The cars are free to the public," he contended stubbornly.

"But the one I shall take will not be free to you. Goodbye," she said, extending her hand.

"Goodbye," he replied smilingly, giving her hand a quick clasp, "until we meet again—tomorrow night—if not sooner."

VI.
CONNECTING LINKS

Thursday morning again brought two letters. The one to Mrs. Thayer stated that Cushing's mission had been so far successful that Wentworth was now amenable to reason though in a physical condition that rendered it unwise to bring him home before Thursday evening. They would take the late afternoon train but would not arrive in Boston in time for Cushing to accompany the ladies to Mrs. Archer's reception.

The note to Evelyn was couched in tenderer language. He was impatient at his absence; he longed to be near her. He begged her to wear the flowers he had ordered sent, and also another token which would reach her from New York during the day, and hoped that she might think of him at least once during the evening.

"What does he say, Evelyn?" inquired her mother, after having read her own letter.

By way of reply Evelyn handed her the sheet.

This simple action impressed Mrs. Thayer unpleasantly, and a glance at the letter strengthened the impression. So far, at least, Evelyn was not in love with Cushing, or she would never have handed over her first formal love letter with so much unconcern. She would have answered her mother's question and kept her letter to herself. But Mrs. Thayer was confident that in time Cushing would evoke the love which every true woman instinctively feels should accompany and sanctify the married relation. In her heart of hearts she did not see how any woman, with the least encouragement, could help but love a man who combined so many ideal qualities.

"How thoughtful he is, Evelyn!" she said with an involuntary sigh.

"Yes, he's awfully good," assented Evelyn cheerfully.

The letter had given Evelyn more pleasure than her mother suspected, and a very different sort of pleasure from what the writer had intended. Her heart had distinctly lightened at the implied assurance that Cushing would not be present at the ball. She may not have put this proposition squarely to herself. Had the charge been made, she would have denied it indignantly, and might have believed in her own denial. But whether confessed or not, it is certain that Cushing's expected absence brought her no regret, and all day long she looked eagerly forward to the evening and never thought of him at all, except when his presents came or when her mother mentioned his name.

Wentworth Thayer had been his mother's greatest joy, and was her severest trial. In childhood he had been amiable, docile, and obedient, and a source of much pride to his mother. It had been her hope that he might grow to useful manhood and redeem the family fortunes. But with the first faint down upon his lip his dominant appetite awoke. He developed an eager and indiscriminate love of pleasure. For a while he was able to conceal his irregularities, but when the inevitable exposure came, he promised to do better. He kept his promise for several months, and meantime made good progress in his school work, winning golden opinions. Then suddenly he disappeared from home and from school, to return, at the end of several days, repentant and anxious to retrieve his disgrace. A man's authority, properly exerted, might have kept these errant proclivities in check, for the same weakness which yielded so easily to temptation would have been amenable to a strong influence for good. Vastly more men and women go to the devil from weakness than from wickedness. But unfortunately, at the time when a strong hand would have been most effective in shaping the lad's character, Cushing was absent for several years, upon a journey around the world. When Mrs. Thayer was most anxious about her son, she would receive long letters from her friend, describing the Taj Mahal, the Mosque at Delhi, or reporting an interview with some interesting Chinese or Hindoo celebrity.

Returning to Boston and being informed of the facts, Cushing reproached himself for his neglect, and began to take a more serious notion of his guardianship. To his long-time friendship for the family was now added a dawning interest in Evelyn as a beautiful and desirable woman, and a correspondingly nearer interest in her brother's welfare.

Wentworth's career at the university had been very uneven. He had entered early, and was now in his Junior year. When he chose to apply himself his progress was rapid. His infractions of the rules had been skilfully concealed, and his occasional absences covered by the plea of illness. He was large and strong and might have made his mark in athletics; but his habits rendering steady training impossible, he was ruled out of the list of eligibles. He had amiable qualities which made him good company; but when in liquor these could not be relied upon, and undergraduate society, tolerant in many things, demanded consistency as a condition of fellowship. He had friends, but was regarded by many as not a good man to know. Shortly before the present time he had formed, during one of his lapses, the acquaintance of a woman, some years his senior, whom he could not possibly have met in any circle which his mother or sister touched. This liaison cost him little, for the woman had abundant means of her own. A few months before he had gone off with her upon a steamer to New London, and had returned a few days later, much the worse for wear, and seemingly unable to give a very clear account of his movements.

Mrs. Thayer recalled with alarm a certain bit of family history—the case of a great uncle who suffered from periodical lapses of memory, during which he wandered long distances from home and remained unconscious of his identity for weeks at a time. Recurring to his medical reading, Cushing, who had pronounced views upon heredity, feared that a predisposition to some such weakness might have come down from some remote ancestor, skipping here and there a generation or two and likely to recur under favorable pathological conditions. Such an influence, however slight, would be stimulated by vicious Indulgence. This bit of family history and Cushing's views upon it were made known to Wentworth, upon whom they made a deep impression. Under his guardian's influence, steadily exerted in many ways, he had led for some months a model life, and Mrs. Thayer, with a mother's hopefulness, had convinced herself of his reformation, when her hopes were suddenly dashed by this outbreak. Begun in a wine supper at a college club, it had run into a lengthy debauch, and had culminated in his departure for New York in the company of the woman already referred to.

Under ordinary circumstances Mrs. Thayer would not have felt equal to a ball while so disturbed about her son; but Cushing's letter had reassured her—she had entire confidence in his wisdom—and she felt it her duty to take Evelyn to Mrs. Archer's. This lady was a life-long friend of Cushing's and a leader of society. Mrs. Thayer owed Mrs. Archer a debt of gratitude for the greatest service one woman can render another. Years before, when Cushing's friendship for the family had been a new thing, there had not been wanting evil minds to note his frequent visits to the widow, nor malicious tongues to seek other motive for his attentions than mere friendship. These whispers had reached Mrs. Archer. She had quietly investigated, and being convinced of their utter falsity, had taken Mrs. Thayer under her protection, than which there could be no better guaranty. About that time Mr. Cushing had gone away, ignorant that any such rumor had been current, and when he came back a year later, there was other food for prurient minds, and the rumor was not resurrected. Since Cushing had never heard it, there had been no self-consciousness upon his part to disturb the harmony of their intercourse; and Mrs. Thayer, strong in the knowledge of her rectitude, and having always a single eye to the welfare of her children, had never sought in any way to limit or restrict his welcome at her house. If she had dreams, she put them bravely aside, and tried to do her duty as she saw it. It was obviously to Evelyn's interest, since her social position was soon to be permanently established upon a high plane, to make her appearance in good houses as often as possible before her marriage, in order that she might not seem to have been unduly exalted, or her husband to have stooped too much. If Mrs. Thayer's pride was involved in this consideration it was a harmless and very proper pride, which tended to enhance Evelyn's value in the eyes of her future husband.

Mrs. Archer's ball was to be the crowning event of a lively season. It marked the opening of her new town house—almost the first to rise in a new fashionable district which had been reclaimed from the marshes. The house had been modeled after a famous French château of the eighteenth century, the theatre of much romantic history. Its construction had been involved in mystery; no society reporter had ever penetrated beyond the high board fence which surrounded the growing structure, and every workman had been solemnly sworn to secrecy, and a percentage of his earnings withheld as a guaranty that he would keep his oath. This ball was society's introduction to the new mansion which was said to rival in luxury and taste its famous prototype. All sorts of extravagant stories were in circulation concerning it, and public expectation was at a high pitch.

In the afternoon the messenger brought two bouquets—for Evelyn roses, and violets for Alice. A second messenger delivered a parcel addressed to Evelyn, which was opened in the presence of the messenger in order that he might take a receipt for the contents, a rarely beautiful pearl necklace.

Mrs. Thayer gave an exclamation of delight. Evelyn was strangely silent.

"How perfectly lovely!" exclaimed Mrs. Thayer. "Evelyn, you ought to be the happiest of girls, as you are the most fortunate. It is a beautiful and costly present!"

She clasped the necklace around Evelyn's throat.

"Edward has such exquisite taste. The pearls will match your gown and set off your neck effectively. You will make a sensation, and Edward will be pleased that others should appreciate his choice."

Still Evelyn had nothing to say. A week before, this munificent present, worth twice her mother's annual income, would have given her keenest pleasure; she loved beautiful things and had always longed to possess a pearl necklace. But now, because of its significance, the gift seemed embarrassing. She had not thought of Cushing since his letter of the morning; she foresaw that he would occupy her thoughts but little during the evening. She was guiltily conscious now, if she had not been before, that in her heart of hearts she was rejoicing at his absence. Her conscience smote her; for Evelyn, as we have seen, had been carefully reared and possessed fine intuitions. She had shaken off for the day her bonds. This collar, though of jewels, would be the badge of her servitude, which already she was finding irksome. It ought to be the token of her loyalty, but it was not; to wear it otherwise was disloyal.

"Must I wear it, mother?" she asked, with palpable reluctance. "Are we rich enough for me to wear such an ornament without making talk? People would wonder where I got it."

"Don't be absurd, Evelyn. Your engagement will be announced in a few days, when any vulgar curiosity about your affairs, if there should be any, will be fully satisfied. It was Edward's wish and mine to let our friends know of the engagement tonight, had he been here. The pearls were in honor of the event."

Evelyn now exulted in Cushing's absence. The evil day would be put off for a little while. Tonight, at least, she would be free. She had read in a newspaper that morning the story of a man who, having been released from prison after serving a long sentence, was allowed half a day's liberty, under surveillance, and then rearrested for an old offence. She felt as this man must have felt. This ball, and the few days for which she could keep Cushing at bay, was her brief hour of freedom.

VII.
THE ANNOUNCEMENT

Simpson brought the carriage around at nine o'clock, and the ladies arrived at Mrs. Archer's at the hour best calculated for an effective entrance. Mrs. Thayer was anxious that Evelyn, on the eve of her promotion, should make an impression which would justify Cushing's choice. They arrived at a moment when the rooms were comfortably full and yet not so crowded as to hide the individual in the mass. There was still room enough for a beautiful or well-gowned woman to turn around so that she might be studied by the appreciative eyes as a complete picture as well as in detail. Another reason why Mrs. Thayer was anxious that Evelyn should shine was that she had determined upon a coup d'état this evening which should force her daughter's hand. There could be no better occasion upon which to announce the engagement, and she intended that it should be done before the reception was over. She knew that Cushing was willing and had looked forward to the event. It would have been better to have him there, but his presence was not indispensable. Alice was not without sympathy with Evelyn's hesitation to name her wedding day, thereby yielding the right to exercise the power which she had only just discovered herself to possess. She would not however, deprive Evelyn of one more evening of the adulation due to a beautiful debutante. Toward the close of the evening she would tell Mrs. Archer and few others, in confidence, and the news would spread rapidly enough.

They had no sooner entered the ballroom than Mr. Rice came forward with beaming alacrity. For a moment he was convinced that he had met his fate. Miss Thayer should be his future wife, Mrs. Thayer his future mother-in-law.

"Miss Thayer, you don't really know, don't you know—you could n't really appreciate how charming you are tonight!"

Alice came in for her share of compliments.

"And really, Mrs. Thayer, a stranger would certainly take you for Miss Evelyn's sister, don't you know. You grow younger every day."

Mrs. Thayer received this amiable platitude with smiling complacency. Mr. Rice was a good young man, if not a very deep one; if it were not for Edward, he would make a nice husband for Evelyn.

"It was so good of both of you to look at my plans and to like them. I am delighted. How many dances may I have?"

He took both their cards, and made a judicious selection from each, for Mrs. Thayer was only less fond of dancing than her daughter. Even as he wrote his old instinct of prudence awoke; it would be well for him to look before he leaped. The numbers he chose upon Evelyn's list were far enough apart to enable him to test his first impression. If it should outlast the evening, he would make up his mind and propose to her in the near future.

The reception was largely attended. Few people in Boston would have felt inclined to slight an invitation from Mrs. Archer at any time; and public curiosity in regard to the new house had been lively enough to bring society out early and in great force.

Mr. Rice enjoyed his monopoly only a moment, for the two ladies were soon surrounded. Several ladies spoke to Mrs. Thayer, and Evelyn soon became the center of a group of young men, all clamorous for dances. A white-haired gentleman with a distinguished face and a very erect bearing, came up to Mrs. Thayer and put out his hand.

"My dear Mrs. Thayer," he said, "I'm sure you're well, unless your looks belie you. And your charming daughter is a picture of youth triumphant. She should be painted somewhere in the Public Library—Sargent or Abbey should perpetuate her in a fresco, so that she might be preserved as an edition de luxe of one of nature's masterpieces."

"Ah, Mr. Sterling, she will hear you, and you will spoil her."

Mr. Sterling was a leading architect, whose talent had found expression, during a generation past, in the solid and dignified style which had preceded the later and more artistic development of domestic and business architecture. He had been associated with Henry Thayer in the enterprise which had brought fortune to them both and to Cushing. Mr. Sterling had shared Thayer's disaster, but had long since retrieved his losses and had stood for many years at the head of his profession.

"Yes indeed," he sighed, "if I were thirty years younger, and single, I would give those boys a hard run."

Mrs. Thayer understood the sigh. A fervent admirer of beauty, Mr. Sterling had married for her money, a plain and stupid woman. He had been justly punished for his crime against his finer self. He found an artist's pleasure in beauty and health. His two daughters were replicas of their mother. His wife had long been querulous, while her fortune had been swallowed up in an unfortunate speculation.

Mrs. Thayer's ripened beauty and well-known conversational charm attracted gentlemen of maturer mind than those who flocked about Evelyn. Among those who sought her were a famous litterateur, who had written many delightful books and from the lecture platform had charmed many a cultivated audience with his patriotic reminiscences of the war period; and a certain venerable Unitarian minister whose cheerful optimism and charming character made him popular alike among orthodox and heterodox—if any one in Boston could draw the line between the two. Among those to whom she was introduced was a famous American sculptor, resident in Paris, but present in the city for the installation of a monument to a local hero, whose fame, of national scope, would be perpetuated by a work of art no less noble than the life and death of him in whose honor it was erected. In the company were other celebrities, musical, artistic or literary: the stately daughter of a famous poet; a living bard of the lesser magnitude; a venerable philanthropist, who had devoted her life to the cause of her downtrodden sex, divided in opinion as to whether they are downtrodden or not;— certainly they were queens and princesses on this occasion, and it is questionable whether one of them would have yielded her crown for the right to vote.

These were the intellectual stars. They shone brilliantly in conversation, but went into partial eclipse when the dancing began. This part of the evening belonged to the hosts of wealth and fashion, of youth and beauty, who found in pleasure an enjoyment as keen as intellectual delights; who looked forward and not back, and who saw in the brilliant scene around them, nothing to envy or to regret; it was but the threshold of glorious life.

When Evelyn's program was half-full she began to look around restlessly, but her face lit up when she saw Manson coming across the room, with his eyes fixed eagerly upon her.

"Am I too late?" he asked, making his way to her side. "I have been talking architecture to a patron—not from choice, but because I could n't escape—and I finally ran away in sheer desperation, for I had seen you coming up the stairs."

He took possession of Evelyn's card, and without a word of protest, filled up most of the remaining spaces.

"I want to see as much of you as possible," he murmured.

The other young men, perceiving Evelyn's immediate absorption in the newcomer, whose tall, stalwart figure towered above them all, had moved away disconsolate, and left them for a moment alone.

"I have thought of scarcely anything else since I saw you yesterday," he went on, in a low voice. "You have filled my mind ever since your face first dawned upon me the other night at the opera."

"And you have nearly filled my program," returned Evelyn, with outward flippancy, but inward delight. Her lover's boldness of the day before had started her, but the effect of the shock had already worn off, and while she had meant to be on her guard and keep him at his distance, she already felt herself yielding to the compelling power of his eye. The vibrations of his voice swept through her in delicious little waves of feeling. This night, she reasoned recklessly, she was free; her appearance was a marked success; she would enjoy herself without stint.

A half hour later, Mrs. Thayer had just finished a waltz with Mr. Rice, who had been sounding her as a possible mother-in-law when they were joined by old Mr. Sterling, who had been wandering aimlessly about.

"Mrs. Thayer," he inquired, "who is that unusually big and unusually handsome young man who is dancing with your beautiful daughter? I never saw a more perfectly mated couple."

"I guess it's Manson," returned Rice. "I saw them waltzing together in the other room."

"I must go to her a minute, if you gentlemen will excuse me," said Mrs. Thayer anxiously. She had no desire that Evelyn's name should be coupled with Manson's, or that either her daughter or the young man should discover how admirably they were matched. The gentlemen simultaneously offered to accompany her.

"No, thank you, I wish to speak to her alone."

"Manson is a very clever fellow, Mr. Sterling," said Rice, when they were left together, "quite a genius, in fact. He is designing a house for me. He has new ideas, and an unerring taste."

"Where did he come from?" asked the old gentleman, with interest.

"Dropped from the skies, I guess. He's not a man of family, is of rather humble origin, and, from his accent, I suspect from somewhere in the South. He's a college man—worked his way through, you know. A little crude, but good stuff at bottom."

"Ah, yes," said Mr. Sterling. "I've heard of him. He was with Wharton and Starr for a while. If you see him, bring him to me; I should like to meet him. I might do him a service."

Mrs. Thayer found Evelyn standing with her hand on Manson's arm, before a mantel in the style of Louis XV., which, it had been whispered among the guests, had once adorned the boudoir of a royal favorite, and had been brought from a French château, at a cost, including the duty, of more than ten thousand dollars. Mrs. Thayer's heart quickened with alarm as she perceived that, while Manson's eye was on the mantel-piece, the beauties of which he seemed to be describing, Evelyn's eyes were blind to everything except Manson's face, upon which they rested with an expression singularly like that of a woman in love—certainly not the expression with which an engaged woman should look upon a man who was not to be her husband.

Mrs. Thayer looked around from Evelyn to speak to some one who had come up behind her. When she looked back Evelyn and Manson had disappeared. As soon as Mrs. Thayer could get rid of her interlocutor she went in search of them.

Manson had suggested that they look through the house; Evelyn assented readily. They had inspected several beautiful rooms when they came upon Mrs. Thayer.

"I was wondering what had become of you, Evelyn," she said with an expression of relief still tinctured with anxiety, "I've been looking for you everywhere."

"Mr. Manson has been showing me the house," returned Evelyn, "and explaining everything so beautifully! It's perfectly lovely; there's nothing like it in Boston. Come along with us, mamma; you'll find no better guide."

"Yes, Mrs. Thayer, do join our class in Louis Quinze decorations," added Manson, gallantly supporting Evelyn's volubility. "Miss Thayer is appreciative, but a larger audience may inspire me to greater efforts. It's fine—magnificent! Mrs. Archer has covered herself with glory."

"I think you had better come with me, Evelyn," said her mother.

"Oh no, mamma," said Evelyn, moving forward, "we really must finish. Come along with us. The dancing will commence in half an hour, and we must hurry in order to get through."

Evelyn moved off with a determination that surprised her mother, and caused that lady to shut her lips tightly, while an unaccustomed gleam shone in her eye. Nevertheless she followed with outward calmness, determined that she would at least keep her eye on Evelyn while with this very enterprising young man. It was quite time, she reasoned, that Evelyn's engagement was announced, and the date of her marriage set. Marriage was a very effective germicide for incipient flirtations.

When the dancing began again, Evelyn was fully occupied for an hour, during which she danced with Manson only once. She saw him watching her disconsolately through the wide doorway, in conversation, in the next room with old Mr. Sterling, to whom Rice had presented him, and now and then her eyes met his in a flash of sympathy. A little later there was a lancers in which she and Mr. Rice stood up opposite Manson and another young woman. The touch of his hand in the movements of the dance, and the gleam of his eye, which never seemed to leave her face, relieved the tedium of the delay which must elapse until their next round dance together.

"Old Mr. Sterling has taken quite a fancy to Manson," said Rice during one of their pauses. "It would be a great thing for Manson if the old gentleman would take him into partnership."

Evelyn had always liked Mr. Sterling, who often called at the house and had paid her many pretty compliments. She determined that upon the first opportunity she would encourage him to speak of Manson, and use her influence in the young architect's favor. She had already learned that praise from red lips had greater weight even with grey heads. Her instincts were already aroused for Manson's advancement.

There was an intermission, and Evelyn went down to supper with an elderly millionaire whom Mrs. Thayer had deftly produced at the right moment. Since Evelyn was to marry a man of middle age, her position required that she seem not too young. To be seen with elderly men would aid in taking off the edge of any incongruity which shallow people might affect to discover in her union with a man more than old enough to be her father.

There was a waltz, a long delicious, dreamy waltz, in which Evelyn felt herself floating around the room in a pair of strong arms to whose guidance she yielded herself with a delicious abandonment. She wondered where this Kentucky mountaineer had learned to dance so divinely. Perhaps the gift was inspiration, like his eye for beauty his frank and joyous face, and the shrewdness which had found so many opportunities for their meeting within two days of acquaintance. Manson was in fact, merely keeping good time, and that with conscious effort; but Evelyn was in a mood to idealize whatever he might say or do.

She danced with him once more, a little later, after there was an improvised German, in which he secured her for a partner. When they were ordered to their seats at the end of the first figure Manson said:—

"It's awfully warm! Let's look for a cool place until our turn comes again. Have you seen the conservatory? It is a dream of beauty."

"No. Show it to me."

They left the brilliant ballroom and were soon amid the cool green foliage of the orangery, to which a tropical grove seemed to have been bodily transplanted. Here and there a fountain played a delicate spray, and incandescent lights in vari-colored globes, skilfully disposed among the foliage, lent to the scene a fairy-like fascination. Evelyn was quite willing to leave the throbbing ballroom behind and, leaning upon Manson's arm, to wander by his side in the shaded coolness of this leafy retreat, which was the nearest to romantic woodland glade, which the exigences of city life would permit.

Mrs. Thayer had missed her daughter again. Evelyn had never before behaved in so unaccountable a manner. The time had come, in Mrs. Thayer's opinion, to inform Mrs. Archer of Evelyn's engagement. Moving about the rooms in search of her daughter, she met Mr. Rice.

"Have you seen Evelyn?" she asked.

"Miss Thayer? She was dancing with Manson in the German a moment ago," he said somewhat ruefully. "I've looked for her several times myself, but Manson doesn't give any other fellow a show."

Rice was already beginning to doubt whether Evelyn would quite suit him. If the marked attentions of a wealthy young man were ignored for those of a penniless architect, query: Was a young woman with so little sense of proportion a fit wife for such wealthy young man? He was inclined to feel doubtful upon the subject. Miss Thayer was stunningly beautiful, but marriage was a serious step, which should not be taken without due and careful deliberation.

Mrs. Thayer could not find her among the dancers, nor was Manson anywhere visible. A hasty tour of the main rooms showing no trace of them, she turned her footsteps toward the conservatory.

"I wonder I had n't thought of it before," she murmured.

She passed several couples. Gay laughter had characterized the conversation of the ballroom. The air here was full of sentiment. Steps were slow, tones were low. Mrs. Thayer had seen nothing of Evelyn, and was about to retrace her steps when a gleam of white from behind a clump of palms caught her eye. As she approached, a low murmur of voices reached her ear—a male voice, deep, passionate, subdued—the other Evelyn's voice.

Mrs. Thayer drew nearer noiselessly. No uncomfortable thought of anything surreptitious deterred her. It was her duty to watch over Evelyn, to protect her from this sudden rebellion of a nature supposed to be disciplined. It was her duty and her privilege to guard her daughter jealously for her friend; to give her to Edward Cushing, since she would not bring him passionate love, with a clean white mind, upon which to write his name. Otherwise she would not be paying their debt, or would be paying it in spurious coin, and merely adding to its total.

So softly had she approached, so completely absorbed were Evelyn and Manson, that Mrs. Thayer by reaching her hand through the leafy screen between them, could have touched them with her fan. Evelyn was speaking.

"I am engaged," she said, "I ought not to listen to you; it is not right."

"It might not be right if you loved him," declared Manson, "but you do not. You love *me*—believe me, child, I know love when I see it, and I don't misread your eyes—and you do not deny it!"

Evelyn did not deny it and silence was confession. His arm sought her waist. Mrs. Thayer, fascinated, stood looking at them. It recalled long dormant memories of the time, many years before, when she had been wooed by a strong man, to whom she had given her young heart.

"I am coming to see you," he said, "and make you break off this engagement. It is a sin to sell you to an old man for his money. I shall come tomorrow."

"But my mother—"

"Your mother must yield. She has no right to force you. No, Evelyn, you are mine; I seal our betrothal with this kiss."

Mrs. Thayer awoke to a sense of her own remissness. She should have interrupted them sooner; she would have given much to have prevented this act, but was too late, for their lips had met, and at their first touch Evelyn's arms, in an abandonment of love, had sought his neck, ere Mrs. Thayer could step backward—it was no part of her plan to create a scene or give Manson a chance to speak—and approach them from the front.

"Evelyn!" she called, sharply, but softly, "Evelyn!"

"Yes, mamma! is that you?"

"Oh, you are here! I've been looking everywhere for you. It is late; we must be getting ready to go."

Evelyn showed no sign of embarrassment, except a slight start. Women are more adept than men at concealment, it is an art of defense, a resource of the weak. Manson, who by his own argument had nothing to be ashamed of, had flushed furiously. "Is it so late?" he stammered.

Mrs. Thayer paid not the slightest attention to his question, but ignoring his presence completely, took Evelyn by the arm and led her away. Manson followed them feeling like a schoolboy caught in some breach of the rules. It was easy to sneer at convention from a safe distance. It was more difficult to brave its behests in one of its own temples, in the presence of the Brahmins who waited upon its altars.

Evelyn's mood was more complex. The firm but gentle authority that had guided her life was strained almost to breaking. Had this rebellious mood been less novel, or had Manson spoken out, upon her mother's appearance, she would have been equal to declaring then and there that she would not marry Cushing; that she would not sacrifice her youth to an old man's vanity and selfishness for the benefit of her family; that she was entitled to live her own life in her own way; that she would marry no man that she did not love; that she had accepted Cushing in ignorance of what love was, but that her eyes had been opened, and she must be freed from her promise. Even now she might speak! But they had left the quiet corner and the air was filled with the throbbing of the music, and gay laughter, and the hum of conversation. It was not time or place for confidences, or disputes, or anything but smiling lips, though hearts might be sore. Her mother's constrained smile did not deceive her. She foresaw that she would not win her liberty without a struggle, from which, now that the support of Manson's presence was removed she shrank in dismay. His presence might have nerved her to anything; without it, she felt her courage oozing from her fingertips.

Mrs. Thayer led Evelyn directly to Mrs. Archer whom they were fortunate enough to find alone for a moment.

"Well, my dear," said that lady, graciously tapping Evelyn on the arm with her fan, "you have been the belle of the ball. I am quite proud of you. Have you enjoyed yourself?"

"Very much indeed, Mrs. Archer. I've had a delightful evening."

There was a touch of preoccupation in her manner, which Mrs. Archer noticed with her keen eyes. Mrs. Thayer, equally observant, perceived Mrs. Archer's questioning look. There could be no more appropriate occasion to crush Mr. Manson's pretensions, to nip Evelyn's folly in the bud, and to surround her engagement with the social safeguards which no properly reared young woman would dare to transgress.

"Yes, Mrs. Archer," she said, "Evelyn has enjoyed the evening as much as she could, in view of her disappointment."

"Her disappointment?" said Mrs. Archer, lifting her eyebrows.

Evelyn's cheek paled with apprehension. Under her mother's soft tones she heard the challenge to combat, and saw in her eyes, beneath the smile of maternal pride assumed for Mrs. Archer's benefit, the prospect of impending battle.

"Yes, her very great disappointment. Evelyn is engaged to Mr. Cushing, and he had expected to be here tonight; but was called away to New York suddenly."

Evelyn was crushed; her frail castle of defense had collapsed at the first onslaught. Mrs. Thayer observed her confusion and covered it, for it was no part of her plan to embarrass Evelyn;—to commit her was sufficient. This accomplished, she would help Evelyn to bear gracefully the honors from which she shrank. She had no thought but for the girl's welfare; it was inconceivable that Evelyn should not see that her happiness was bound up in this marriage.

"It was a deep disappointment to both of them," she went on smoothly. "Evelyn and he had thought it would be so beautiful to have the announcement made at your reception, in your beautiful house! And even now, though Edward is away, Evelyn thinks she ought to tell you, first of all, as our dearest friend."

"My darling child," exclaimed the lady with genuine enthusiasm, drawing Evelyn toward her and kissing her impulsively. "I am so glad! Edward is, as you know, one of my most intimate friends. I've always told him that he'd never be happy until he was married and settled. It is a duty he owes to himself, to his name, to society. The Cushings are an old family, with a fine history; it would be a sin to let them die out—there are so few old families who can keep their heads above water. He could not have made a finer choice, my dear, and I hope you will be very happy."

Mrs. Archer had always liked Mrs. Thayer, whose fight for position against narrow means she had admired and aided. She now felt for her a very considerable enhancement of respect. To have secured Edward Cushing as a husband for a portionless daughter was a decided social triumph. It would elevate Alice Thayer immensely, in the estimation of the body of matrons with marriageable daughters. For in society, as elsewhere, success is the test of merit; and envy, the vice of small souls, is a tribute paid to success. Mrs. Archer, too, would reap the reward of merit: as patroness of Mrs. Thayer and her daughter, her social refulgence, already dazzling, would be heightened by an additional ray.

Evelyn, her heart cold as ice, forced the smile demanded by the occasion. Her role required her to say but little, and she said no more than necessary, leaving her mother to answer or to parry the questions which naturally followed so important an announcement. She foresaw an uncomfortable interview with her mother, and braced herself for the inevitable.

Mrs. Thayer would have stayed to await the spread of the announcement and to receive congratulations, but Edward was not present to share them; Evelyn was palpably over-wrought, and in no condition to receive them; while the presence of Manson in the house made the situation all too critical. They took their departure quietly, followed by the hearty felicitations of Mrs. Archer, who had imparted the news to her intimate friends before the rumble of Mrs. Thayer's carriage wheels had died away in the distance.

VIII.
PUTTING ON THE SCREWS

Evelyn's expectations were fully met. Her only point of doubt had been whether her mother would begin her lecture at once or wait until they had reached home. Evelyn hoped she might begin immediately, and get through with it.

Mrs. Thayer did nothing of the kind. She had no intention of having the force of what she might say spoiled by the clatter of the horses' hoofs or the swaying of the carriage, or interrupted by their arrival at the house. She sat back in her seat in silence more eloquent than speech and uttered not a word until they reached home.

Leonie had sat up for the ladies, and let them into the house. As soon as she had assisted them to undress, Mrs. Thayer excused her.

"There, Leonie, you may go to bed now. We've kept you up a long time, but we'll all sleep late in the morning. Good night."

Leonie had guessed, from Evelyn's silence and Mrs. Thayer's air of repressed excitement, that there was something unusual between mother and daughter. She appreciated perfectly that Thayer desired to get rid of her. This only strengthened Leonie's curiosity to hear what might be said. She bade the ladies good night, walked somewhat noisily to her own room, which was in the rear of the same floor where the ladies slept, shut her door audibly, opening it at the same instant, and then clicking the key in the lock as though she had fastened the door. She then took off her shoes, put out the light, opened the door wider and stood listening closely for what she might hear.

Mrs. Thayer, having taken down her hair and slipped on a dressing gown, went into her daughter's room. Evelyn was in similar undress, awaiting the attack.

"Evelyn Thayer," said Mrs. Thayer, in clear incisive tones, "I am utterly astonished at your conduct tonight."

Evelyn made no reply. What could she say? Her mother continued in the impressive manner of a judge passing sentence upon a convicted criminal:—

"For the past few days you have acted so unmaidenly, so differently from what have been expected of your training, from what you have always seemed to be, that I don't know what to think of you,—I really do not."

"Why, mamma!" Evelyn exclaimed, weakly, "I—I don't know what you are talking about."

"Your conduct has been disgraceful; there is no other word to describe it. I saw Mr. Manson kiss you in the conservatory, and saw you shamelessly put your arms around his neck."

Evelyn's cheeks flamed, and she cowered in the armchair where she had taken her seat. She had not known until now that her mother had seen so much;—she had evidently witnessed the whole scene in the conservatory.

"You are bound by your promise," Mrs. Thayer went on mercilessly, "to the noblest and best of men. He has committed his honor into your hands, and yet with that sacred charge to guard, you act in a manner which even a serving maid would consider improper. You have actually been throwing yourself at this underbred young man's head."

"Oh, mamma!" exclaimed Evelyn, stung to the quick, "you speak as though I were married already! And I am not; I am still mistress of my own person. When you saw us in the conservatory my engagement was not even announced— and it was not I that announced it!"

"You had given your word! You were as good as married: you are bound in honor, which does not depend upon publicity. To help you to do your duty, I took pains to make your engagement known. To marry Edward Cushing ought to make you the happiest woman in Boston; there is not an unengaged girl at Mrs. Archer's tonight who would not be flattered by his choice, and few would refuse him."

"I wish," said Evelyn, desperately, "that he had asked one of them—any one of them—or all of them—and not me!"

"Be silent, ungrateful girl! Do you know where Edward is at this moment? He is taking care of your brother, Wentworth, who has again disgraced himself, and who, but for Edward, might long ago have brought us to shame. While you are flirting brazenly with another man, your future husband is spending his time and sacrificing his comfort for your sake."

Evelyn's defiance evaporated immediately. She loved her brother deeply. In spite of his faults they had been very dear to each other.

"Oh, mamma, he is good, if only he would n't—if only he did n't want to marry me!"

Leonie had been listening with breathless curiosity. Mrs. Thayer's voice had been at first low, and Leonie had only been able to make out that her mistress was scolding Miss Evelyn about a man. It was as much as her place was worth to be caught eavesdropping, for Mrs. Thayer had found fault with her several times of late; but curiosity overcame discretion, and she left her room and stepped softly down the hall to where she could hear more distinctly.

"Listen, Evelyn," continued Mrs. Thayer, more kindly. "I must tell you what I have never yet whispered to a living soul. All that you have and are you owe to Edward Cushing,—the food you have eaten, the clothes you have worn, your shelter, your education, your social position—you owe it all to Edward Cushing."

Evelyn uttered a cry of astonishment. "But my father's estate!"

"Your father's estate was a dream, an invention of Edward Cushing's, set up as a screen for his benevolence and a protection to my pride. Your father failed disastrously. Edward Cushing was named as his executor. Had he presented against the estate notes of your father's for money borrowed of himself, we should have been obliged to live on the charity of relatives, or to work for our living."

"Oh, how could you let him do such a thing!" exclaimed Evelyn. "It does n't seem like you! You are lecturing me on the point of honor. It would have been more—honorable to work than to live on his bounty. I would rather have taught school or—given music lessons," she concluded somewhat lamely.

"You would not have had the opportunity to teach! You would much more likely have been a sewing-girl, or a saleswoman or a manicure. I should n't have been able to give you an education. As to honor—I did not suspect, for two full years, that the 'estate' that your father left was given to us outright by Edward Cushing. True, it was only a small part of what your father had been the occasion of his acquiring; but we had no claim upon it. If he had continued to follow your father's advice, he would have been as poor as we!"

Mrs. Thayer had felt the more than implied reproach of Evelyn's attitude. She could not confess her own weakness to Evelyn, and yet she was anxious to justify herself.

"When I discovered the truth," she went on almost pleadingly, "it would have been difficult to return the gift, and equally difficult to acknowledge it. Edward does not suspect that I know his carefully guarded secret. Since you have grown up, I have hoped to repay, through you, who have been their joint beneficiary, these heaped-up gifts. Evelyn, if you do not marry Edward, I shall never get over it—I should feel ashamed and humiliated all my life."

Evelyn listened as though almost stupefied by this revelation. Duty commanded gratitude and sacrifice. Youth and love resented the burden of an obligation imposed without her knowledge or consent. Her mother went on.

"It has been very hard, Evelyn, to live on his bounty all these years, with a heart full of gratitude, and yet for the sake of one's self-respect, and for one's children's sake, not to be able to express it. Were you to add to this burden by disappointing and wounding our benefactor, I should never get over the disgrace—I could never hold up my head again. We could not expect to retain Edward's friendship, or the countenance of his friends. Mrs. Archer, to whom I owe more than I could ever tell you, Evelyn, would cut us dead. Edward is the sole barrier between your brother, your poor, weak brother and ruin, and without knowing it, is risking his own happiness to save him. When this Mr. Manson came to our box the other night—Edward's box!—Edward was at the telephone, inquiring about Wentworth, who had gone to New York with that—creature. And tonight when you went to this ball in Edward's carriage, wearing his jewels, carrying his flowers, to let this impudent young man make love to you, Edward was trying to save your brother and to protect our good name. To throw him over for another would be the basest ingratitude. You should marry him, quickly, gratefully; and thank God that he gave you such a man for a husband."

The stress of the conflicting emotions of the evening had been too much for Evelyn. She burst into a passion of tears.

"There, there, dear," said her mother, softening still more, "calm yourself. You are going to do the right thing, and the honorable thing, and marry Edward, and be happy, and make him happy. I'll get the sal volatile—it's in my room."

Mrs. Thayer's room was across the hall. Leonie fled incontinently and escaped discovery. She had not heard everything, and some things not distinctly, but she had learned that Mr. Cushing had been keeping the family. She had suspected as much for a long time, and now she knew it.

"Ladies think they're awful smart," she soliloquized between the sheets, "but they're not too smart but their maids gets next to 'em. To think of it—all these years the mother!—an' now he's goin' to marry Miss Evelyn! Life in this house is goin' to be interestin' from now on. I wonder who the young man is that Miss Evelyn's been makin' love to? My, if Mr. Cushing knew!"

Mrs. Thayer's method of treatment, by which she had at first overwhelmed Evelyn with reproaches, and had then appealed to her finer emotions, seemed entirely efficacious. Evelyn's own pride awoke. If by marriage with her guardian she could repay the debt which burdened them, she would drive from her heart this sudden love, this delight to which she had just awakened. It had possessed some of the bitter sweetness of a forbidden thing. She could now look forward to the exquisite suffering of the martyr; it would be some compensation. To Evelyn all violent emotions were new, and pain would be only less interesting than pleasure; she was sane and vigorous, and could endure a great deal of both and be none the worse for either. Life is so organized that pleasure exceeds pain, but pain is sometimes good for discipline.

With a heavy heart she sat down to her desk next morning and wrote a brief, formal note to Mr. Manson in which she regretted that her mother and she would not be able to receive him that evening, and that their engagements would probably occupy all their time for several weeks.

In the humility of her surrender she showed this note to her mother. Mrs. Thayer's first impulse was to tell her not to send it; she doubted whether Manson would call. If so, he could be told that they were not at home, and the rebuff would be sufficient. On second thoughts she let it go. It would encourage Evelyn in her new and better mood, and would terminate the affair conclusively. She kissed her daughter, and thanked her, and praised her.

Evelyn went out and mailed the letter at the box upon the corner. Her hand trembled as she dropped it in, but she returned to the house with an easier conscience—with more, indeed. She felt something of the glow of self-esteem which follows an act of renunciation.

IX.

EVELYN'S MARRIAGE

Mr. Cushing came at ten o'clock next morning, with Wentworth, pale and nerveless, but submissive and repentant. They had arrived by the midnight train, and Cushing had kept Wentworth at his own house until morning. Wentworth sought his own room, after his mother had kissed and embraced him. Evelyn had not yet appeared, so Cushing was left alone with Mrs. Thayer. He gave her the details of his experience with Wentworth. As they suspected, there had been a touch of his former trouble. The moral weakness had reacted upon the physical, more strongly than before. The boy would require careful handling, as the difficulty was likely to increase with each recurrence.

"I've thrashed it out with him," said Cushing. "He confesses his faults and appreciates the danger. If he can harness self-restraint to good resolutions, we may hope for the best."

"Our hope lies in you, Edward," said Mrs. Thayer. "I could do nothing alone with Wentworth. I can never repay what you have done for me and mine."

He supposed her more ignorant than she was of his benefactions. Her gratitude was therefore all the more touching.

"My dear Alice," he replied amiably, "he is the son of my dead friend, and of you, and he is Evelyn's brother. So far as lies in my power to influence it, I charge myself with his future."

"You are too good to us," she replied, with a qualm of conscience at the mention of Evelyn's name. "No, I can never repay you."

"You owe me nothing Alice, unless it be reproaches. Had I looked after Henry's son as I promised him, Wentworth might never have gone astray. If you have felt yourself under any debt to me for a promise so poorly kept, you have more than made it good in giving me your daughter. I sometimes tremble, Alice, at the thought that her fresh young beauty, her virgin heart, as yet unstirred by the thought of any other man, are to be entrusted to me. And yet so strong is my love for her that I do not fear, but welcome the responsibility. Bring her to me Alice. I yearn for her; I must take her to my home. She must fix our wedding day!"

A twinge of remorse contracted Mrs. Thayer's heart at the thought that Evelyn did not merit the supreme confidence reposed in her by this honorable gentleman. Yet Alice could not tell him of it. But she took comfort in the thought that Evelyn's infatuation for the young architect was but a fleeting fancy, which would be forgotten in the excitement of the wedding preparations.

"She is not very well, today," replied Mrs. Thayer. "She woke up this morning with a violent headache."

"Ah, poor child, I had not thought! My love is selfish; I was considering only myself. Of course the dear girl is fatigued after her night of pleasure. I can go away and come again, in the afternoon."

"Oh, no, she is up and dressed, and has breakfasted. She is already better; it was merely the reaction from the excitement of last night."

"I hope she enjoyed herself," murmured Cushing with a smile.

"She could not help it. She had everything to make her happy, except your presence. Your flowers were splendid—thank you for my own as well, and for the carriage—and the pearls were superb. Oh, Edward, you overwhelm us."

"It is nothing, Alice; I love her and I am going to give her all I possess, with a single encumbrance—myself."

"I told Mrs. Archer of the engagement. I was sure you would not mind."

"Mind? I would have published it in the newspaper a month ago, had I been permitted. I hope all Boston knows it by now, and I should like the announcement of the marriage to follow close upon the heels of the other. If you are sure that she can stand it I should like to see her for a moment."

Mrs. Thayer went to fetch her daughter. Evelyn was seated in her own room, pale and *distrait*, dreading the interview, which she knew was imminent. Having resigned herself to the inevitable, there was no further hope of escape, and therefore no reason for putting off the evil day. Since she must marry Cushing, the sooner she should marry him the better; she could not then be tempted by the face or voice of the other. She knew she did not love Cushing as instinct taught her that a woman should love her husband. Surely so old and so wise a man as he must have divined as much. If so, and he still insisted, it was his own act. Once married, she would do her duty, so far as in her lay; more she could not do. He might command her person; she might not be able to control her own heart.

"Evelyn," said her mother gently but firmly, "Edward is here and wishes to see you. He is delighted that we told Mrs. Archer; and he wants to thank you for making the engagement known. Be kind to him, Evelyn—we owe him so much. Our poor boy—'As Evelyn's brother,' he said, 'I charge myself with his future.'"

Evelyn's feet seemed made of lead as she followed her mother to the reception room. Cushing greeted her warmly, with a decorous kiss upon the cheek which invoked a vivid memory. It was indeed scarcely an act of memory to recall Manson's ardent caress; she seemed still to feel his lips upon her own, and was glad that Cushing's kiss had sought her cheek; upon her lips it would have seemed like sacrilege, at least so soon.

"But my dear child," her lover said, holding her arm's length and looking solicitously at her pale cheeks and downcast eyes, "you are not well. The excitement of last evening was too much for you. We must not let your roses fade. An ocean voyage will make them bloom, Evelyn, and fix their bloom permanently—a long, leisurely voyage—London and the Abbey; Paris and the Louvre—and the Bon Marché; the Alps, Rome Venice, Athens—the storied Nile—would you not like the trip, Evelyn?"

It had been the dream of her life, and now that it was within her reach, and thrust upon her, it seemed a punishment instead of a pleasure.

"It would be very beautiful," she said bravely.

"A month from now," he said, "in July would be an excellent time to start. Will you not take the trip with me, dear Evelyn?"

"If you wish it," she whispered with an effort; after which she thanked him for the flowers and the pearls.

"They belonged to my mother," he told her. "they were in several pieces, but I had them made into a necklace by Tiffany, for you. They have never been worn except by the two women whom I have loved the best."

Mrs. Thayer came in; she had not wished to intrude, but was anxious as to how Evelyn might act. She had paved the way for her as well as she could, and was relieved when Cushing spoke.

"Alice," he cried, "congratulate me, I am the happiest man alive. In one month Evelyn and I will start together for Europe."

Alice folded her daughter in a warm embrace, which subtly conveyed to Evelyn her mother's thanks. Then she gave both her hands to Cushing, strong and shapely hands, which trembled ever so slightly.

"I too am happy," she declared and believed it. "The time is short, but—"

"It seems very long, Alice. Can we not shorten it?"

"It is very short. There are things to be done, preparations to be made. Your wife must come to you clothed suitably for your wife's station."

"Were I a king and she a beggar maid, I would take her just the same. As you will then; a month—but no longer. The days will be long between now and then."

The preparations for the wedding went forward rapidly, as such things always do where there is will and energy, and the tradesmen, milliners and dressmakers are complaisant, as they always are when there is plenty of money. Mrs. Thayer spared no expense to give her daughter a handsome outfit. She was spending Edward's money nor would she need so much when Evelyn was provided for. Cushing engaged a suite on the best steamer sailing at the end of the month, and arranged his affairs for a long absence.

For several days after the announcement of her engagement, Evelyn remained at home, conscientiously avoiding any opportunity to meet Manson. She did not wish to see him. She had finally given him up; and yet she dreaded the prospect of meeting him somewhere, casually, alone, where

she could not escape. He had exercised, she knew, a dangerous fascination upon her. The sight of his face, the sound of
his voice, drew her with a strength difficult to resist. She felt
that if they met even once, her struggle must all be made
over again, and that if they met often, it might even yet prove
unavailing. She was only so strong as it was vouchsafed for
her to be strong; beyond her powers she could not go, hence
the prudent desire to avoid temptation.

Manson, on the other hand, had not given up hope. True
to his theory that no woman was bound until the final vows
were spoken, and that then the heart should have the right of
way, he did not relinquish his suit, but accepted obstacles as a
part of courtship which merely rendered it more exciting.
After several fruitless attempts to meet Evelyn, during which
he called twice at the house and was told that the ladies were
not at home, he had recourse to letter-writing. But Mrs. Thayer
was vigilant and experienced. Leonie had strict orders to
bring her the mail. Suspecting their source, she opened the
first of Manson's letters. Her action was against the law, but
quite, she argued, in the line of her duty. The letter remained
unanswered. The half dozen in the same hand that followed
were returned unopened.

Manson firmly believed that Evelyn could not have
remained unmoved by his letters, and suspected that they had
never reached her hands. He was a young man of resources.
If Miss Thayer was not under lock and key there must be
some way of reaching her. He took the necessary steps to get
speech with Leonie. By arguments that were convincing to a

romantic and mercenary nature, he converted Leonie to his cause, and through her conveyed a letter to Evelyn's own hand.

The answer was brief, incoherent and unconvincing, marked indeed by the hesitation which invites attack. Manson smiled and wrote another letter; and then another and then one every day, whether he received a reply or not. Meanwhile he sent one through the mails occasionally, which was always promptly returned.

Evelyn's trousseau was well nigh completed. The invitations to the wedding had been issued and many handsome presents were pouring in. The ceremony was to take place at Trinity Church, of which the bride and her mother and Cushing, were members.

Cushing came as often as he was permitted—a few minutes at least every day. He sent Evelyn gifts of many kinds,— flowers, jewels, whatever he thought might please her fancy. The autumnal awakening of his heart increased in fervor every day, and he looked forward to long years of happiness.

Evelyn's cheeks, when she met him, burned with feverish glow, the distress signal of an outraged conscience which protested against the surreptitious and futile correspondence in which she was weakly engaged. She had even been disingenuous enough to write notes without date, address, or signature, not out of an overflowing heart that scorned these as immaterial details, but merely by way of precaution. Cushing and Mrs. Thayer attributed her agitation to the excitement of the approaching event. The thought that he had evoked these maidenly flutterings was inexpressibly pleasing to Cushing.

All his doubts and fears vanished, and a rosy future beckoned him to a renewal of his youth. There was nothing, he resolved, that he would not do to make Evelyn happy. He spent much of his time, during the month which he must wait, in making elaborate plans for redecorating and refurnishing his house during their absence, holding frequent private conferences with Mrs. Thayer upon the subject of Evelyn's tastes and preferences, and even arranging with her to supervise the work while they were absent on their wedding tour.

"Of course, Alice," he said, "upon such an occasion, you will make your home with us."

Much as she loved her daughter, Alice declined his offer. That they might be happy was her fervent wish, but to live with them was an ordeal from which she shrank.

"No, Edward," she said, "I do n't think it best. I know you'd like to have me, and after while perhaps I may come, if you still wish it. Evelyn will enjoy her married life much better if I am not too near—at the beginning. Let me, too, retain my—independence"—the word came hard—"a while longer."

"As you please, Alice, as you please! I only wish to make you happy. A suite of rooms shall be fitted up for you, and remain at your disposal. You may occupy it an hour at a time, or a day, or a year, or for life, and you will always be welcome. I have no wish in gaining a wife to lose a friend, so dear and of so long a standing."

He pressed her hand cordially, and went away.

Alice wondered, sadly, why the same words meant such different things in the mouths of different men. One who knew Cushing but slightly, would have wondered why this fervid friendship had not long ago ripened into a more intimate relation. Why it had not, Alice herself did not know;—certainly not from any unwillingness on her part. A certain shyness there had been, a part of her Puritan inheritance,—a certain reticence about her innermost emotions. A warmer, more impulsive woman would in some womanly way, have put her own fate to the test years before, when there had seemed some ground for hope. But even this friendship was precious; and while, for Evelyn's sake, and because Edward wished it, she was willing to give Evelyn into his arms, she had no desire to become a mere appendage to her daughter. She wished this friendship to remain a thing apart; she would indeed rather lose it and retain only the precious memory, than to merge it into the commonplaceness of her new relationship.

Evelyn held out to the last day. On the morning of her wedding day Leonie brought her a letter from Manson. He pleaded eloquently, passionately, for one last word. He had met her four times and he would love her forever. When she went to the altar of marriage, his heart would go to the altar of sacrifice. He did not know if he would care to live, or what desperate step he might take. Surely she would not refuse the condemned one word, one last look. He knew he had no right to ask it—he simply threw himself upon the generosity of a noble heart which he would always remember had for a few brief and glorious moments beat in unison with his own. He wished only to bid her farewell and then he would try to accept his fate. At twelve o'clock he would be at a certain inconspicuous corner in the neighborhood. If she would contrive to pass by there at that hour, it would be his opportunity, for which he would be humbly grateful.

Evelyn was deeply stirred by this letter, which could not have been more skilfully calculated to play upon her overstrained emotions. Her reason taught her that it was unwise to meet him, and that the meeting would be of doubtful propriety. Her heart pleaded that to refuse so slight a thing would be cruel, and that it was better to be kind. Nor was there any danger—there could be no danger; a few words in the open street could do no harm to any one.

A slow drizzling rain set in, toward noon, to mar what had promised to be a perfect day, but was now more in harmony with Evelyn's heavy heart. At five minutes of twelve she slipped on her rubbers, threw a gray rain coat around her, drew a veil over her face and left the house unperceived. She would speak one word to him, one last word, and then hurry back, or she would be missed. The hair dresser would be in attendance at one o'clock.

Manson was waiting at the designated place. He wore no overcoat and carried no umbrella, seemingly oblivious of the slow, chilly look of one who had not slept for several days.

She gave him her hand, and they walked along slowly side by side. At the touch of his fingers she felt the influence of his power over her, sweet but terrible, dangerous but irresistible; every word he uttered served only to strengthen.

They turned off the street into a narrower, quieter thoroughfare, little more indeed, than a paved alley-way. By the time he had broken her heart with his eloquent sorrow, they reached a point where a closed carriage stood waiting, with the door open.

"This is mine," he said, drawing her toward it. "Come with me, Evelyn, for one brief half hour—one last half hour of parting. No one need ever know it."

Evelyn entered the carriage like one entranced; Manson followed her and closed the door.

Evelyn had been gone only a few minutes when Mrs. Thayer missed her. No one knew what had become of the bride. A hurried search of the premises failed to reveal her whereabouts.

"She has doubtless gone out for a breath of fresh air," said her mother. "She will be back soon, for she expects the hairdresser at one."

The hairdresser came before Evelyn, and Mrs. Thayer grew well nigh hysterical with suspense, suspecting some vague evil, fearing at last the worst. At two o'clock, when her nerves were on the ragged edge, a note addressed to her was delivered at the house by a special messenger. Her lips went white as she recognized the handwriting of the superscription, and her hands trembled to such an extent that she tore the envelope open with difficulty.

"Dear Madam:
"Permit me to inform you that your daughter Evelyn and I were married, at one o'clock this afternoon, by Rev. John

W. Smith, of the Clark Street Methodist Church. Evelyn joins me in regrets for the pain and inconvenience this will cause you, but any other course would have caused us still greater suffering. Yours will soon be over, and ours would have lasted for life. I am writing this at the South Station, whence we leave for New York at two o'clock. Try to think as kindly as you can of us until we return to ask your forgiveness in person.

> "Respectfully,
>
> "Hugh Manson."

Mrs. Thayer had read no further than the statement that Evelyn was married, when her overwrought nerves gave way. A doctor was called, who ordered her immediately to bed, and Mr. Cushing was hastily summoned.

There was much hurried telephoning, and many notes were sent out by messengers hastily got together. There was no wedding at Trinity Church, but, instead, a nine days wonder. Mr. Cushing sailed for Europe alone, and scarcely emerged from his stateroom during the voyage.

X.

A SUCCESSFUL MAN

A year slips quietly by, so quietly at times that busy men and women scarcely realize that one-fortieth or more of an average lifetimes is gone. To perfect happiness a year will pass and bring no change, for perfection cannot be improved, and if a change for the worse, it is no longer perfection. To wretchedness there is a similar dead level:—often a year brings no change for the better, except that there is one year less of unhappiness. Life offers most to those whose fate lies between these two extremes; they are not cloyed with happiness nor crushed with misery.

Such had been the lot of more of the actors in this drama, during the year which succeeded Evelyn's choice of a husband. Of them all, Cushing had perhaps suffered for a time most keenly. Not only had his pride been outraged by Evelyn's desertion at the very altar; not only had he been made by the thoughtless a butt of ridicule; not only had he been gibbeted in the daily newspapers as a jilted elderly Adonis and slandered by an atrocious woodcut; not only had he been, even to his friends, an object of a pity dangerously near contempt; but the shock to his affections had been a severe one. He had loved for the first time, with a deep and he had thought an abiding passion. He had been rudely awakened from his dream of happiness. His last state, unfortunately, was worst than his first; the wound healed slowly and left an ugly scar. His faith in woman could have been shaken to its foundations. His attitude toward good women, prior to this melancholy experience, had been less that of the cynical bachelor of forty-five, disillusioned by experience, than that of the *preux chevalier*, who in a more romantic age was willing to give battle for the honor of all women. He had admired and respected them, in varying degrees; and if he had sought no one of them in marriage, it was because the attractions of no single one of them had been strong enough to overcome the restlessness which had sent him wandering about the earth. His admiration for the sex had taken the form of an esthetic penchant for them, rather than an overmastering passion for any one. Many women had called him friend; until he met Evelyn he had wished no woman to call him more. Now he was skeptical even of their friendship, and this cynicism often found reflection in his speech. He remained abroad for nearly a year after Evelyn's marriage, excepting one or two necessary visits to Boston, which he made as short as possible. So deeply had his pride been wounded, that while at home he made no calls, drove about in a closed carriage, and if perchance he met an acquaintance, turned his head away.

Evelyn and her husband had left the city for a brief wedding journey, returning at the end of a week, since Manson could be spared no longer from his office. They had begun housekeeping upon a modest scale in a flat where they had remained ever since.

For several weeks after their marriage Mrs. Thayer had refused to see Evelyn, but natural feeling had at length prevailed and the mother had consented to meet her daughter, and after the first tearful and reproachful interview, had permitted a formal call from Manson. She had been righteously indignant. Her pride too had been injured; her plan of compensation had failed; her triumph had become a rout. The hiss of envy, which she could have borne with equanimity, had become the cackle of ill concealed delight, and mock condolence, or an equally significant silence had replaced the expected congratulations. If she forgave the young people all this it was not solely from maternal love. Alice's own heart was Evelyn's best advocate.

An invitation to Mrs. Thayer to become a part of the new family was not accepted. The relations of the two households, while openly amicable had not yet become quite cordial. Alice had liked Cushing too well to have lived in his house; she liked Manson too little, to reside in his. In her own home she might retain Cushing's friendship, when time should have blunted the edge of his disappointment and soothed his wounded vanity; in Manson's house it was scarcely likely that he would ever set his foot. Then she still had her son to look after.

Since his New York escapade, Wentworth had shown a decided growth in self-control, and in spite of severe temptation had maintained his conduct above reproach. He had been as keenly sensible as Mrs. Thayer herself of the injury done to Cushing's feelings, and of the reflection cast upon the honor of his own family by Evelyn's defection. Certain information which at this juncture Mrs. Thayer had felt constrained to give him, had so appealed to his finer nature that he had thrown himself feverishly into study, in the hope that he might soon be able to assume the support of his mother, and earn the wherewithal to return with interest the capital she had enjoyed so long.

Mrs. Thayer would have been willing after Evelyn's marriage, to give up her handsome flat, to lodge in one or two rooms, and to seek some method of earning her own living. But to do this now was to acknowledge that she had knowingly accepted Cushing's bounty for all the past years. This might lower her in his estimation, and certainly it would not save her pride. The money should be regarded as a loan, of which her son must now assume the obligation. He would be able to discover some way of paying the debt without humiliation to her. Wentworth's conduct had for nearly a year been above reproach. In a month he would graduate. They had friends who might give him some business opportunity, and he would need nothing more. He had reached his majority during the year, thus terminating Cushing's guardianship, from which Evelyn's marriage had already partially released him.

There is an essential element of dependence in the female character, and Mrs. Thayer now pinned her hopes to Wentworth as passionately as she had fixed them upon Evelyn. It would have been hard to give up her position, precarious as it was, and to lose the friends whom she could only hope to retain while she might meet them on a plane of equality. It had always required close management to hold her own. Less income would have rendered it impossible, and her pride would not have permitted her to accept entertainment which she could not return. To her independent spirit, even hampered though it was by the consciousness of her secret dependence, the semblance of equality was an essential of friendship. That this pride could exist alongside of the knowledge of the source of her income was only explainable by the complexity of motives growing out of her relations with their benefactor—the difference of sex— the hope, at first, that she might repay him with her own devotion—then that Evelyn might satisfy the debt—now that her son might lift the burden.

During Cushing's year of absence she had heard from him several times. He had not mentioned Evelyn. Replying, she had tried to express, in guarded language, which should not wound his self-love, her own grief that he should have been so betrayed, in the house of his friends. He had begged her not to speak of the matter. It was no fault of hers. It had profoundly altered his views of life and human nature, but had not at all affected his friendship for her, Alice, a friendship which had stood the test of time. He hoped that Wentworth was doing well, and wished to be kept informed of his plans for life. He had not forgotten his promise to befriend the boy—for his father's and mother's sake.

His letters could not have been better. They were those of a sensitive spirit tempered somewhat by philosophy—not the expressions of one quick to forgive; or likely to forget, but of one whose self-respect was paramount, and sure to lead him in the end, to the proper and dignified course. To what extent his nature might be swayed by unused emotions she could not know. The warmth of his passion for Evelyn had surprised her. What depths of feeling yet remained unfathomed in his bosom, she could not know. His letters gave no sign.

Evelyn's married life had been, to her mind, for the first few months, well-nigh ideal. The match had seemed a perfect one, a union of souls made for each other. But, very naturally, there had come, after a while, a reaction from the violent passion which in bringing them together had swept everything else from its path. The pendulum did not swing as far back as it had come, for the married relation had created new and strong ties; but there was reaction enough for Evelyn to appreciate something of the pain her conduct must have caused her mother and Cushing, and to make her sorry that she had been compelled to wound them. This, however, was her sole regret. She had married where she loved, and as long as she loved, could never question the wisdom of the step which had saved her from a loveless union.

That Evelyn should ever cease to love her husband was inconceivable to her, except in the equally unthinkable event that he should cease to love her. Her feeling upon the subject was hardly to be dignified by the name of reasoning; it was, rather, an instinctive part of her nature. She had not loved Manson solely because he had loved her; but a mutuality of sentiment had been necessary to complete her love. Hers was a love that fed on love, and would have starved without it. Manson's love was more primitive. To him Evelyn was a woman—*the* woman, of course, the one woman—to be loved and cherished; but, after all, merely subsidiary to her husband; an object to be sought, but, once she had become his, to be held in assured possession while the man put his energies at work to acquire other and more serious things—wealth, reputation, social position. Wives are not hard to find, for the qualified man who seeks one: a man may marry several—consecutively, of course, with the entire approval of society. He can scarcely hope to make more than one reputation; and it is rarely that having gained and lost wealth or social standing, he can regain either. There are instances, but they are rare as stems of four-leaved clover. As between Evelyn and her husband it was the old story—she found her life in her love; to him love was only one of life's prizes, all of which he sought; those which he had not seeming the most desirable; for he brought to life the zest of the talented parvenu, whose fresh blood had not been diluted by the wine of luxury in past generations. Hence, since Evelyn gave him all her heart and all her thought, time came when there grew up in her mind a slowly ripening consciousness that she gave more than she received, and with this an incipient feeling of resentment. It was not a fair bargain; she was entitled to as much as she gave.

Toward the end of the first year of their marriage, this feeling, to which she had given no utterance, had gained a dangerous ascendency over her thoughts. Her pride would not permit her to mention it; she would have bitten out her tongue before she would have acknowledged herself jealous: but a student of human nature who had so diagnosed the complaint would not have been far wrong.

For Manson the year which had elapsed had been one of uninterrupted prosperity. Success in love had seemed to bring with it every other kind of good fortune; indeed, to one of his buoyant temperament, the elation of success in any form was the strongest incentive to further effort. The stimulus of hope had carried him through the hardships of youth; the dawning consciousness of power had nerved him to the struggles of early manhood.

"I can," he had said stubbornly, when his funds were low and his outlook dark, "I can and I will."

But when he had passed the era of preparation and entered upon that of performance, his nature demanded, as its spring of effort, his mood of appreciation, of applause and of substantial reward. The laborer he believed, was worthy of his hire.

All that he had asked had been forthcoming. Rome was not built in a day, nor could one make a great reputation or a substantial fortune in a year. But he had laid foundations deep enough, and broad enough, it seemed, to withstand any test to which they might be subjected.

Shortly after his marriage, Manson received a message from Mr. Sterling, the architect whom he had met at Mrs. Archer's reception. Mr. Sterling requested him to call at his office between certain hours, or at some other convenient time.

Manson put in his appearance promptly. Mr. Sterling received him cordially.

"I want," he said, "a partner. My associate for many years past is ill, and compelled to retire. I myself am growing old. The firm needs fresh blood. You have youth and energy, and, let me assure you, a very fine talent. I have looked into some of your work and have heard of more."

This offer was Manson's golden opportunity. To accept it was to have all his initial difficulties cleared away, and to give him the personal guaranty of the head of his profession. It was at the dawn of an era of rapid civic development, when a new architecture was being evolved to meet the conditions of modern life, an architecture adapted to modern building materials, to the value of land in congested cities, to the demands of a strenuous climate and commercial age, in which was discernible the first vague, uncertain movements of a national taste which would no longer be content with the architectural monstrosities which had satisfied a former generation. Such an architecture could not be entirely new. Human thought and human learning were, like the ancient cities of the East, superimposed upon the buried ruins of the past. Hence no new thing was conceivable in any old art, and architecture was one of the oldest. Yet there was born, now and then, an original mind, which could select and adapt and combine the old so as to give it all the effect of a novel creation. Such a mind old Mr. Sterling had recognized in Manson, and, with a wisdom born of experience, had offered him a partnership.

Manson accepted the proffered partnership promptly and gratefully. He was indeed profuse in his thanks.

"It is a recognition for which I could hardly have hoped. I assure you that you shall never regret it."

"That's all right, my boy. I quite fell in love with you at first sight. I never saw a prettier couple in my life than your wife and you at Mrs. Archer's famous reception. The same thing seems to have occurred to you. I was sorry for Cushing when you cut him out—but it was much more suitable. Youth should mate youth."

Curiously enough, Manson's marriage with Evelyn had furthered his material fortunes in other ways as well. Society seemed to have a certain respect for the young freebooter who had stormed its citadel, and carried off the affianced bride of one of its ornaments. Manson became the vogue; the new firm had more than they could do.

An important matter which had lately occupied much of Manson's attention was the design for a new group of county buildings. A series of articles from his pen, begun before his marriage, when he had leisure to write them, and published soon after the announcement of the new firm, had given birth to a movement for the beautifying of municipalities. The beautiful, he argued, was equally valuable with the good; indeed, only the beautiful could be the perfectly good.

It was fitting that a community noted for its civic pride should be among the first to make a practical application of this new doctrine, thus setting an example to less favored cities. A comprehensive scheme of municipal improvement having been outlined, and the preliminary legislation secured, it was equally appropriate that the prophet of the new ideal should be asked to submit designs. There would be competition of course. The best architects of the country were invited to try their fortune. Even the unsuccessful would be compensated for their labor. To the successful competitor would be given the contract for the architectural supervision of the various structures. An expenditure of many millions was involved, the commissions upon which alone would make the supervising architect a rich man, in a reasonable sense of the word.

The conception and working out of the Sterling & Manson plans had been left entirely to the junior partner. A few months before the decision was to be made, a sudden attack of illness had driven Mr. Sterling abroad for several months, during which the entire management and supervision of the firm's affairs had devolved upon Manson. Had not the office been well organized, he would hardly have been equal to the task; and even as things were, he had little time for his own private affairs.

Manson was very hopeful of success in the competition. He knew what might be reasonably expected from his rivals, and there was no element of surprise against which he need guard. He had friends, too, upon the commission with which the decision rested. As a singular instance of the manner in which fate intermingles the destinies of mankind, Edward Cushing had been a member of the commission, but, upon Evelyn's marriage, had resigned the office before going abroad. Manson wondered what chance he would have stood in the competition had his rival in the field of love remained upon the commission.

With his advancing prosperity Manson had cherished a secret design for Evelyn's happiness. They had lived since their marriage in a modest apartment in a quiet neighborhood, their household consisting of Manson, Evelyn and two servants, of whom Leonie was one. Mrs. Thayer, after Evelyn's marriage, had charged Leonie with her perfidy. Leonie, with a characteristic disregard of truth, had denied the accusation. The facts had been brought home to her, unmistakably, and Mrs. Thayer had dismissed her from her service. Evelyn could scarcely do less than take in this sufferer in her behalf; though her presence in the house continued to be a thorn in Mrs. Thayer's flesh, and Leonie, as well as Evelyn, knew that if perfect cordiality was ever to exist between mother and daughter, Leonie would have to go. The place was a good one, however, and Leonie hoped to defer the evil day. There was, moreover, a secret reason why she wished to remain in the house.

The Mansons kept a carriage at a neighboring livery stable. Evelyn, knowing of her husband's prosperity, had of late expressed a wish for a house of their own, and a larger establishment. Manson had secretly planned, as a birthday present for her, a beautiful home in a choice location,—a house which should contain every appliance to make it convenient and comfortable, enshrined in a framework which should embody in purest form his own ideas of architectural beauty in a city residence. Evelyn's birthday would be reached in a few months, and upon it he wished to present her with this home, completed, furnished, and ready for occupancy. Had he told Evelyn this, it would have saved her some heartburnings, and Manson some trouble, and would have rendered this story impossible.

The expense attendant upon this undertaking was considerable, and required a careful husbanding of resources. The vigilant and loving supervision which Manson gave the work consumed all the time he could spare from his business. Manson was naturally free-handed, and Evelyn knew that his income was, for a professional man, a large one. A suddenly developed and unexplained closeness in money matters; a deep absorption in affairs concerning which she was too proud to ask and upon which he did not enlighten her, gave rise to a vague discontent upon Evelyn's part. When to this was added a certain amount of neglect inseparable from an occupation which for the time being occupied her husband all day long and several evenings a week, it was not strange that Evelyn should at times wonder if there might not be some attraction for him elsewhere of which she was ignorant. She found herself wondering now and then, if her husband's ardent and impressionable temperament, so susceptible to beauty, would prove reliable in the long-drawn out daily association of marriage? In all of these thoughts, for which she was herself ashamed, she did Manson an injustice. But she never voiced her doubts, Manson never suspected them; he therefore had no opportunity to correct them, and the mischief went steadily forward to the resulting catastrophe.

Still another element, of which he said nothing to Evelyn, entered into Manson's preoccupation. The country was in the full tide of a prosperity which had passed all former bounds, and to which a people becoming almost as mercurial as those of ancient Athens or modern Paris, seemed to set no limit. Manson had not escaped the prevailing enthusiasm. He had recently bought through a firm of responsible brokers, a large amount of a certain stock, which he had left on deposit as collateral for the greater part of its purchase price. It was essentially a purchase on margin, though neither party called it by that name. Manson had friends upon the inside, upon whom he thought he could rely for safe advice. The stock was a good one, but subject to manipulation, and therefore liable to severe fluctuations. His friends had promised to let him know when to sell. Already the stock showed a handsome profit, but a still larger advance was promised, and he was expecting, at any moment, the signal to unload.

Such was the condition of Manson's affairs toward the end of May, 189–, when he remained out until two o'clock one Tuesday night, at a meeting of the Architects' Club, of which he was a leading member.

XI.

A BOLT FROM A CLEAR SKY

On this particular evening Evelyn had planned a special dinner for her husband. He did not appear at six o'clock, but telephoned that he would take dinner down town with a friend, and would not be at home until eight, when he would only have time to dress hurriedly in order to attend the monthly meeting of the Architects' Club, at which there was an important matter to be discussed.

Evelyn had not taken the disappointment in very good part. It seemed to her that she was neglected. Her pique led her to a somewhat unusual step. She laid out her husband's things for him, and went, after dinner, to pay a visit to her mother. There, much to her surprise, she found Cushing. He had returned from Europe a few days before. The unexpected meeting was embarrassing, more embarrassing to Evelyn than to Cushing, who made no reference to their engagement, but directed the conversation along an entirely different channel. When Evelyn rose to return home, he accompanied her to her own door, a fifteen-minute walk, during which they were engaged in earnest conversation. She opened the door with a latch-key and bade her escort good-night.

Manson was somewhat surprised, when he reached home a little after eight, to learn from Leonie that his wife was absent.

"Was there anything the matter at Mrs. Thayer's," he asked, "that should call her there?"

"No, sir," answered the maid. "She was a little put out I think because you did n't come home to dinner."

Manson made no reply. He had been detained down town upon affairs concerning the new house, and was slightly irritated that Evelyn should have chosen such an occasion to display resentment at his absence. This was a perfectly irrational idea, since Evelyn knew nothing of the reasons for his absence. As between the two, she had the better excuse.

It was Manson's custom to return home early from his club meetings, but upon this occasion he remained until midnight, and after the meeting adjourned went to a restaurant with several friends, where they remained for an hour or two longer. He suspected that Evelyn would be uneasy, but she would be none the worse for a lesson. They were to live together for many years: it might as well be understood, now as at any other time, who was at the head of the household. He had no manner of doubt upon the subject; it was well enough that Evelyn should be equally informed.

Upon returning home, he went into his wife's room; but she seemed asleep, and gave no sign, so he went to bed, for the first time since his marriage, without having spoken to his wife for twenty hours, which, before morning had lengthened into a full day.

They met at breakfast, with a slight feeling of constraint which found expression in greater formality of greetings than was usual between them. An explosion would have been much more healthy. Manson indeed felt a little ashamed of his irritation of the night before.

"How did you find your mother?" he inquired, with an attempt at his usual cheerfulness.

"Quite well, thank you," answered Evelyn, in the tone as well as the language of formal politeness.

Manson made another effort.

"Did she have company?"

"A little—not any one that you would care for."

Evelyn took up the morning paper, and Manson's mind reverted to his business of the day, which was pressing and important, and destined to have a great influence upon his career. He would have spoken of his hopes and expectations to Evelyn, had she seemed responsive; but she did not, and he concluded to wait until he could bring her a story of success. Impulsive by nature, his early struggles had taught him how to wait. Frankly egotistical, he had been obliged to work so long before any one had cared to hear him speak about himself, that he had learned self-denial in the exercise of even this facile pleasure.

There was a postman's ring, and Leonie brought in the mail. There were several letters for Manson, and two or three for Evelyn.

Evelyn opened one of hers and glanced over the contents. She displayed signs of agitation which were noticed by Leonie, who was waiting on the table and had already recognized the handwriting upon the envelope. Evelyn's agitation must have been apparent to her husband, had he not at the moment been absorbed in a letter of his own; and even when he laid down the sheet he noticed the change in her expression.

"Is there anything the matter?" he asked amicably.

"Nothing that would interest you," she replied with an effort at indifference assumed to conceal her emotion.

One of Manson's letters sent him at once to the columns of the morning paper. He had already glanced over the financial column, but this letter directed his attention to another page. It contained an article relative to certain anticipated movements in the stock in which he was interested, which was showing signs of restlessness, and, it was predicted, was likely to go higher or lower within a day or two. It would require careful watching, and he must hurry down town so as to be in close touch with his financial advisers.

"Hugh," said Evelyn, as he rose to go, "I wish you would let me have a hundred dollars this morning."

"What for, my dear?" he asked.

"I have a use for it," she replied, "I do not care to state just now what it is."

Her letter had evidently been from some importunate dressmaker or milliner, or some one of the sort, who could very easily wait.

"My dear Evelyn," he said easily, "I have n't the money with me just now."

"Can't you send it up by a messenger?" she asked, with some persistency, and a gleam in her eye, which a man less absorbed might have diagnosed as dangerous, but which Manson did not perceive.

"Really, Evelyn" he returned, "I have got to make some large payments today, and would rather not deplete my bank account. If you can wait a day or two, I can let you have as much as you want. Meantime, let the tradesmen wait, and if you want anything, have it charged."

"Very well," replied Evelyn, with a face and a voice utterly devoid of expression.

Manson hurried away intent upon his own affairs. Evelyn was probably offended, but she would get over it; and he would have a story of prosperity to tell her at night that would remove any little irritation she might feel.

His morning was a busy one. A hasty visit to his financial adviser elicited the injunction that he watch the market carefully. The chances were that it would go up, but after it reached a certain point Manson was advised to sell.

Another matter which demanded his attention was the renewal of a note at the bank, temporarily secured by a lien upon the new house. The cashier called him up over the telephone.

"Mr. Manson," he asked, "how about the insurance on the house securing your loan? You remember it expires today."

Manson remembered receiving the notice.

"Yes," he replied, "I've been too busy to attend to it. I'll call up the agent and have the policy renewed right away."

In the mail delivered during the morning came a note from his friend on the municipal improvement commission:

"My dear Manson:—

"I am in a position to say that your design for the public building group stands highest in favor, Howell & Baker's of New York being a good second. The committee meets today at one o'clock for their final decision, and you are requested to be present for consultation. I may say privately that if you will consent to certain modifications in the plans, the decision will be in your favor. Howell & Baker have several friends upon the commission, but your plans are so manifestly superior that your presence and acquiescence will almost certainly turn the scale in your favor. Don't fail to be on hand in good time."

This note from his friend gave Manson much pleasure.

"Things are coming my way," he said to himself with a glow of satisfaction. There was merely enough uncertainty to make the competition interesting.

The price of his stock had been rising steadily all the morning.

"Watch it closely," telephoned his financial friend, "and sell on the slightest reaction. When it begins to go, it will slump off as rapidly as it went up."

Toward noon he received an unexpected remittance of a thousand dollars. With this much of ready money in his pocket, the renewal of his note provided for, and the prospect of a large profit on the sale of his stock, he felt very well indeed.

"Things are still coming my way," he said.

At twelve o'clock he thought of Evelyn, and remembered her request for a hundred dollars.

"Bless her heart!" he said. "She was annoyed with me last night, no doubt, and I'm not quite sure how she took my putting her off this morning. I'll take a cab and run home for lunch. I'll give her the money, and a kiss, and be back in ample time to meet the commission."

He called a hansom, and on the way home indulged in a pleasant little dream of Evelyn's delight, a few weeks hence, when he would ask her to visit a certain house, as he had several times taken her to inspect and admire his creations. He pictured her praise of its comfort, its convenience, the charm of its location, the beauty of its style, the luxury of its fittings, her wish that she might have one like it, and her surprise and delight when he should tell her that it was hers. Perhaps he had been the least bit neglectful of late; but it was for her, after all, and, when enlightened in regard to the facts, she would appreciate his forethought and his love. He had fitted up in the new house a charming room for Mrs. Thayer, whom he hoped that Evelyn might still induce to come and live with them.

Just before reaching home he recalled that he had forgotten to have the insurance policy renewed. It should be done by three o'clock, before the bank closed, or his note might go to protest.

"I'll call up as soon as I reach the house," he said to himself, "and ask them to make out the new policy immediately, and send it over to the bank."

Requesting the cabman to wait, Manson ran up the steps and rang the bell. He might have used his latch-key, but if the maid were in the front part of the house he was likely to get in sooner by ringing.

"Is luncheon ready, Leonie?" he asked, as he threw off his hat and overcoat.

"Why, no, sir, we were not expecting you."

"Surely Mrs. Manson will lunch at the usual hour?" he said, in some surprise.

"We have had no orders, sir," returned Leonie. "Mrs. Manson has been gone an hour. She said nothing about returning—at all," she added with a meaning smile, after a pause just long enough to be significant.

"What do you mean?" demanded Manson, frowning darkly.

"She took a valise, sir, and her jewels."

"Did she go to her mother's?"

"I think not, sir. She went with a gentleman."

"What gentleman?"

"Mr. Cushing, sir."

For a moment Manson stood like one bereft of speech, a confused flood of ideas running through his mind. Where had Cushing come from? He had supposed him to be in Europe. What business could Evelyn have with the man whom she had jilted?

"Is Mrs. Thayer ill?"

"No, sir; Mrs. Thayer is quite well. She is out of town."

Leonie watched her master keenly, like a cat watching a mouse.

"And Mrs. Manson left no word?"

"She left this letter, sir."

She handed him an envelope, which he tore open. It enclosed a note which ran as follows:

"Hugh:—I am going away. I seem to fill so small a part in your life of late that doubtless you will not miss me. I am going where I can be of some service, and where I shall be appreciated.

"Evelyn."

Manson dropped the note in a sheer bewilderment, beneath which, however, a note of anger was beginning to make itself felt. Leonie, who, thanks to her natural talent for intrigue, had read the letter, though it had been delivered sealed, kept upon her master a watchful eye, which lost no phase of her expression.

"Tell me," he demanded, "everything that has happened since I went away this morning."

Leonie was prepared to comply in her most dramatic manner. There was such a situation in the novel she was reading, the latest production of Martha L. Mudd, a popular department store bargain, and for other reasons as well, Leonie did not let her story lack for color.

"Mrs. Manson received a letter at breakfast, sir. You were busy with the morning paper, sir, or you would have seen her tremble and turn pale."

He recalled her having read a letter, of which she had said nothing. No, she had lied; she had said that the letter contained nothing that would interest him. It was a bad sign.

"She left the letter in her desk, sir. I found it while cleaning her room, and recognized the handwriting—I've seen it very often, sir."

"Bring it here," commanded Manson. He stepped into the parlor and flung himself into the nearest armchair to confront this crisis in his life. That his wife should leave him would have seemed, an hour before, as wildly improbable as a tale of the Arabian Nights. It was still incomprehensible. There must be some simple explanation, even for the note to himself, written doubtless in a moment of ill-humor. That this enigmatical note fit in so well with the base suspicion of a servant's corrupt imagination was a mere coincidence. Doubtless the letter Leonie had gone to fetch would hold the key to this mystery. Only a year, a brief year, had passed since Evelyn had braved public opinion, had risked social odium, had renounced the certainty of wealth and position, for love of him. That she should face squarely about, so soon, without provocation, and with no sign of warning, revealed a recklessness or a duplicity of which he could not believe her capable.

Leonie brought him the note.

"Dear Evelyn,—It must be this morning, or perhaps never. I shall be ready to leave by the one o'clock train. If I have anything to say to you in the meantime, I will telephone. At one o'clock—remember."

Manson crumpled this note in his hand with an involuntary grip. He recalled that his wife had received a letter while at the breakfast table; and that she had asked him, with some signs of agitation, for money, a hundred dollars. Her manner he had ascribed to the events of the night previous. Her demand for money, he had supposed, had grown out of her frame of mind—that of an angry woman seeking fresh cause of offense. This letter, equally as unexplainable as the first, except upon one sickening hypothesis, strengthened the probability of that explanation. But he would not entertain so incredible a proposition until there was no possible escape from it.

Leonie was watching him furtively. A very clever woman was Leonie, in a shrewd, ignorant, animal sort of way. In the gay society of an eighteenth century court, her talent for intrigue would have gained her a fortune or lost her her head, or her right hand, or some other useful member.

"Mr. Cushing came home with her last night, sir," she said. "It was my night off, and I was coming home, and I saw them in front of me, locked arms, and talking low. They did n't know that I saw them."

Manson swore profanely.

"Where have they gone?" he demanded, having relieved his mind somewhat. "They said so much that they must have dropped some clew."

"I think sir," replied Leonie, "that I could guess where they went."

"Where?" demanded Manson eagerly.

"They spoke of the train for New York, and something was said about a steamer tomorrow."

"What steamer, and for what port?"

"That I did n't hear, sir."

"What else did you hear? You heard so much—you must have heard more. I wish to know everything!"

"After I heard the first few words, by accident entirely—"

"Go on, go on! never mind how you heard it!"

"After the first few words I guessed there was something wrong. You see I knew Miss Evelyn before you did, sir."

"Never mind that now! Go on!"

"I felt that you ought to know what was going on, sir, so I listened. I knew how fond they used to be of one another, sir, and how he had supported the family and given her nearly everything she had before you married her. I suspected it for a long time, and then I heard Mrs. Thayer say so with her own mouth."

Manson let Leonie talk, and by a question now and then drew out a skilful mixture of fact and imagination, truth and deliberate falsehood, by which Cushing's long and unselfish friendship for the widow and her children was insidiously attributed to the basest motives. Her insinuations spared neither mother or daughter, and painted Cushing in colors which made Manson, himself no purist, curse beneath his breath.

The girl might have exaggerated things somewhat, he argued; she might be something of a liar; but she was no fool. She had lived with the family five years, and had had full opportunity to observe. Her deductions accorded with human experience, and seemed borne out by the events of the morning. That a wealthy bachelor should have maintained innocent and high-minded relations of intimacy with a young and attractive widow, and should have heaped her with benefits for twenty years with no return, was scarcely more thinkable to Manson than to Leonie—they were both simple, direct and primitive in their reasoning.

That Evelyn had been disloyal to him since her marriage and until her flight Manson had no idea. But she had been reared in an unhealthy atmosphere. Even her hasty marriage to himself took on a new aspect in the light of this suddenly acquired knowledge. Her desertion of Cushing had seemed a tribute to his own superior powers of fascination. Now it seemed that vows of any kind sat lightly upon Evelyn. To have married where one loved had seemed to Manson a triumph of reasonableness; to have married without love would have been bad enough; to have married, loving elsewhere, would have been worse; to love elsewhere after marriage was no less than monstrous. The case seemed clear. Leonie's word alone would not have sufficed to convince him; but there lay the proof, the damning proof, in the handwriting of the guilty couple. In such affairs the husband was always the last to know the truth.

XII.
CLOSE PURSUIT

When Manson looked back, a year later, to the events of the next day, they seemed like the vague happenings of a dream, through which, nevertheless, ran a well-defined purpose. Had his mind not been dominated by a single thought, which eclipsed for the time being every other, it is inconceivable that a shrewd and careful business man should have permitted the series of disastrous events which combined, within the next twenty-four hours to make him a penniless wanderer upon the face of the earth.

What he remembered was that having heard Leonie's story and having reached by the logic of circumstances, assisted by a jealous temperament for the first time stirred, the conclusion that his wife had fled with Cushing, he knew but one thought, which was to follow them. Conviction seemed to take the form of a thick wall which suddenly grew up on either side of him. Down the lane between these walls had gone his wife and her companion. All his emotions resolved themselves in an overwhelming impulse to follow a blind instinct, which did not stop to count the cost of pursuit, or formulate the course to be taken when he found them.

He recalled, when reviewing this episode later on, that he had told Leonie to take care of the house until his return. He then rushed from the house and ordered the driver to hasten to the railroad station. Throwing himself back upon the seat, he plunged into reflection so deep and somber that he did not notice that the cab was going toward the North Station.

The cab drew up before the entrance. Manson threw the driver a coin and rushed into the station.

"Where is the one o'clock train for New York?" he inquired of the first man in uniform he encountered.

"South Station, for New York," replied the ticket agent. "There's no one o'clock train for New York at this station. South Station for New York."

Manson awoke from his trance long enough to curse the driver's stupidity. It was then fifteen minutes of one. The cab in which he had come was still standing at the entrance, along with several others. He hurled a curse at the driver and chose a different cab.

"How long will it take you to drive to the South Station?" he asked.

"About fifteen minutes, sir."

"Can you make it in ten for a double fare?"

"I can make it in nine, yer 'anner."

"Very well. A dollar for every minute under ten."

Manson sprang into the cab and slammed the door. The driver whipped up his horse, and the cab rattled over the pavement.

For the first half of the distance the way was comparatively clear. Manson, now thoroughly awake, with his watch in his hand checked off the intervening space by the flying seconds. The cabman figured upon saving time by passing through a certain narrow street which cut off a considerable distance. But Fate had otherwise determined. The cabman had seen from a glance, as he reached the end of the street, that it was clear of obstructions. But no sooner had he turned into it and got well under way for a spurt of speed that an immense wagon, drawn by two heavy horses and loaded with beer-kegs, emerged from an alley and squarely blocked the road. The cabman yelled. The driver of the wagon, calm in the impregnability of his fortress, vouchsafed no reply, and instead of making an effort to clear the street, backed deliberately to the sidewalk, which he evidently meant to obstruct until he should have delivered a portion of his load.

The cabman's paroxysm of profanity was of no avail. There was no policeman in sight, and no alternative except to turn at some inconvenience, go back to the street which they had left, and continue by the more roundabout route.

This involved a loss of fully three minutes. When the cab dashed up to the station entrance, Manson sprang out and threw the cabman a five-dollar note. He rushed into the station and demanded of an officer dignifiedly pacing the lobby, from what track the one o'clock train for New York left.

"Track 16 today."

Track 16 was near the farther end of the station. Manson hastened in that direction. The crowd was dense; several incoming trains were pouring their passengers into the station at different gates and at times it was difficult to make his way through the press. At one point his efforts to make progress brought him into violent contact with several other people and called down upon him the reproof of a station officer. He reached gate 16.

"Which is the New York train?" he demanded of the gateman.

"Track 6 for New York."

The station clock was pointing to the hour. Manson rushed frantically back toward the other gate. The crowd had grown denser and seemed densest as he neared the gate. He could see the train standing upon the track and a belated passenger hurrying toward it. He was near enough to see that the gate to track six was still open, though the gateman stood with his hand upon it. He was almost in reach of the gate when the crowd again delayed him. He could see the train starting, with the slow and gliding movement with which modern science overcomes the momentum of standing cars. At the same moment a man came out of the rear door of the receding train and looked toward the gate. It was Cushing. Manson's despairing eye ran along the side of the car, to which a line from his own position still formed an angle. He saw a white face looking out and backwards.

A cry burst from Manson's lips. It was drowned by an unearthly cacophony which at the same instant proceeded from a group of young men who were going through the next gate. The crowd laughed at the college yell, which kept up until the train was out of the station. Manson had reached the gate just as the iron bars came together.

"Let me through, let me through!" he shrieked, grasping the gate and shaking it in his excitement.

"Too late," said the gate-keeper, imperturbably. "Stand back. The second section will leave in ten minutes. It will pull in upon the track as soon as the first section gets out of the way."

The shock of his disappointment at missing the car, coupled with the sight of Evelyn's face at the car-window, reäcted curiously upon Manson's mood. He was no longer in suspense; he had seen with his own eyes. He must follow them, of course, and when the pursuit began, the suspense would be even greater. But for the present there were five idle minutes. He wondered vaguely whether his plans had been accepted by the Public Group Commission. A few hours before this had been the most important concern of his life. To his mind at present it presented an interest scarcely less academic than that of the nebular hypothesis or the origin of species. He waited at the nearest public telephone until some one ahead of him was through, and then called up the clerk of the Municipal Improvement Commission.

"Were Sterling and Manson's plans accepted?" he inquired.

"No," came the answer. "Mr. Manson was not present—"

There was some confusion on the wire, but Manson did not care to hear any more, and hung up the receiver. An hour before, this announcement would have been a severe blow. Now it seemed a matter of very little consequence. He bought a ticket to New York and a few minutes later was following at fifty miles an hour the train which was bearing his wife and Cushing toward New York.

He bought half a dozen newspapers from a boy who came through the train, but the attempt to read was a failure. At the end of a column he knew no more of its contents than if he never looked at the sheet. After an hour or two he put his hand into his breast pocket for some purpose, and felt there the fire insurance policy which he had neglected to renew. Without it his note had doubtless already gone to protest. Well, no matter. In the presence of superior misfortune the loss of credit was a trifle.

When the train reached New Haven, at half past four, he bought another newspaper. The first page gave an account of a sensational slump in A. & B. For the first time since reaching home and finding Evelyn gone, Manson recalled that he had put up heavy margins against a large block of this stock, which by this unexpected decline were entirely wiped out. The next column announced a destructive fire by which a handsome building, in process of construction by the eminent architects Sterling and Manson, for an unnamed client, had been reduced to ashes. The amount of insurance had not been ascertained.

Manson knew very well that there was no insurance. The policy had expired at noon, and had not been renewed. This completed his ruin. Beyond the $500 which he had in his pocket he was without resources—he was indeed worth about $100,000 less than nothing; and he had lost his wife, who at this supreme moment of his destiny, was worth more than all the rest combined. Not one moment did it occur to him to relinquish his pursuit in order to see if he might not possibly snatch something from the wreck. If he could but reach New York in time to save Evelyn and punish her seducer, the rest might go. With Evelyn, these other things were a large part of his life; bereft of Evelyn, they were no more than a frame without a picture—no more than kindling wood.

Manson reached New York in the early evening. He had no baggage, not even a hand satchel, and therefore did not go at once to a hotel. He had eaten nothing since breakfast. There had been no dining-car upon the train and he was conscious of a ravenous appetite. One's mental or spiritual side may be neglected, sometimes indefinitely, without discomfort; indeed, there are those who find decided satisfaction in such neglect. But physical needs are more insistent, and soon clamor shamelessly for attention in the midst of the greatest emotional crisis.

When he had satisfied his hunger he set about the investigation which he had outlined during his journey. Hailing a cab at the curb, he engaged it by the hour. Beginning at the nearest, he set out to visit the hotels of the city in search of Cushing and Evelyn. This occupied him until nearly midnight, without success. That Cushing was in New York he had every reason to believe, but that he had put up at any well known hotel seemed improbable. Beginning at length to feel the effects of the strain of the last twelve hours Manson drove to the hotel of his choice, dismissed the cab and registered for the night. He would resume the search in the morning under better conditions which would afford a more reasonable hope of success. No steamer had sailed from New York Harbor since the arrival of the train which had brought Evelyn and her companion to the city, and no European liner was scheduled to leave before noon of the following day. He would therefore have six hours of daylight in which to continue the search. Evelyn had been a good woman. Perhaps there would be time, even yet, to save her from the worst consequences of her escapade. If he could find them before the steamer sailed, and if she could make the proper assurances, he could take her home with no strain upon her reputation, no real injury to himself. But every hour that elapsed until then would pile up a debt against Cushing, which should be collected to the last farthing. And if he were too late—if they got away, he would follow them to the ends of the earth.

"I will send him to hell," he said to himself, "if I have to follow him there. No man can take my wife from me and live!"

Having reached this decision, he went into the café, ate a hearty luncheon, went to bed, and slept soundly. His nerves were under perfect control. He had a task to perform, and meant to have strength to perform it.

Manson left orders to be called at six o'clock in the morning. He awoke at five with his brain clear and active. A shower of cold water sent the red blood coursing through his veins. And with it came a sudden sense of freedom, as though he were shaking off a weight. The very completeness of his ruin appealed in a way to the innate simplicity of his nature. His state of mind was comparable to that of a red man of the forest, who, having seen his wigwam in ashes, his squaw and children butchered, and his winter stores carried off, merely draws his belt the tighter, sharpens his tomahawk the keener, and sets out upon his evening's trail, finding in the anticipation of revenge a bitter pleasure that replaces and in a measure compensates him for his ruined happiness.

In the conflict of emotions which yesterday had made of his heart a battleground, the sense of loss and injury had predominated. This morning the sense of justice controlled his mood. He had suffered an injury which in all probability was already deadly and irreparable. His fathers and grandfathers had revenged wrong by bloodshed. It was the simple, natural, logical method. An eye for an eye, a tooth for a tooth, was good scriptural doctrine. He was familiar with the

Bible:—it had furnished a large part of the course of study at Berea College.

He descended to the hotel office without waiting for the elevator, only to find that he might as well have slept an hour or two later. Breakfast was not yet ready and a few abortive attempts to telephone revealed that the machinery of the business world was not yet in motion. So complete, for the moment, was his sense of separation from his past, that it did not even occur to him to buy a newspaper. He walked a block or two, and inquired at several nearby hotels in the hope that the fugitives might have registered after midnight, but found no trace of them. Returning to his hotel, he went into breakfast, as soon as the dining room was open, and then addressed himself to the work which he had laid out for the morning. This involved a visit to several inquiry offices and detective agencies at each of which he left a description of the runaways, with orders that no effort be spared to locate them as speedily as possible.

Manson's next step was to make a round of the steamship offices on Broadway and scan the passenger lists, in none of which, however, did Cushing's name appear, nor was the booking agent at any office able to recollect selling a ticket to such a person as Manson described. Indeed, Cushing, as a veteran traveler, was well-known at most of the offices, and it seemed reasonably clear that he could not have personally secured passage on any boat even under an assumed name without having been recognized. There was a possibility, however, that he had bought his tickets through a third person—a not unlikely proceeding, in view of his companion, and the nature of their association. Two Atlantic liners sailed that day, one at eleven o'clock and one at noon. Manson kept in touch with his agents during the morning, but without result. At ten o'clock he was present at the wharf of the steamer first to sail. By liberal use of money he learned who had gone on board, and that those he sought were not among them. An agent was employed in like manner at the neighboring dock from which the other steamer was to leave. Manson remained by the gang-plank until the steamer sailed, scanning each arrival closely, but in vain.

During the morning he had bought a revolver, which he had loaded carefully and hidden upon his person. Once or twice as he saw a couple alight from a carriage at the head of the pier, his heart had leaped to his throat, and his hand had sought his weapon instinctively. But when the gang-plank was drawn in, he was certain that neither Cushing nor Evelyn had entered the ship.

Leaving the pier, while the band played a stirring march, Manson sprang into a cab and hurried to the other steamer's wharf. Only a few people had gone on board, he was informed, and among them no persons answering the description of Evelyn and Cushing. An hour's watch of the arriving passengers was no more successful than that at the first steamer. So far as human probabilities went, the fugitives had not sailed for Europe during that day.

Manson had assumed, upon the information furnished by Leonie, that Cushing would take Evelyn to Europe. Having with his usual directness pursued this assumption to a fruitless end, he turned his thoughts elsewhere. The couple might be in New York city. But Cushing had spoken of a steamer. Cushing was a veteran globe-trotter. Was it not likely that, anticipating pursuit, he might have taken Evelyn, by some less frequented route, to some quiet spot where there would be less danger of interruption than upon the main highways of travel?

"I am a fool," he groaned, "not to have thought of it sooner. It is the most natural thing for them to do—the coward, the dastard! He would go into hiding, of course! His guilty conscience will tell him that I am on his track."

Thoroughly imbued with this idea, born full-grown, he proceeded at once to follow it up with his agents. The telephone, the telegraph, the electric car, made it possible to do this without further loss of time. At half past two o'clock, as he sat waiting in the lobby of an uptown hotel, he received a message that Mr. Edward Cushing had engaged passage for two, for whom he had secured a whole stateroom, upon the Lambert & Hall Steamer *Bolivar*, which would leave her dock at Martin's stores, Brooklyn, for Pernambuco, Bahia, Rio de Janeiro and other South American ports, at three o'clock in the afternoon.

Manson inquired of the clerk at the desk where Martin's stores might be. The clerk had never heard of them. A hurried consultation of a map and a directory disclosed that Martin's stores were in Brooklyn, below Battery Park. The clerk thought that barring accidents he might get there in three-quarters of an hour.

"Take the Elevated to South Ferry Station and take the ferry; or, go to the City Hall and cross the bridge, and take a cab on the other side. You can make it, if you hurry."

Manson paid his bill and took a cab for the nearest elevated station. The train made its usual speed, but seemed to Manson to creep with wormlike slowness. He asked a man on the train, who looked as though he might be a sailor and who proved to be one, which was the nearest route, and by his advice got off at the City Hall and crossed the bridge. By good fortune he found a disengaged cab at the terminus, and springing into it gave the order to be driven to the Lambert & Hall wharf at Martin's stores. His drive was beset by none of the accidents which had caused him to miss the train at Boston. And his watch still lacked ten minutes of the hour when he drove up to the office at the end of the pier.

"Where," he asked, "is the steamer for South America which sails today?"

The man looked at him with surprise.

"She's gone," he said "sailed twenty minutes ago. You can see her down the bay," he said with a wave of his hand.

"I thought she sailed at two," said Manson.

"So she did," said the clerk, "marine time, which is half an hour faster than standard time. She is generally a little late; but everything was ready today—cargo loaded, and passengers and mail aboard, captain and crew on hand. She really got away a few minutes early. Did you mean to sail on her?"

"No," said Manson, "I wished to see if certain passengers were on board—and to speak to them."

"I think the whole list was accounted for," replied the clerk. "Here's a good glass," he said amiably. "The passengers generally stand around the stern as the steamer goes out. You may at least see the people you want."

Manson thanked him, and seizing the glass lifted it to his eyes and leveled it at the receding steamer. The passengers were standing about the after deck, most of them with their faces turned toward the city. Men on land may sometimes long for the sea, but men at sea turn instinctively to the land, for man is a terrestrial animal. Manson swept the deck with his glass until it rested upon a couple who were standing a little apart from the rest, upon the starboard quarter. In the man he at once recognized Edward Cushing, whose face he knew very well. Beside him stood a woman. She was turned away so that her face was not visible, but her attitude, her dress, the turn of her head were those of Evelyn. It could be none other; it must be Evelyn; it was Evelyn!

Manson dropped the glass with a groan, and hurried back to the office.

"They are on the steamer," he said, "is there any possible way to overtake it?"

"You might charter the tug *Rocket* lying in the slip yonder," suggested the clerk, "although the *Bolivar's* had half an hour's start—and she's a clipper. There's no flies on the *Bolivar*—but I guess the *Rocket* can catch her."

Manson ran for the adjoining dock. The captain of the *Rocket*, a somewhat phlegmatic man in a blue suit, was seated on a stool, leaning against the deck-house, and smoking a pipe.

"I wish," said Manson, "to catch the *Bolivar*. Can you do it?"

The captain looked up from his pipe to a wild-eyed man in a state of intense excitement—too marked an excitement, the captain thought, for a sane and honest man.

"I might and I might n't," he said. The captain sized up his passenger. He was very much agitated, and desperately anxious to overhaul the *Bolivar*. That any one should want to catch a South American steamer was proof of some sort of weakness, mental or moral. Any reasonable white American would be glad of an excuse for missing a steamer to such a country.

"Can you pay for it if I can?"

Manson thrust his hand into his pocket.

"How much will it be?"

The captain wondered just *how* anxious the stranger might be to catch the South American steamer, and how much he might be willing to pay for the accommodation. There were no extradition treaties with several of the South American republics; they were convenient places in which to disappear,—especially if a steamer could be caught after the passenger list had been printed and she had left the dock.

The man wore good clothes, and the stone upon his finger, if genuine, was a valuable one. A man who could wear such a jewel ought to be able to pay.

"One hundred dollars," said the captain.

Manson had thrust his hand into his pocket to encounter only emptiness. He had last drawn out the roll of bills to pay his bill at the hotel, after which he still had about two hundred dollars of the money with which he had left Boston. His expenses for carfare and cab-hire had been paid out of the loose change in his pocket. He dimly remembered having been jostled in the crowd at the New York end of the suspension bridge.

Fate was against him, but he had one more resource.

"My pocket has been picked," he declared. "I'll give you this ring to take me to the *Bolivar*."

The captain's point of view underwent a change. From a rich embezzler his bird had become a mere murderer, or some other sort of vulgar criminal, to escape a felon's cell. Had he been sure of the ring, he might have accepted it, turned it into money, paid the Tug Company the regular fee, (which, by the way, would not have been anything near a hundred dollars), and pocketed a handsome surplus. But if the gem happened to be spurious—which seemed likely enough, since he seemed so willing to part with it—he might have to account for the use of the tug himself, which would leave him out of pocket. With the disappearance of any prospect of profit, his sense of rectitude became forthwith paramount.

"Look here, my fine fellow," he said severely, "I suspect I could get more than a hundred dollars by keeping you right here until I could send for a policeman. I'm not in the business of helping criminals away to South America. I should advise you to look further, before I buy a paper from that lad on the pier yonder and find out what reward has been offered for you. I should think a bird of your feather ought to be worth five hundred to cage, eh?"

Manson realized that it was too late to overtake the steamer. She was already disappearing in the distance, and before he could turn his watch and ring into money, would be beyond the verge of overtaking.

He retraced his steps to the Lambert & Hall pier, and addressed himself to the obliging clerk at the office.

"I could n't make it," he announced dejectedly. "When does the next steamer leave for the same ports?"

"Two weeks from today," replied the clerk. "I'm sorry you were n't sooner. There was plenty of room and good company."

It was apparent, from the would-be passenger's dejected air, that he was greatly disappointed. The clerk was a young man, just engaged to be married. His thoughts gave color to his conjectures. The gentleman's disappointment had probably grown out of a love affair.

"Are you anxious to make the trip sooner?" he asked sympathetically.

"Desperately anxious—more anxious than for any earthly thing—more anxious even than for life."

"There's a Red Star steamer leaves from Pearl Street across the river, a week from today," said the clerk. "We divide the traffic. Ours is the better line and it's worth waiting for, but of course if you start a week sooner you'll get there quicker, even by the opposite line. We can beat 'em a day, but not a week."

"I must go by the first boat," returned Manson. "It is a matter of life and death."

The clerk reflected for a moment.

"There's a tramp steamer loading for Pernambuco and Rio, at Willson and Wilcox's dock below here," he continued. "She's a good sailor, and I don't mind saying that she'll probably get to Pernambuco as soon as the *Bolivar*. I think she sails this afternoon. She don't carry passengers, but you might make a dicker with the captain for a berth in his room. I guess you can persuade him, if it's a matter of life and death."

Manson thanked the accommodating clerk, and hurried away with renewed hope. He found the steamer. The captain was on the dock. All was confusion on the deck, where the first officer was swearing at the men, who were lowering and stowing the bales and boxes which the longshoremen were wheeling on board.

Manson made known his wish and without stating the nature of his errand, gave a strong impression of its urgency. The captain was bluff of manner, but kind of heart.

"It's nothing crooked?" he asked, with a keen glance at Manson. "You're not running away—from the law, for instance?"

"No," said Manson, "it's just the other way; I'm pursuing a criminal."

"Oh, you're an officer?"

"No, an injured man. A passenger on the *Bolivar*, which left the dock an hour ago, has wronged and robbed me, and got away with his plunder."

"Ah, that's different. I despise a thief. Perhaps I can give you the berth, if you're willing to take ship's luck. We're not provisioned for passengers. We sail at five o'clock."

There was further talk, about terms. The captain made some suggestions about an outfit, and Manson made his way back across the river and disposed of his watch and his diamond ring, for much less than their value, but for enough to answer his purpose; and he had no time for haggling. He purchased some light clothing, suitable for the tropics, and a valise to receive his purchases—he had left Boston with nothing but the clothes in which he stood—and at half-past four found himself at the steamer's wharf. He paid his passage money in advance. At five o'clock the *Adelaide* threw off her moorings and started down the bay, in tow of the very tug which had refused to help Manson catch the *Bolivar*.

XIII.
SHIPWRECK

The *Adelaide*, designed originally for a line vessel, had been run for many years in the regular traffic between New York and the West Indies. She had been staunchly built; her lines were graceful; she still made good speed, and looked sound enough as she lay at her moorings in a smart coat of fresh paint. But beneath the surface her plates were badly rusted, and patched in many places. Both steamer and cargo were heavily insured.

Captain Pennock, of the *Adelaide*, was a bluff, hearty seaman, whose one vice, that of inopportune intoxication, had caused him to be broken as master of a line steamer. This, however, was not altogether a disqualification, to owners of a vessel for the loss of which the insurance would have been adequate compensation. Of course these good men would not have imperilled human life or defrauded an insurance company—they would have repudiated any suggestion of the sort with righteous anger. They might have said justly that the *Adelaide* had been examined by the steamboat inspectors and given a certificate that she was sound and staunch and seaworthy. But the fact remained that from the counting-room standpoint the loss of the *Adelaide* would not have been an unmixed misfortune.

The Captain knew the steamer and took his chances. He was down on his luck, and glad to get a berth. The perils of the sea were well known. Did we not pray weekly for those that go down to the sea in ships? One must take chances everywhere. The man who tried to cross the street at Broadway and Union Square was undertaking a more dangerous trip than that from New York to Rio de Janeiro, upon which the *Adelaide* had set out. The steamer could make the voyage quickly and securely in ordinary weather. In the event of a severe storm—well, severe storms were dangerous to the staunchest vessels. Stormy weather was one of the hazards of the sailor's life.

Manson became sea-sick almost as soon as the steamer reached the open water, and was several days recovering. A child of the mountains, he did not love the sea, which returned his antipathy with interest, as the sequel showed.

Nevertheless, after Manson was able to eat his meals and go on deck, the sea and he hid their mutual dislike, for a day or two, under a mask of smiling good humor. The weather was fine. The placid water showed scarcely a ripple. A clear blue sky, a golden sun; the silver moon, the spangled vault of heaven, the varied charms of the open sea, appealed to the innate love for the beautiful which marked the man. But neither sea-sickness nor the beauties of nature at all affected his feelings or intentions toward the objects of his pursuit; nor, since he was possessed of healthy animal instincts, did his fixity of purpose interfere with his susceptibility to physical pain or esthetic pleasure.

He was thrown mostly upon his own thoughts for company. The seamen were mostly lewd fellows of the baser sort, the dregs of the craft, men not able to get a billet on a better boat. Manson was a democrat, in theory; but in practice he was rather select of his company. Not all of his judgments were correct; some of his tastes lacked refinement, but for beauty of form or feature, he had an unerring instinct, and a corresponding aversion for the base and ugly. The sailors were offensive to his sight, and offered no attraction to his mind. That he might find, beneath their dull eyes and weatherbeaten faces, hearts that thrilled with like passions as his own, did not occur to him,—would not, in these men, have interested him. This self-concentration, this unconscious selfishness, born of the early struggles which had thrown him back upon himself, was curiously evident now and then, to others. For instance, he had never had the slightest perception that Evelyn's conduct in throwing Cushing over upon his wedding-day, had been concerned in any way with the point of honor. To Evelyn, in the first months of her marriage, the consciousness that she had broken faith had been the sole drawback to her happiness. The debt of gratitude which the family owed to Cushing remained unsettled, and when the fire of passion had subsided, she had felt something like the sting of remorse. But Manson had not even argued, to himself or to Evelyn, whether or not a bad promise is sometimes better broken than kept. At least it had been his doctrine that a woman, being unmarried, might marry whom she pleased—an argument which she had accepted at the crucial moment, knowing all that such a course involved, and having been, for the month which had elapsed since their meeting, controlled by entirely different considerations. Manson would not have admitted that Evelyn's conduct had been even constructively dishonorable, and he would have regarded as a sheer imbecility the suggestion that his own course was in any way open to criticism. Indeed he gloried in it. He was entirely convinced that in taking Evelyn away from Cushing he had done, as he would have expressed it, "a mighty fine thing." To a mind constituted like Evelyn's, to recognize a debt to honor was in itself the beginning of payment. In Manson, the payment had preceded any consciousness of the debt—he was paying, with compound interest, a bill which had not even been presented.

Captain Pennock had furnished Manson some company. The captain had been for many years in the West Indian trade and knew much of the islands and their customs, and of the strange mixed peoples of tropical America, with tales of whom he beguiled many tedious hours. At other times, he was silent and self-absorbed and perfectly sober. But on the afternoon of the fifth day out, when the steamer had passed the 20th parallel and was somewhat to the eastward of the Caribbean Sea, Captain Pennock paused beside Manson's chair where he was sitting, near noon, under an awning which tempered the growing heat, and Manson became aware of the sickly odor of brandy, perceiving it more keenly because he seldom drank strong liquors.

"How beautifully calm the sea is, Captain!" exclaimed Manson.

"Much too calm, sir," returned the captain. "The glass has been falling steadily for the last two hours. If it does n't blow a gale before night, then I'm no sailor."

The captain's watch was succeeded by that of the first officer,—a great, blonde Norwegian, whose face would have been fair had it not been tanned by the sea air, a head like Olympian Jove, shoulders like Atlas, arms like Vulcan, legs like the columns of a Greek temple. Outlined against sea and sky, he needed only a change of costume to become a Viking standing at the prow of his vessel, pushing on into unknown seas in search of booty or new lands. He was in fact as mild-tempered a mate as ever swore at an able seaman or knocked a malingerer down with a belaying-pin; a good officer, after his kind.

"The captain predicts bad weather, Mr. Nelson," said Manson, as the mate passed by.

"Ay, ay, sir, ve vill haf a storm pime-py. I must make tose tam foremast hands get the teck cleart off and the hatches pattened town."

Captain Pennock's prediction was verified. In half an hour the wind began to rise, and soon became a gale, and increased to a hurricane. It was Captain Pennock's unhappy fate that his disability advanced as the weather grew more dangerous. By the time the wind had risen to a gale, the captain was unable to navigate across the deck. The first officer did all that a man could do, to help the ship ride out the storm. When the gale increased to a hurricane, Captain Pennock, at the moment when judgment and decision were of more value than mere technical seamanship, was dead drunk in his berth.

The great storm of that season is a matter of marine history. It is written in the records of insurance companies, some of which kept no more records thereafter. It is written in the registers of almshouses, and asylums for sailors' orphans. It worked widespread havoc, after the manner of Nature when she wishes to assert herself and teach man his true place in creation; and among other things, it sunk the *Adelaide*.

Not, however, all at once. The steamer was a thoroughbred. She weathered the storm, and, had she been staunch, would have reached her destination. The first officer did his best, luck did the rest, and they were saved, for the time being, at least, from destruction. But the strain had been too much for the old greyhound's battered frame. When the storm had lulled, the vessel was found to be leaking. Then a shaft broke. The steamer drifted for a week under such slender canvas as she carried. The leaks grew worse, the pumps proved inadequate, and in the end it became necessary to abandon the ship.

The captain was now sober, alert, and fully equal to the emergency. It was his fate, when misfortune might be met and overcome, to be incapable of service; but where disaster was inevitable, no one could lead a more orderly retreat than Captain Pennock. Under his directions the boats were provisioned, and supplied otherwise, as fully as there was room and probable need.

Manson had his choice between a boat in command of the captain and one in charge of the first officer. He chose the latter. They left the ship to her fate, hoping to be picked up by a passing steamer and meantime directing their course toward the nearest land, which lay several hundred miles to the westward.

The boats kept together for a day. During the first night the wind rose again, and ere morning they were separated. For a week Manson and his companions toiled at the oars, making a snail-like progress westward, watching the horizon in vain for the ship which should rescue them. For a week liberal rations were served out, and hope ran high. Still there was no ship in sight. The supply of food was cut down one-half. Still no ship appeared, and hope declined. Three days more and starvation threatened them. There was still no ship, and no land in sight, and grim despair showed his face among them, and growing bolder, did battle with hope. One man sickened and died. The plunge of his body as it was dropped into the sea cast a deeper gloom over the rest; it seemed too clearly the doom that awaited them all.

Throughout this trying time, Manson was the life of the party. Borne up by the confident belief that he would live to accomplish his revenge, he succeeded for a few days in warding off the terrible despondency which threatened his party. But nature, as in the storm, was again stronger than the human will. Exerting her power from within or without, she could command victory. The food gave out, then the water. Of the five men left in the boat, two fought desperately with two others for the last few drops, and two of the four, locked in a deadly embrace, fell overboard and were drowned. Those who were left were too weak to rescue them. Manson managed to settle the dispute, and divided the remaining water equitably. Of the crew, thus reduced to three, one became delirious the following night and threw himself into the sea.

Manson and the mate Nelson were now all of the crew that were left. They had ceased any attempt to row. Nelson had lashed the tiller amidships and sat in a stupor at the stern of the boat. Suddenly he roused himself, seized a tin cup which lay in the bottom of the boat, plunged it into the sea, drank greedily of the water, and then relapsed again into stupor. Manson was past remonstrance. He still clung desperately to his own life: his interest in that of others had become a mere dull curiosity. When the copper sun had sunk into the sea of lead, followed by sudden night, Manson slept—a restless doze, from which he awoke during the night to find his companion bending over him, with a bucket poised in his hand. Manson could not see the light of madness in his eyes, but he heard his stertorous breathing, he saw the uplifted object, and divined the mate's fell purpose. Before Manson could rise to defend himself, before he could do more than throw up his arms instinctively, the bucket crushed heavily upon his head. At the same moment Nelson, with a maniac's wild yell, sprang headlong into the sea.

When Manson recovered consciousness he was alone. He bound up his wounded head as best he could with a sleeve of his shirt, which he tore out for the purpose. In the morning it rained, and he spread his handkerchief and squeezed it into his mouth, thus quenching his thirst. A flying fish which dropped into the boat gave him food for the day. Again night came, and there was no land in sight, and no ship on the horizon. He began to notice, too, that his head hurt, and there were shooting pains in his eyes. Obeying an intuition, he lashed himself to the boat. If he should dream—such dreams as come to starving men—he might do himself an injury. For a while the pain kept him awake, but finally he fell asleep, and since his hunger and thirst had been partly satisfied, slept soundly during several hours.

When he awoke it was dark—very dark, he thought, but that was natural enough to one suddenly awakened from sleep during the nighttime. It seemed strange, however, that it should be so densely dark, unless indeed the sky were cloudy. But there had been no sign of a cloud in the air when he had fallen asleep, and even a cloudy sky would scarcely blot out the light so completely that not a star, not the edge of a cloud, not the shimmering crest of a wave would be discernible by a pair of good eyes!

Suddenly the dull throbbing of the wound on his head, behind the eyes, gave place to acute pain, and he uttered a terrible cry, which there was no one to hear—the involuntary expression of the terror which seized him, the terror that had walked by night, the terror of impenetrable darkness. He was alone, on the boundless expanse of ocean, in a small boat, without food or water,—and blind!

Alone at sea, and blind! If food should come within his reach he could not grasp it. If a ship were at hand he could make no sign. His boat might drift past the land, when a mere turn of the rudder would mean rescue, life, revenge! Men go mad in solitary confinement, when there are other men at least near them. The loneliness of a prison is populous beside of the loneliness of the sea; only hope keeps one alive and sane when abandoned to it. But for what could a blind man hope? Even under the best conditions the fate of the blind is tragically wretched, but they can at least have human companionship, and feel the solid earth beneath their feet. Manson was alone, with only a frail plank beneath him and the fathomless depths of the ocean. And yet such is the power of the human heart, that in the breast of this man, who a few weeks before had seemed almost at the summit of human happiness, with long years of wealth, love and honor before him, and who now found himself bereft of all that had constituted his happiness, and reduced to the most abject depth of misery conceivable, the spark of hope still burned, faintly perhaps, but kept alive by a passion for revenge like that of the ancient Greeks, whose shades, even after death had claimed their bodies, carried their earthly hatreds with them into the gloom of Hades itself.

XIV.

A GOOD SAMARITAN

The eastern extremity of Brazil, just below which lies the harbor of Pernambuco, or Recife, is, as may be seen upon the map or any sailing chart, almost directly southeast of New York, with a clear stretch of water intervening; so that steamers running between these ports strike out from New York upon a straight compass course, stopping perhaps at the Bermudas, which lie immediately in their path; continuing thence upon their course until they reach Cape St. Roque, whence they bear southward to their port of destination. This course lies several hundred miles to the eastward of the Leeward Islands, and crosses the equator about five hundred miles from the nearest mainland.

The vast expanse of ocean, stretching from Cape St. Roque to the Gulf of Guinea, unbroken, except for St. Helena and Ascension Island, contains here and there, nearer the South American coast, a few points of land, mainly of volcanic origin, which, because of their unproductiveness, remoteness from the mainland, or insignificant size—or perhaps from all three combined—are left uninhabited. If one perchance is found to contain guano, it is carried away and the island left to the birds. Now and then the lone schooner of some beachcomber may call at the island in the hope of some sort of treasure trove, but for months it may be left untouched by the foot of man. In the seventeenth and eighteenth centuries, when buccaneers swarmed the Spanish Main, such islands were very useful—as places of rendezvous for pirates, as hiding places for ill-gotten wealth, or as prisons upon which to maroon recalcitrant sailors, or passengers whose room, after they had been parted from any portable property which may have been shipped with them, was deemed preferable to their company. Nowadays they serve, sometimes, as a refuge for the shipwrecked; or, when the hurricane rages and the waters near them are not well-known, their hidden reefs help to swell the hosts of those who lie in dreamless and eternal slumber at the bottom of the sea.

Upon such an islet, a well-nigh barren, altogether cheerless spot, a mere speck upon the waste of waters, a tall and slender white man, whose cheeks were bronzed by exposure, stood looking out over the sea. A gentleman, accustomed to a life of luxury, he had lived here alone for two weeks, without shelter, except that of a rude, improvised shack, thatched with leaves from the few straggling palms on the island—fortunately it had not been cold; without clothes, except what he wore upon his person—a shirt, a pair of light trousers suitable for a hot climate, a pair of pumps, well-nigh shapeless from a long soaking in the water, and a sort of hat made of leaves fastened together with thorns; without food, except the shell-fish and turtles' eggs which he had been able to gather upon the beach. Of water he had fortunately had plenty. There was a clear, running spring half-way up the hill of which the island consisted; for, although the shore was somewhat diversified, the island was scarcely a mile across, and rose in the form of a low and somewhat symmetrical cone, with its highest point in the center, from which rose a solitary blasted palm, like a flagstaff crowning a fortification. Here and there were scattered small clumps of palms, and a considerable extent of dense thorny underbrush or chaparral.

Two weeks upon the island had emphasized its loneliness. There was not even a goat that the solitary inhabitant might tame or a parrot that he might teach to speak. The Caribs, who had once inhabited the presumably adjacent mainland, had long since perished from the earth, and he might therefore hope for no Man Friday to rescue from a cannibal feast and make into a companion.

On this clear, hot summer morning, the solitary inhabitant stood upon a hillside, and shading his eyes with his hand, scanned the horizon, and wondered in a bored but still philosophical way, how long his exile would endure. Two weeks before this island had been the most welcome spot on earth; it had offered the alternative of *terra firma* to the unstable element which had supported him for several anxious days, and never had solid ground been more acceptable. To the eastward, some rods from the shore, a long line of breakers marked a dangerous reef, with a narrow opening through which a vessel would scarcely seek to penetrate, at the risk of shipwreck, except in a case of great emergency. The loneliness of the place, after two weeks of solitude, was depressing beyond expression.

"I could welcome," said the tall man, speaking aloud merely to hear the sound of his own voice, so that he might not forget what human speech was like, "I could welcome the devil himself, or my worst enemy. It would at least break this monotony."

This utterance merely voiced his discontent; for he did not believe in the devil, and while there were men whom he did not love, and one at least toward whom he cherished a deep and abiding sense of injury, he was not aware that he had an enemy in the world, in the sense of one who would like to do him harm.

Having scanned the horizon without result, the man sighed, and turned his eyes upon the beach at his feet. He was somewhat long-sighted, and had lost his eyeglasses, and while nature, thrown upon her own resources, had corrected the fault in some degree, it was a moment or two before his vision was so focused that he perceived an empty boat, lying with her nose to the beach, against which she was pounding slightly. He ran hastily down the hill. This boat, which had drifted from he knew not whence, must be secured; it might furnish the means of escape from his island prison.

When he reached the boat he found, to his surprise, a man lying in the bottom, at first sight scarcely more than the skeleton of a man, so terribly was he emaciated. His scanty clothing hung loosely upon his wasted frame. His eyes were closed; his purple lips were blistered and swollen; his face was covered with a disfiguring stubble. He lay perfectly still, upon his back, in the bottom of the boat. Appearance, attitude, everything, indicated that another had been added to the endless roll of the victims of the sea.

With a quick sympathy, for which his own minor sufferings had laid the foundation, the inhabitant dragged the boat up upon the beach, lest it should be washed away by the tide, which was nearing its ebb. It was a heavy boat, and his strength could make but little impression upon it. When he had drawn it as high up as he could, he took the line which he had found in the bottom of the boat, and fastened it around a near-by boulder. This would hold it for a while, and when the tide came in again, it could be drawn farther up upon the beach and fastened more securely.

Having thus temporarily secured this possible means of escape, he turned his attention to the body in the boat. There had been no visible signs of life; but by applying his hand over the castaway's heart, with the manner of one not altogether ignorant of what he was about, the man in possession discovered a faint movement which indicated that life was not yet extinct, though the stranger was perilously near death by starvation.

"Poor devil!" he soliloquized. The expression was purely idiomatic, and had no conscious reference to the author of evil, whom he had a moment before been ready to welcome— "Poor devil, I sympathize with him, I've been on the ragged edge myself, but not quite so nearly over!"

The first inhabitant, no longer solitary, since chance had thus doubled the population of the island, after this remark picked up the wooden pail which lay in the bottom of the boat, and hastened up the hill. Returning in a few minutes, he dipped out some water with the tin cup which was part of the boat's equipment, and held it to the lips of the unconscious stranger, the muscles of whose throat contracted automatically to swallow the life-giving fluid as soon as it had passed between the swollen lips.

"If I only had some whiskey," he muttered, "I could bring him round easily. But such is life! Where liquor is n't needed, and brings death and destruction in his train, there's too much of it. Here where it might save a life, there's none to be had."

He lifted the stranger's body from the boat—an easy task for it was light and limp—and deposited it upon the soft sand.

"The man is starved! He should be fed on warm milk and beef tea. The proper thing would be to send to the drug-store for a jar of extract of beef. But here we have, unfortunately, neither drug store, beef nor fire. I never appreciated quite so much as during my sojourn on this island, the advantages of civilization of which I was beginning to tire. By Jove!" he exclaimed, as a sudden thought struck him, "why had n't that occurred to me before? It's once chance in a million, but—"

He sank to his knees beside the unconscious stranger, and went rapidly through his pockets. When he drew out of one a revolver wrapped in an oilskin cover, he merely felt the outside to ascertain the contents, and then laid it aside. The remainder of his search produced only a pocketbook, which he also laid aside, and a metal matchbox, which he grasped with a joyful exclamation.

"Ah! here it is! Let us hope it's full."

His hope was doomed to disappointment. There were several matches in the box, but the water in which the man had been lying, at the bottom of the boat, had penetrated between the body of the box and the lid and ruined every one. Moreover, it had soaked the heads entirely away; it was not even possible to dry them in the sun, with the hope that one of them might ignite.

A look of deep dejection settled over the islander's face.

"Old fellow," he said reflectively, "you are pretty far gone, and unless I can get into your starved stomach some nourishment that it can assimilate, I fear you will soon be as dead as you look. By the way," he added with a sudden tightening of his brows, "where have I met you?"

There was of course no answer. The islander stared curiously down into the unconscious face, but while it dimly suggested the features of some one he had met, memory did not come at once to his aid. After a brief inspection of the other's features, his eyes wandered to the revolver in its oilskin cover, lying on the sand where he had dropped it.

"Eureka!" he exclaimed, stooping to catch it up. "I have it—if this is loaded and dry!"

He tore off the cover—the manner in which it was wrapped gave him hope. The revolver proved to be loaded, and the cartridges had been kept dry. He handled the weapon curiously.

"You were made," he said, still speaking aloud to himself as lonely men are apt to do, "you were made as a instrument of death. I will turn you, if I am fortunate enough, into a means of life."

Leaving the revolver upon the sand, he walked over to where the beach joined the underbrush, and gathering dry grass and bits of driftwood, heaped them into a little pile. Then cocking the revolver, he stuck the muzzle into the heap and pulled the trigger. There was no resulting explosion.

A second attempt was more successful; the cartridge exploded, but the tinder did not ignite.

The islander began to grow anxious. After the next shot he waited a moment, and as a faint smoke first appeared, followed by a thin flame, hardly visible in the ardent sunlight, his face cleared and beamed with satisfaction. As the fire grew he fed it carefully, and when it was well started, heaped on heavier pieces of the driftwood with which the beach was sparsely strewn.

When the fire was burning well enough to take care of itself for a few moments, he picked up the tin cup, went a short way along the beach, and stooping down from time to time, extracted from the sand, at various intervals, certain small round objects, until having collected a dozen of these, he returned to the fire. Gathering a couple of small stones from the beach and drawing some of the hot coals to one side, he emptied the tin cup on the sand, dipped some water into it, and set it over the fire. When it boiled, he dropped in a couple of the turtle's eggs which he had collected, mashed them with a stick, and in a few minutes had some warm and nourishing broth.

The odor of cooked food which he had not tasted for several weeks, was so seductive that it was only with an effort that he could restrain himself from devouring it. He did so, however, and having lifted off the cup and left it on the ground to cool, set about finding something with which to feed the broth to the patient. It was easily found; there was a great confusion of sea-shells near at hand, ranging from the huge conch to the most delicate spiral, many of them rare and curious. A simple clam shell, however, was best adapted for his purpose, and made a very good spoon. The broth being still hot, he cooled it with a little water from the pail, lifted the head of the unconscious man and fed him a few drops at a time, with the life-giving liquid.

The result was soon apparent. When the islander had given him enough, for a beginning, he laid the stranger down, and felt of his heart. It was beating more strongly already and a faint pulse was discernible in his wrist. Seeing the stranger on the road to recovery, the islander momentarily turned his attention to his own wants, and in a few minutes had cooked and eaten, with huge satisfaction, all the turtle eggs that were left.

The meal ended, the islander replenished the fire in a manner to keep it alive for some time, and then set about removing the sick man to a place of shelter; for the hot tropical sun was now beginning to beat down fiercely, and would soon become well-nigh unendurable, except in the shade.

Out of bits of driftwood and the trunks of such saplings as he had been able to cut down with a clasp-knife, the islander had built against the overhanging side of the rock a rude hut, which sheltered him from the heat by day and the chill that sometimes came at night. To this he now carried the rescued man, who was still unconscious. The transfer was not made without considerable effort, for, while the stranger was greatly emaciated, he was of larger frame than the islander, who, in spite of his height, was a man of slight build. When he had laid the sick man down upon the couch of dry grass which had formed his own bed, and had disposed him as comfortably as was possible, under the circumstances, the islander returned to the beach. It was about time, he reasoned, to give the patient something more to eat.

When he had gathered and prepared some more turtles' eggs, he replenished the fire on the beach below, and bringing with him a burning piece of wood, started another fire on the hillside, near the hut. It was but a matter of a few minutes to prepare the food, with which he again fed the rescued man, who by this time showed rapid improvement, and some signs of returning consciousness.

After completing this task, the islander set out with the pail for more water. When he neared the hut upon his return, the stranger was talking, with a shrill and rapid flow of words. The islander needed only to approach and listen, to discover that the utterances were those of delirium.

"I'll kill him on sight, like a mad dog. As for her, she is a woman and over-persuaded. The scoundrel that did it must die. An eye for an eye, a tooth for a tooth. I'll kill him! This weapon shall never leave my person until I have unloaded it into his."

"Quite interesting!" mused the islander, as he looked down upon the other, who was moving restlessly but feebly. "I'm evidently on the track of a tragedy. It never rains but it pours. I've been a traveler for twenty years and never had an adventure. Now within a couple of weeks I've been lost at sea, in a most unusual way, and cast on an uninhabited island, where I seemed to be doomed to remain alone indefinitely; I've rescued a man in much worse case than myself, and I am on the track of a tragedy designed to end in blood. I'll be able to write a book when I get away from this island—if I ever do."

The newcomer was resting more quietly. The islander went over and give him some more water, which he swallowed greedily, making a faint but ineffectual effort to reach the cup with his hands. After drinking he seemed to fall asleep, whereupon the islander left him, and climbed to the highest point of the island, about half a mile away, where he had rigged a signal to the blasted palm-tree. He had been a much travelled man, and knew how savages climb tall trees with ease. By weaving around the trunk of the tree a strong hoop or circlet of flexible vines, of sufficient size to admit his body and leave room for a purchase, he had been able, bracing his waist against one side of the hoop, and placing his feet against the tree, by successive shifts of the hoop to work his way upward to the top of the tree, where he had fastened one of his few garments as a signal of distress to any vessel approaching the island.

When he had seen that his signal was securely fast, and had ascertained, by scanning the horizon, that no ship was yet in sight, he went back to his hut. He observed that the stranger still seemed asleep, and as a precaution carefully covered up with ashes the embers of the fire. It was now near noon, and growing very hot. He was tired from his unusual exertions and the excitement attending the stranger's arrival. It was time for a siesta. He lay down on the shady side of the hut, and himself soon fell asleep.

XV.
TEMPTATION

"Evelyn!"

The islander stirred in his sleep, then awoke and sat up.

"I was dreaming, no doubt," he murmured, "and called out her name in my sleep. But I cannot remember my dream, not any of it at all."

"Evelyn—"

He was not dreaming now, nor was it he who had spoken. The voice came from within the hut. In a moment the stranger was talking volubly while the islander listened intently.

"Ah, Evelyn," he was saying, "you will marry no one but me! We were made for each other; the proof lies in this, that from our first meeting our hearts have beat but for each other!"

"Her name is Evelyn," sighed the islander. "Poor fellow! Our fates seemed to have paralleled each other at more points than one."

"No, Evelyn—let me call you Evelyn!—it is a sweet name, and since it is your name, there is no sweeter—no, Evelyn, you cannot marry that poor weak creature! He is old, Evelyn, and we are young! He is rich, but what is wealth without love? And I shall make money—it is easy enough. He hasn't even made money. You are not for him, Evelyn; I want you and I mean to have you. As to him, he is a mere clothes-horse, Evelyn, a mere frame to hang coats on. I've learned all about him. He's never done anything but bear his honored name—honored because his ancestors did things—and wander up and down the earth. He's done nothing to justify his right to live—except to be born, which he could not help, and for which he's been amply enough rewarded. You were made for a man, Evelyn, and for a mother of men!"

The islander frowned and listened even more intently. This might be delirium—it was very obviously delirium—but there seemed to be method in it—method which brought a cold frown to the islander's brow and a hostile look into his eyes,—which brought him to his feet and led him toward the shack.

"Your word? That you have given him your word is nothing! To extort it from you was a cowardly outrage! He is fifty, if a day, and he offers to buy you with his gold, and chain your glorious youth to his decrepitude. He should have married years ago; it was a duty he owed to society. Now, after he has wasted his youth, now that he needs not a wife but a nurse, he has selected you for that worthy office; the Sultan has thrown his handkerchief. Bah, Evelyn, the thought sickens me!—sickens you darling, for I feel you shudder in my arms. You are mine, Evelyn, mine forever. Your heart is mine already, you shall be all mine tomorrow, and once mine, always mine, for what I once possess, dear heart, I never yield! Forget this old and musty Cushing, Evelyn, and kiss me, kiss me, darling, once more before we part! Soon we shall part no more!"

The islander had risen to his feet, and was peering into the open door of the hut, and into the wide-open, staring eyes of the sick man, who, with fever-flushed face, was tossing in delirium, but gave no sign of seeing the man who stood over him, frowning heavily.

"Why!" exclaimed the islander, with astonishment pictured upon his face, "it's the fellow himself. I thought I had seen that face somewhere. But what a coincidence! How, in the name of heaven, came he here?"

The mystery was soon solved, as Manson—the stranger was Evelyn's husband—in the delirium of fever unfolded, incoherently, disconnectedly, the links in the chain of events of the past few weeks—the discovery of his wife's flight, her letter, Leonie's revelations, his fruitless pursuit, the ruin of his fortunes, his deadly and undying purpose. Curiously enough, his disordered fancy did not touch the events of his voyage, but dealt entirely with the period anterior to his taking ship. And, curiously also, the islander followed this incoherent revelation, re-arranged its disordered sequence, and bridged over the gaps, as easily as though he were familiar with the whole history. All the while, his face marked distinctly, though there was no one to see it, surprise becoming wonder, and wonder astonishment, anger barely escaping rage, and settling into contempt, scorn and a certain bitter humor at Manson's wild goose chase and his present bitter predicament.

When he had heard enough, or as much as he could endure, the islander, or to drop a thin disguise, Edward Cushing, rose and walked away beyond the range of the sick man's ravings. In the struggle between good and evil forces which now took place in Cushing's mind evil had all the preliminary advantage. The cold eye, the stern set lips, the pale cheeks were indubitable marks of hostile feeling. Cushing's nature, like that of other men, was a mixture of good and evil. Self-love had not blinded him to that fact;—if no man is a hero to his valet, still less is any thoroughly sane man a hero to himself. Cushing had never been so self-centered as to believe himself perfect; but on the other hand, he had never been subjected, even in his self-searching moods, to so merciless an analysis as Manson had unconsciously made of him. It was unjust, but contained enough of truth to make it rankle. The primal instinct, which had impelled him to feel, a year before in the full tide of his newborn passion, that he could kill anyone who should rob him of Evelyn, now returned with redoubled force. He had been robbed and wronged, infamously wronged. By what freak of fate must he be compelled to act the Good Samaritan, not to a stranger, but to the only man he thoroughly detested, and who awoke all his baser instincts? He wished neither speech nor any other association with the fellow. He should be supplied with food for a few days, and then he would do well to keep his distance. Solitude, and remoteness from civilization were not conducive to self-restraint; primal instincts might easily assert themselves, and Cushing would not answer for himself indefinitely.

He watched the horizon carefully. If a ship should come to-day, it would relieve him from an unenviable situation. But no distant speck marred the perfect line where sky and water met, and at the end of an hour, when his mood had softened somewhat, Cushing returned to the hut. He approached it at a backward angle from the opening which served as doorway, so that he was not visible from within, and he stepped softly so that his approach might not be audible. The sick man's fever was due to exposure and star-vation; it might disappear when hunger had been long enough appeased. Cushing wished to know whether his patient were asleep, delirious or fully conscious—or dead, which he might easily be; he had been perilously near it, and a slight reaction might snuff out his life like a candle flame. Cushing paused and listened now and then but there was no sound. When within reach he cautiously parted two of the branches form-ing the side of the hut, and peered through the opening.

The patient had risen half way from a recumbent posture, and with his hands stretched out, was feeling round him, like one in the dark. While Cushing looked on curiously, Manson rose unsteadily to his feet, and began to grope his way about the hut.

"Where am I?" he muttered, "and is it day or night? Hello! Hello! Hello!" and Manson's only reply was the echo of his own voice. Cushing made no sound, but advanced noiselessly toward the front of the hut until he faced the door, from which at the same moment Manson emerged with an uncertain step.

"I'm on land, thank God," he muttered, "and yet I smell the sea, and hear its murmuring. How I hate the sea! I've been lying on the grass, and when I put out my hand it touches leaves and branches; and yet the grass is dry and thick, as though it had been gathered a long time, and the branches form a shelter, to keep off the sea-breeze. I must have had food and drink, for I'm not thirsty, nor quite so hungry. I smell burning wood, so there must be fire somewhere about; and where there's fire there must be men. Hello! Hello!"

He was facing Cushing with eyes wide open and staring; but Cushing knew that he did not see him—knew that he was blind.

"Hello!" repeated Manson, and there being no response, raised his voice almost to a shriek. But the silence remained unbroken save by the sound of his own voice, and the constant murmur of the sea.

The only man who could have answered him moved cautiously and noiselessly away for a distance of several rods. Having gone far enough to suit his purpose, he sat down with his back against a tree, and his face toward the blind man, and renewed the conflict from which he had just emerged.

Edward Cushing was a fair type of the cultivated man. In his family, plain humanity had been overlaid by several generations of culture, and in his particular case, by a lifetime of study, of travel, of thought, of human intercourse. He had imagined himself charitable, humane, generous. He had spent much time and money in the service of others. If he had been narrow and too much self-contained; if he had helped others subjectively—for his own self-satisfaction, more than for that of humanity, he had not known it. He had imagined his benefactions, including those to Henry Thayer's family, to be a rather fine thing; and he had tested the Scriptural doctrine that it was more blessed to give than to receive. Until his experience with Evelyn Thayer, he had passed through no great emotional experience—had endured no great loss, sorrow or temptation. He had not lived to be past forty without several earnest friendships, among which he reckoned that with Alice Thayer, although it was rooted in his affection for her dead husband, and always partaken of the nature of a legacy. He had looked upon passionate love, with its offspring of jealousy, hatred and revenge, as something for the vulgar, who did not possess the resources of culture or the consolations of philosophy. His sudden passion for Evelyn had been his first awakening, and had so completely filled his heart for the time being, that he had no time to think of it as a reversal of his whole theory of life. His misfortune, and a subsequent year of opportunity for reflection, had made clear to him that love, with all its attendant passions, was a very real and vital thing, so real, that, once stirred to action, it might, whether fortunate or unsuccessful, determine the course of a man's life.

Evelyn's defection had still further shaken his moral foundations. He had tasted the bitterness of defeat, the humiliation of a man esteeming himself and esteemed by others, deserted for a younger man. He had felt the sting of pity, and had divined the jeers of contempt. He had rankled under a fierce and gnawing jealousy; he had felt the poison of hatred, the animal longing for revenge. He had gone away for a year, and then, too proud to condemn himself to exile for a false woman, had come back meaning to resume his place in the world where he belonged, and with some vague idea of utilizing the talents he had let lie fallow for so long. He had met Evelyn unintentionally, unexpectedly, and had felt some revival of his former passion, mingled with a melancholy regret. Her husband he had until then never spoken to, nor did he wish to know a man whose character, judged by his conduct, was entirely devoid of honor. That he possessed a certain talent, amounting almost to genius and serviceable to his generation, was probably true enough. Whether he knew anything else than his trade Cushing neither knew nor cared. He had wished Evelyn no harm, but could hardly be expected to concern himself greatly about her happiness. He had rigidly suppressed his feelings and schooled himself to meet her if his continued friendship with her mother should make it impossible to avoid the daughter; and he found the task easier than he thought, than he had deemed possible.

Then had supervened the events of the past three weeks, and now fate had brought Evelyn's husband and himself to this lonely island, had revived all these settled issues and placed his rival in his power. They were far from civilization, which, by the common experience of mankind, seems to lose its force with the square of the distance from its strongholds. Cushing was absolutely at liberty to act, with no restraint except such as his own will might impose; with no responsibility, except to his own conscience.

His enemy—and why was Manson not his enemy?—had robbed him of his bride, of his one love, almost at the very altar—his enemy was in his power, bound hand and foot. Three weeks of solitude and shipwreck do not strengthen the moral fibre. Forced to live like primitive man, one would revert to primeval savagery; and Cushing had gone far enough, an hour before, to weigh in his own mind, the question of letting this man starve, or of going back, armed with Manson's weapon, and inviting the attack which Manson had set out from home to make upon him. Of the issue there could be no doubt, and he would be justified, if, in self-defense, he should kill the other. Manson, who had come two thousand miles, to kill him, would ask for no explanations; his delirium had made this much clear, and Cushing owed him none. To fight Manson would be a pleasure; to kill him might bring its reward.

This impulse conquered, he had come back to the camp to reconnoiter, before deciding upon any definite course. The man might die from natural causes, which would relieve any embarrassment. He was not dead, and Cushing was assailed by the same temptation in a different and much stronger form.

The man was blind, and therefore absolutely helpless! Even Cushing, in possession of all his faculties, had not found it easy to maintain life on this tiny island. Clothing and shelter, in a tropical climate, in the dry season, had been of slight importance; but to procure food had tested his powers to the utmost, and for fire he had been dependent upon the accident which had brought his enemy. Manson was blind; by himself he could find nothing; without succor he must inevitably face the death by starvation from which he had so lately escaped. Cushing did not need to lift his hand. His presence on the island need not be known to the blind man. If he chose, he might watch his sufferings and gloat over them; or if this were distasteful, he might merely keep away from Manson until the inevitable end. Revenge was sweet! The man had come to kill him: it would be no more than even-handed justice to let the would-be murderer die;—the man had wronged him; he ought to suffer for it!

Then too, there was Evelyn! Were this man out of the way, she would be entirely free. She might well be sorry for her former treachery. A touch of poverty would strengthen her remorse. That he would soon get away from the island there could be no doubt. It was inconceivable that an island in the Atlantic Ocean, every mile of which must have been surveyed and charted, could long remain unvisited by some ship. Evelyn, free and repentant, would be glad to seek refuge in his arms.

The blind man had wandered a little farther from the hut. He was struck by a sudden and terrible fear of loneliness. Perhaps there was no one there. His boat might have drifted on a barren island. In delirium he might have wandered into a wood and lain down upon the grass within the leafy covert. He may not have eaten, he may not have drunk—it might all have been a mere hallucination.

"Hello! Hello! Hello!" he cried, continuing with a long yodeling mountain call of his boyhood. A faint echo came back, that was all; and on every side was the restless, ceaseless booming of the sea.

"God in heaven," he muttered, despairingly, "do I merely dream that I have eaten and drunk; and am I alone and blind?"

That Cushing should have been tempted was natural enough. Under the circumstances it was inevitable that to an active, imaginative mind, smarting with a sense of outrage, every selfish consideration should present itself with unnatural force.

But it was equally inevitable, after the first fierce struggle had spent itself, that Cushing should do none of the things he had considered. His race, his civilization, his training, all constrained him to do otherwise. He bore the man no love, but he could not see him starve. To succor him was an elementary duty, as to destroy him had been an elementary impulse; and in Edward Cushing the developed altruism of the race was the stronger feeling. It was civilization against barbarism, in a mind where civilization, being in possession, was bound to win against barbarism, so long banished as to be merely an invader. He must speak to Manson, and must supply his wants, within his power to do so.

So far Cushing would go, but, for the time being, no farther. He did not love Manson. He had no desire to make him happy. That Manson might suffer mental anguish, growing out of his own folly, was no concern of Cushing's. If Manson's marriage with Evelyn had brought these woes in its train, let him suffer! It was no more just. He, Cushing, was under no moral obligation to relieve Hugh Manson of any merited punishment. There was a law of compensation in nature; those who sinned against others should expiate their sins. Cushing had suffered most horribly at Manson's hands, for no fault of his own, unless his engagement might be called a mistake of judgment. He would feed and shelter and tend this man, because he was a man; but Manson might continue to suffer any purely mental anguish he may have brought upon himself, until they were rescued from their prison. Cushing would not usurp the place of providence, by seeking to increase Manson's punishment, nor would he presume to interfere to lessen it.

To Cushing this seemed but justice, and he was not at the moment equal to more. The matter was entirely in his own hands, and he might choose his own course. Any deception he might practice, any reservations he might make, for what he deemed sufficient reasons, were easy of accomplishment. None are so helpless as the blind, and never was blind man so helpless as Manson.

XVI.

DAVID AND JONATHAN—WITH A DIFFERENCE

The blind man had felt his way back to the hut, over the outside of which he was running his hand vaguely. Cushing rose and walked toward him.

Manson caught the sound.

"Hello!" he called again anxiously.

"Hello!" replied Cushing, in an ordinary tone.

"Thank God!" exclaimed Manson fervently, "a man, a white man, and an American, if I can trust my hearing."

"You're not discreet," responded Cushing drily. "It's safe enough to assume that I am a man. But I might have been a negro, with whom these waters abound, and most of whom speak English; or I might have been a European. Possible neither would have been flattered by your exclamation."

"Ah, my friend," said Manson, "I care not what you are, so that you be my friend; for never was man in harder case than I, or needed a friend worse. I was ruined before I started on my voyage, and now, in addition, I am shipwrecked, starved and blind. The last I knew of myself I was alone, wounded and sightless in an open boat at sea. Now, I am on dry land, have been fed by you, I suppose,—though I'm still outrageously hungry,—and am face to face with a friend; for whoever would n't befriend one in my predicament would have to be less than human, and your voice has the ring of a true man. Where am I, friend?"

"You've stated the situation almost as well as though you could see," returned Cushing. "You're on land, quite true, but the land is a small island, about a mile across, and evidently of volcanic origin. It is the only land in sight, and I have felt it shake once or twice beneath me, so I cannot vouch for its permanent solidity."

"It's better than the sea," returned the blind man. "If it shakes occasionally, the sea moves all the time. I hate the sea! What is the name of this island?"

"I don't know," returned Cushing. "It has a name, no doubt, for there are no uncharted seas in this part of the world, but what it is I've no idea."

"Have you been here long?" asked Manson.

"Two weeks," rejoined the other.

"And you've not inquired of any one the name of the island? But perhaps you don't speak their language? There can't be very many inhabitants, on so small an island."

"The only language spoken on this island is English," replied Cushing, "and you and I are the only ones who speak it."

"What!" exclaimed the blind man, "we are shipwrecked on a desert island?"

"Not exactly a desert island, for it has water enough, and food, in moderation; an uninhabited island, except for us. But it cannot be far from the mainland, and doubtless some ship will call, in the course of time, and take us off. But who are you, and how came you here? Of course I know you came in a boat—but before that? You must have quite a story to tell."

"My name is Manson—Hugh Manson. I was a passenger on the steamer *Adelaide*, bound for Pernambuco, Bahia and Rio de Janeiro. We rode out the great storm of three weeks ago, but emerged too badly battered to keep afloat. The crew and I, the only passenger, abandoned the ship and took to the boats. Of one boatload I am the sole survivor; and I have lost, I hope not forever, my most valuable part, for what is a man without eyes? A mere useless lump of clay. If I had not found you here I should have been dead already. May I ask your name?"

Cushing had anticipated the question. Clearly the blind man did not suspect in the slightest degree to whom he was speaking. He had never heard Cushing's voice, or, if so, but seldom, and it meant no more to him than any stranger's. Cushing, having decided to keep Manson in the dark as to his identity, had no scruples about the method. In ordinary dealings between man and man he would have scorned a lie; he would even have hesitated at it with a woman. But this was a different case; there being no obligation, there was no obstacle.

"I call myself Singleton," he said. "I was a passenger on the steamer *Notre Dame de los Remedios* bound from Rio to Havana. We were caught in the same storm, and I reached this island—alone. For the rest, ask the sea: it will hardly give up its secrets."

"It's a wonderful coincidence," said Manson. "Though I was brought up in the Baptist Church, and know the Bible by heart, I've never really taken much stock in religion. There's too much to be done in this world, to spend much time upon the other. But who could deny the finger of Providence in this? I am cast on these shores, alone and blind, and you are here to succor me! You have given me food and drink, and company without which I must have died. I have a mission, too, and my rescue stamps it with God's approval. Otherwise why should I alone, of all my party, have been miraculously spared?"

"A mission?"

"Yes, to rid the world of a scoundrel, who is n't fit to live. Did I have a revolver when I came ashore?"

"Yes, I've taken care of it!"

"Keep it for me. I shall need it yet, Singleton,—my friend."

Cushing smiled cynically. To him, Edward Cushing, a gentleman, a scholar, a philosopher, Evelyn had preferred this shallow fool, this poor ignoramus, who could imagine that a merciful, all-wise and all-powerful God had interfered with the natural sequence of cause and effect, in order that some one might be in readiness to receive this fool upon an unpeopled island, in order that he might be sustained and comforted and carried forward in a murderous enterprise. To such a fellow Evelyn was tied. She must long since have recognized his limitations, and Cushing already had reason to suspect that she had not been perfectly happy.

"I know your story," said Cushing. "You were delirious this morning, and talked a great deal."

"Ah, well! then I need n't tell you any more. And now Singleton, my friend—for your voice tells me that you *are* my friend, tell me something more about our predicament—where we are, what our chances of escape are, and how, if at all, I can help myself or you?"

There was a certain frank directness about Manson which from the very beginning of their acquaintance, struck Cushing favorably in spite of his prejudice. It might of course be merely superficial, but Cushing could easily imagine that it might have proved attractive to an impressionable young woman, especially if used as the vehicle for impassioned love-making. Cushing himself was unconsciously so influenced by it as to find himself, a moment later detailing quite freely to the blind man his views of the island's location, its resources, and his own speculations, as to the probability of their speedy rescue.

"We are on an island in the Atlantic," returned Cushing, "somewhere between the equator on the south and the tropic of Cancer on the North, and between the Carribean sea and the northwest coast of Africa. The island is something less than a mile in diameter, is of volcanic origin, and is likely to end as it began if certain tremors that have shaken it during my brief residence have any serious meaning. I hope it may last as long as we stay."

"It might do that, and blow up, or sink in the sea, tomorrow."

"Quite true; I stand corrected—I hope it may outlast our stay. It is uninhabited, except for us. The sources of food consist of one clump of banana trees, the fruit of which I have practically used up, until the green bananas ripen; and the turtle's eggs which I may be able to find along the beach. Our chances for getting away are indefinite; I have no data on which to calculate them. It is three weeks since I saw a sail, and that was on my own ship, and was not a sail, but a naked mast, backed by a smokestack. There is no land in sight, and I have no idea how far we are from the nearest place where civilized men live. Our ship had been driven somewhat out of her course by the storm. I don't know her latitude when I last saw her, but imagine, from the time I was in the water, that she was not more than twenty-five miles from this island."

"How did you come ashore, in a boat?"

"No, in a life preserver."

"Your steamer was wrecked in the storm?"

"Probably; but not at the time I left her. I jumped overboard."

"On purpose?"

"Yes."

"Why? You don't talk like a fool."

"All men are fools; at least no man is wise. 'At thirty man suspects himself a fool; knows it at forty.' "

"Quite right, Singleton, and sometimes learns it sooner. You too have felt the sea, I see! Give me your hand—I should like to shake it on that proposition. But you had some reason for jumping overboard."

"I was standing by another passenger. This other passenger, a—friend of mine, was sick of melancholia—life had no charm; death seemed an easy solution of a hard problem. As I turned away, my friend, seizing this unguarded moment, sprang into the sea. I turned, and seeing a vacant place where my friend had stood, looked instinctively over the rail, and saw a body struggling in the water. I seized a life preserver, threw it outward, and then grasping another, leaped overboard."

"And did you save your friend?"

"No."

"And the steamer left you there? The captain should be shot!"

"I imagine we were not missed for some time. I kept afloat until the steamer disappeared, and then I drifted to this island. My friend, of whom I saw no more, was probably drowned."

"I am sorry. I have tasted death upon the sea; I should have died of it but for you. I hate the sea. I sympathize with you, Singleton. I suppose you loved your friend."

"Yes, the relation was more than that of friendship; there was a nearer tie."

"I think there is no finer feeling than friendship, Singleton. During my childhood I never had a friend. In youth and early manhood I knew a man who was more than a friend. He reached down and lifted me up, and he died before I had grown to a stature which would have permitted me to call him by that sacred name; I loved him, but I could never be familiar with him. I like your voice, Singleton, and I feel that we're going to be friends. You are already my benefactor. I am blind, and what can a blind man do on a desert island, where there is not even a surgeon who can tell him whether he shall ever see again? I *must* see, Singleton; I have a sacred duty to perform, which, if I were to remain blind might prove difficult of accomplishment."

"When and how did you lose your sight?" asked Cushing.

Manson related the circumstances of the attack in the boat, premising it with a brief recital of prior events. Cushing was struck by the simplicity, force and directness of his language, and by his dramatic power of statement. In spite of a strong antipathy to this blind rival, he was involuntarily drawn along in the current of the story; he felt the pangs of hunger and of thirst, the dejection, the incipient madness; the terror of blindness, the impending hopelessness of despair; and beneath them all, superior to them all, the strong will, the dominant purpose, the fire of energy which would not be extinguished. He could understand how a young and impressionable woman, like Evelyn, might be moved by this unconscious eloquence, reinforced by a mutual passion. A dangerous man to be at large, unless a good man. His course with regard to Evelyn demonstrated that he was lacking in the sense of honor. If he could steal a man's bride at the altar, would he hesitate, when his passion cooled, to steal anything else that he might covet, to disregard any ties, violate any obligations, however sacred?

Nevertheless, Cushing felt compelled to do for Manson whatever lay within the limitations Cushing had prescribed for himself. This consideration prompted his next remark.

"Do your eyes give you any pain?" he asked as the other had finished his narrative. "I know something of medicine and surgery."

"Singleton, I know from your voice that you're a man of feeling, who can sympathize with another's misfortune. Every now and then my eyes pain me most damnably."

"I'm no oculist, and there are neither instruments nor drugs upon this island. But I might know enough about the eye to form an opinion of the nature of the injury. Describe your symptoms."

Manson gave the history of his affliction; it was brief, clear, succinct, a marvel of lucid statement.

"I imagine your blindness is due to some very simple thing," returned Cushing; "perhaps a mere pressure on the optic nerve, resulting from the injury. A very simple operation, by a competent person, might relieve it. It may pass away itself, in time."

"Ah, Singleton, you have given me life and now you bring me hope. None but the blind know how terrible an affliction is blindness. Why, to see is my life! I love the world because it is beautiful. When you give me hope, it is the next best thing to restoring my sight. We cannot remain long upon this island; there are too many ships in these waters. I wonder how far we may be from the mainland, or from some inhabited island? Have you noticed the wind, Singleton?"

"The wind is from the west."

"That is as it should be in this latitude. Have you seen any birds alight on the island?"

"Yonder is one now. He has perched on the top of my lookout. He sits still, as though he were tired."

"Keep your eye on him."

Five minutes later. "How is the bird?"

"He still sits there. He might be carved in stone."

"He must have come a long way, Singleton," said Manson with a sigh.

"We have your boat," returned the other.

Manson shuddered. "I could not get in that boat again, nor trust myself at sea without a staunch ship under my feet. I have just come through hell in a small boat. If we should put to sea, and anything should happen to you, it would be the same thing over again for me. We shall have to wait for a ship. I could n't go in the boat, and you would n't desert me. Your voice tells me that."

Such an attitude seemed to Cushing the personification of selfishness; but blindness, he knew, narrowed the world to a very small circle. This fellow Manson evidently regarded himself as the center of the universe, the other activities of which were valuable exactly as they were related to the gratification of his own desires. That he was deprived of a sense, merely limited the scale of his desires and thereby intensified his selfishness;—what was lost in extent was gained in strength. Cushing foresaw that Manson would be a troublesome companion. Already he resisted stubbornly their most obvious method of departure from the island.

Manson was not entirely useless. It is true that the labor of providing food for them both fell upon Cushing, but Manson made useful suggestions. He taught Cushing how to make a trap to catch the birds which landed on the island, and how to weave, out of splints cut from green wood, a basket-trap for fish, which was set in the little sheltered cove where the rivulet from the spring found its outlet to the sea, where, by the way, Cushing had secured Manson's boat. They found some crayfish, too, which, now that they had fire proved a palatable dish. Cushing had not, for many years, enjoyed the best products of the best kitchens so much as he did these rude repasts of this tropical island, cooked on the embers, served on green leaves, and eaten without knives or forks. Life in the open air brought health and vigor and appetite to them both.

Manson was fond of conversation—or, rather, of talking; he was quite content with a word now and then to show that he had a listener. They were seated one day at the food of the dead palm, upon the highest point of the island, from which Cushing could command the whole sweep of the surrounding ocean. Manson cast his sightless eyes upward.

"Is our signal flying?" he asked.

"Yes, but it doesn't bring any one to our rescue."

"I miss my sight—what is your first name, Singleton? You have never told me."

"Henry."

"I miss my sight, Henry, my friend! You are more than my friend; you are my eyes, my hands, my feet—without my eyes the rest is useless. But my heart is in good working order, and I know how to value such friendship, such devotion as yours!"

There was a thrill in Manson's voice which Cushing thought might easily have imposed upon one who did not really know the speaker well. Upon this occasion, and upon several others, Cushing imagined that in Manson there existed one of the curious but not uncommon characters in whom good and evil exist, not in mingled form, where one may be modified by the other, but side by side, or in strata which could no more mingle than oil and water. A man who could speak in such a tone, with an emotion so apparently sincere, was perhaps capable of friendship. But Cushing could not believe that this friendship could endure any strain of self-interest or self-gratification. And there was always the likelihood, too, that this exaggerated friendliness was rooted in mercenary motives; it might well be that Manson's effusive gratitude was directed as much with an eye to future services as to past benefits.

"I can't help comparing you, Henry, to whom I owe so much, with the fellow I owe a different kind of debt, which I mean to pay in full. Your spirit is a broad and liberal one. His is a mean, narrow, selfish soul—if I do not insult the word by applying it to him! For example, my wife's mother was left a widow, twenty years ago—a young and handsome woman, to whom, in the ordinary and natural course of events, more than one man might have been attracted; yet she has remained unmarried. Why? This fellow, under the guise of friendship, fastened himself upon her household like a leech. For twenty years he had the run of the house, but sat around, and never spoke of marriage, while her very natural hopes grew fainter and fainter. There are lots of such fellows, who are too selfish to marry, and under the guise of friendship steal the affections of good women and enjoy the better pleasures of domestic life, for which they are not men enough to pay the price."

"It must have been interesting to study such a situation," said Cushing. "Of course you knew them intimately for a number of years?"

"Well, no, I can't really say I did. I never saw the fellow very often, and don't know that I ever spoke to him. But that was n't necessary. I know him thoroughly, partly from my wife, partly by intuition, partly from a good, faithful maid who has lived in the family for years, and who helped me to save Evelyn once from this old scoundrel's clutches. And then, having spoiled the mother's life by his failure to do the obviously right thing, he deliberately sets about ruining the daughter's by doing the equally wrong thing. At a time when he ought to have been prepared for the other world—the man must be fifty—he coolly proposed to make that child his wife, to condemn her to his loathsome embraces, to make her the nurse of his decrepitude. Why, it was monstrous!"

Cushing had heard enough for one time. He had begun, in spite of himself, to like the fellow, at least certain sides of his character, but it was impossible for him to sit longer and listen patiently to such a tirade of ignorant and prejudiced nonsense directed at himself. It was a condition of conceal-ment upon which he had not reckoned, and one which it required some self-control to face without challenge.

"I must leave you now," he said abruptly, "and find some-thing for our supper."

He went down to the beach and examined the basket trap, which had been set the day before, and found within it a couple of fish. Seating himself upon the sand beside a flat stone which he used as a table he dressed the fish for their evening meal. Manson's company upon the island was preferable, on the whole, to solitude, but there were occasions when solitude was preferable to Manson's society. Such occasions, for instance, as the last half hour. The fellow had a way of presenting subjects from fresh points of view. Cushing had never been, consciously, a social pirate. The welcome guest of many homes, he had never by word, thought or deed violated the sanctity of any one of them. Less scrupulous men, of equal means and social graces, might have found, in Cushing's position, large possibilities for evil. Indeed, he had always prided himself upon the delicate sense of honor by which he had regulated his intercourse with other men and women. The suggestion, however, that he had been a social parasite, and under the guise of friendship had injured the prospects of Alice Thayer, came to him from Manson's lips with all the force of a novel proposition. Conscious of the generosity of his dealings with the widow and family of his dead friend, Cushing had found no little self-satisfaction in the knowledge of his magnanimity. He was fond of appreciation, and valued his own approval, as that of a man of tact and judgment. He had realized in all these years, in his conduct toward Alice, how much more blessed it was to give than to receive. The suggestion, from this blunt, blind savage who had been thrust upon him by a freakish fate, that his conduct had been mere aesthetic selfishness, he had first indignantly repelled; yet, as he sat there, cleaning fish with a jack-knife, he was uncomfortably conscious that to the outside, uninformed world, his conduct, if ever brought into question, *might* be open to some such construction.

A greater discomfort arose from the novel idea, suggested by Manson, that Alice may have dreamed dreams with regard to him, and suffered disappointment. He had always found her kind, but never too kind, it had seemed to him. Never, that he could recall, upon a review of their past intercourse, had she by work or deed overstepped the limits of a cheerful friendship. Yet as he looked back over the years, and recalled how she had waited upon his footsteps, hung upon his words, consulted his tastes, deferred to his advice, relied, in all important matters, upon his judgment, the question loomed up formidably. Might not her conduct have been influenced by some stronger feeling than mere gratitude? A sense, upon her part, of benefits received, had seemed to him, in his placid role of patron to this attractive widow and her beautiful children, quite sufficient to account for her appreciation. Yet, he asked himself, may he not merely have transferred to her, his own consciousness of benefits conferred? Had he not been crediting her with gratitude for something of which she was not aware? He had never told her the source of her prosperity; not even Evelyn had known it. Perhaps his delicacy had been overdone. Had she known, it was inconceivable that she should have treated him so basely. As he knelt there by the sea, which stretched between them for two thousand miles or more, a certain feeling of regret stole over his spirit, lest by his well-meant but perhaps not well-considered friendship he had caused Alice loss, or pain. This regret, however, was not unmingled with a certain satisfaction at the thought that he might have been the object of something more than mere friendly appreciation on the part of so fine a woman as Alice Thayer. To do him justice, he had never thought of Alice as wife to any one but her dead husband, to whose memory he had believed her so entirely devoted that the idea of a second marriage would have seemed to her like sacrilege. Not once, in all their long association, in the retrospect of which he was now finding these novel emotions, could he recall a single incident which might be construed into forgetfulness of the one he knew she had loved with a great devotion, whose virtue she had discussed with him, whose portrait still held its place of honor in her home—although he recalled with a pleasant thrill, that his own hung where it could be seen quite as often. A strong sense of her loyalty was borne in upon him by the reflection that she had never, for one instant, sacrificed her fealty to the dead for any hope of winning the favor of the living. He honored her for this faithfulness; and yet the thought that this fine, loyal, capable, and handsome woman, for whom he had entertained so profound a respect, might have cherished for him during all these years of their intercourse an untold love, was a very pleasant thought. No man of sensibility could remain unmoved by the knowledge that a woman of beauty and refinement loved him; and

Cushing, even more than most men, basked in the sunlight of appreciation.

But he had loved Evelyn! And Manson's brutal character-ization of his wish to wed her had been so offensive that he had not been able to listen to it longer. He was not yet fifty by several years—was indeed scarcely forty-five. In older lands, where he had spent much of his life, men of his age were looked upon as young, for the serious affairs of life, and their marriage to women much younger than themselves regarded as the natural and proper thing. Unusual beauty was only suitably mated with wealth and standing, and these were possessed by few very young men. Evelyn herself, until she had fallen under the fascination of Manson's voice, had instinctively realized the propriety of Cushing's choice. She was a flower of womankind. He could give her the rich soil in which alone beauty could attain its fullest development.

Cushing had finished cleaning and scaling a fish. With a stroke of his knife he split it down the back, applying more energy than the end in view demanded. The thought that this ideal marriage had been spoiled by the intervention of an uncultured fellow of obscure origin, who had not known how to appreciate his good fortune—as witness his presence on this island and the trail of ruin leading up to it—did not incline Cushing toward any greater friendliness for the blind man who sat awaiting him in impatient loneliness. In the same mood, he tossed the offal from the fish into the sea, thrust a sharpened stick through the severed portions, and went back to the hut. As Manson had sown, so let him reap.

XVII
THE STORM

Cushing raked out the covered embers of the fire and proceeded to broil the fish for the supper. Manson sniffed the odor with evident satisfaction, and ate his portion with an equal relish. He had a keen appetite, and under the influence of regular though frugal meals, was rapidly recovering physical vigor. His beard had grown to a respectable length, and no longer resembled a discarded scrubbing-brush.

"Henry," he said, after he had eaten, "it appals me at times, to think what a burden of obligation you are piling up against me. Why, I should starve to death were it not for you! While you were gone, I was thinking what a marvelous providence it was that brought you here before me! Suppose it had been a different person—my enemy, for instance? He might as easily as you been wrecked in the same storm. How would he have treated me? Imagine him finding my unconscious form in the stranded boat! I can see the unholy joy that would light up his face. I should hardly have recovered consciousness through his help. If, perchance, he had failed to recognize me, and had succored me, and I had not raved, and he had afterwards discovered my blindness, he would have let me starve to death! Or he would have kept me alive to torture me. For he must be a man of small, mean spirit—he could n't be otherwise you know. A man who, having lost a woman in a fair fight—better than a fair fight, for everything was in his favor—can come to that woman, and taking advantage of habit, of old authority, of a momentary discontent, and steal her heart from her husband, making her forget her marriage vows and leave her home—is capable of any baseness. If, to help him carry out some dark scheme of revenge, he let me live, he would try to conceal his identity. He would never have had the manliness to confess the wrong he had done me. His conscience would have made him a coward; he would have been afraid to face even a poor, blind, helpless castaway whom he had wronged. But he could not have deceived me. An unerring intuition would have taught me the truth, and I should have been on my guard. But I shudder to think of the situation—I should have been so entirely at his mercy!"

Cushing listened with a curious expression. He could have laughed aloud at the tricks which Manson's fancy played him—it was literally a game of blind man's buff, in which Manson was now hot, now cold, but never quite touched; so near the truth was he and yet so far from it. It was a rare comedy, which not even Manson's contemptuous estimate of Cushing's character could spoil. Seldom does it fall to the lot of a man to be at one and the same moment loved and hated by the same person—to be simultaneously the object of two great passions which are direct opposites. Had Cushing not been silent for other reasons the strangeness of the situation would have closed his mouth. He counted himself a student of human nature—though his experience with Evelyn, and perhaps with her mother, had somewhat shaken his faith in his own discernment. This situation could not last; sooner or later the island would be visited and they would be taken off. Manson would then learn the truth in regard to Cushing's identity. What might result from the clash of two antagonistic feelings, both in full flower—hatred and friendship, gratitude and revenge, would be a curious problem. What would a man do, who should discover that the friend to whom he owed his life was the enemy whose life he had sworn to take? The problem would interest almost any one. It seemed to Cushing quite as absorbing as any complication of romance—with the advantage of being in real life. The romancer could imagine the outcome, but that was all; he, Cushing, could do the same, and then, as the other could not, might check the fiction by the fact, the imaginary by the real. If the test should come now, hate might prove the stronger passion, for in Manson it seemed full-grown and full-panoplied, and his friendship of only brief duration. But it was impossible to guess how long they might remain upon the island, and Manson's sense of obligation grew day by day, his gratitude increasing proportionately.

Although Cushing had fully determined to treat Manson, so far as the claims of humanity were concerned, precisely as though he were any other human being, and not the one man he detested above all others, he was destined to be put to a test that tried his resolution to the utmost, and at the same time intensified in a very high degree, Manson's friendship, like a hook of steel fastened in a loop of straw.

On the foraging expeditions in which most of his time was spent, Cushing was obliged to go all over the island, in order to make the most of its limited food resources. Manson sometimes accompanied him, but more often remained at the camp, where he sat under the trees, carving into curious shapes with his jack-knife, bits of wood with which Cushing supplied him, as an outlet for his restless energies. Even in this rude handiwork, wrought solely by the touch, his innate love of beauty, and his creative talent, found expression. He could model a ship with graceful lines; a vase, a column, an arch, the figure of an animal, with surprising accuracy. It was the almost spontaneous expression of a natural instinct.

One morning, after they had breakfasted on turtle's eggs gathered the night before, Cushing left Manson to this amusement, and set out for the opposite side of the island, where he hoped, with the aid of a rude net which he had fashioned out of some tough and slender vines, to capture some fish in a little cove where the water was clear and quiet. The wind was rising and there were other signs of bad weather, so that Cushing wished to secure food for the day before the water grew rough. He followed the shore instead of going directly across, which would have carried him past the outlook. He had left the beach at a certain place where a little point jutted sharply into the sea, and was making his way through the shrubbery, across the neck of land, and was nearing his destination when he heard, from beyond the intervening curtain of bushes, the sound of voices. Quickening his footsteps, he soon came out upon the beach. A steamer, flying an American flag, lay off some distance from the shore. There was a boat upon the beach, and several seamen moving about upon the sand.

Cushing ran toward them with a joyful cry. There were signs of answering excitement, and the men moved toward Cushing, headed by a young lieutenant whose uniform betokened his rank.

"Who are you?" demanded the officer, when they stood facing each other on the sand.

"A castaway."

"Your name and ship?"

The officer spoke *de haut en bas*. He was a very young officer, and conscious of his tremendous responsibility. Cushing's appearance, after three weeks upon the island, was not prepossessing. He looked very much at a disadvantage, compared with even the trim sailors under the lieutenant's command; yet he had not used the customary "sir" in replying to the lieutenant's first question. The second had been put with a sharpness which marked resentment at the omission. An officer is a gentleman—which nobody dare deny, and which a common man should not forget. Discipline must be maintained. Democracy is all right on land, but stops at the gunwale of a man-of-war.

Cushing hesitated. His first impulse was to give his real name, but this would be to provoke an explanation with Manson, for which he was not ready. To make known his identity would assure him of courteous treatment, but would also spoil his plans in regard to his companion. He was not a man of prompt decision; he would have liked an hour to think the matter over. But there was no time for reflection. He was compelled to choose his course immediately.

"My name is Singleton—Henry Singleton," he replied.

His hesitation had not gone unnoticed by the officer, whose next question was more sharply put.

"Your ship, and your nationality?"

"I was a passenger on the steamer *Notre Dame de los Remedios*, bound from Havana to Buenos Aires. I am an American."

In reply to other questions, he detailed the same story he had told Manson. He was playing a part, and meant to play it consistently until the moment for complete revelation should arrive.

The young officer having perceived from Cushing's speech that he was a gentleman in distress, condescended to impart some information as to himself.

"We're a detail from the *Oklahoma* yonder," he explained, "which is at present attached to the Coast Survey. We've been here several hours, making soundings on this side of the island,"

"What island is this, may I ask," said Cushing, "and where is it?"

"It is technically one of the Windward Islands, though lying considerably to the eastward of the group, and so utterly insignificant as not to be found on any map except a government sailing chart. It's a breeding-place for turtles, and is visited now and then for the purpose of catching them, when there's a shortage farther west. There's probably an ample supply this year from points along the regular line of travel, which accounts for the island's not having been visited. But we've finished our work and are going on board. You may go with us if you like, and tell your story to the captain, who'll doubtless give you transportation to our next port."

There was another moment of temptation—hardly of temptation, but at least of evil suggestion. He might leave Manson alone on the island. In a week he would inevitably perish of hunger and thirst. Or, if Manson should be taken off the island later by some passing vessel, he would never know that he had been abandoned, and would probably attribute to some accident his companion's disappearance. Should the real facts ever come to his knowledge, he would have only the mythical Singleton to blame for his abandonment. There was absolutely no risk of condemnation for having left a blind man to starve.

But the thought went as quickly as it came. That it should come was due to ordinary human frailty, for which Cushing was not to blame; it was part of his humanity; that it should go so soon was not equally inevitable, and was therefore praiseworthy.

"I'm not alone," he replied. "I have a companion."

"Call your companion."

"He's on the other side of the island, half a mile away. And he is blind. I shall have to go and tell him."

"Make haste then; a storm is coming up, and our anchorage is not safe. We shall put out to sea as soon as our boat returns to the ship."

Cushing darted up the hill and toward the camp. The path was sufficiently defined by constant use, for him to make fair headway, though he could not, of course, travel with the rapidity which would have been possible upon a better road. In twenty minutes, however, he reached the hut. The blind man was not in his usual place nor anywhere visible.

"Manson! Manson!" he called loudly. There was no reply. He repeated the call, louder yet, and there was a faint halloa in response, from the direction of the beach.

Cushing hastened down the hill. Near the bottom he found Manson, seated disconsolately on the ground and rubbing his left ankle.

"Ah! Henry!" he cried, as soon as he heard Cushing's footsteps. "I knew you'd find me. I thought I'd try to help myself a little, and so started down to the beach; but my foot caught in a projecting root, and I fell, and sprained my ankle."

"There's a ship on the north side of the island, and a boat waiting to take us off. Can you walk?"

"Oh, yes, I can walk all right. It's only a slight sprain."

He sprang up, and taking the arm which Cushing extended, walked a few rods without apparent effort. He then began to show involuntary signs of pain, and leaned more heavily on Cushing's arm.

"Let me rest a moment, Henry," he said, with a sharp exclamation. "My ankle pains me most horribly."

Cushing looked anxiously at the sky, already darkened by gathering clouds. The wind was rising rapidly, the sea was booming sullenly against the breakers, and the palms were bending beneath the force of the gale.

"My God! man," he exclaimed, "a storm is coming, and the ship cannot ride it out at her anchorage; she must put to sea. We must hurry. Make another effort, Manson! Never mind the pain. Your ankle can be attended to when we reach the ship."

Manson struggled forward for a few rods farther and then sank helplessly to the ground.

"It's no use, Henry," he said, "we can't make it. You will have to go and get a couple of them to come and carry me."

They were passing the lookout, and through an opening in the trees Cushing saw the ship signalling peremptorily to the boat. An old sailor, he was familiar with the code and knew what the signals meant.

"No," he said, "we have n't the time. The ship is calling off the boat."

"You'll not leave me?" cried Manson in alarm. "Surely, Henry, you'll not desert me?"

"No," replied Cushing desperately, "I'll carry you myself. Climb on my back. It will be the easiest way to bear your weight."

Cushing helped Manson to his feet, and took the blind man on his shoulders, pickaback. Cushing was of slighter build than the other; but Manson had not yet recovered from the emaciation of the long fast in the boat, while Cushing was in fine physical condition. They were now of about equal weight.

Some men weaken and collapse in emergencies; others rise to meet them. Cushing developed a supernatural strength. He staggered forward as rapidly as possible with this Old

Man of the Mountain hanging around his neck. He hated him, and yet he could not leave him.

"Henry," said the blind man, "you are too good to me. I have done nothing to deserve it."

Cushing cursed him silently. It was bad enough to be burdened with his disabled body; his nauseous gratitude was unbearable. He was bound to his enemy by considerations of humanity. He had succored Manson, not for Manson's sake, but for his own. He neither merited nor cared for gratitude: his sole wish at this moment was to escape from this dreary island.

"Shut up," he muttered savagely, "there's no time to talk. The steamer is still signalling."

They were now past the middle of the island. The rest of the path lay through the underbrush. The sky grew darker and darker. A sudden clap of tropical thunder rent the air. The wind was still rising. The whole of the little island seemed to be moaning and throbbing, as though straining at its anchorage in the great deep. The half-mile seemed interminable—it took an age to traverse it. When at length they emerged from the woods upon the beach, they saw the boat some distance from the shore, headed for the ship.

Cushing dropped his burden, and with a cry of rage and despair rushed down to the sea. The men in the boat were deliberately deserting two of their own countrymen upon a barren island, a mere speck of land in a boiling sea, which almost seemed as though it might sweep over and engulf them. They might starve for want of food, or die of illness, for want of medicine, or go insane for want of human companionship! No one knew when the island would be visited again. It might be months. He would not have believed his own countryman capable of such inhumanity. His faith in woman had been shaken, and now his faith in man must follow!

The men in the boat were making signs to him, and over the water, from the distance of half a mile, came the sound of a seaman's voice:—

"Read the note!"

He did not understand until the sentence had been repeated. Looking about him then, he perceived, directly opposite where the boat had lain upon the beach, a stick, stuck upright in the sand, in the cleft end of which a slip of paper had been inserted. In a moment he had withdrawn it and read:—

"Cannot wait longer. Island is dangerous in bad weather. Must put out to sea until storm is over. Will come back for you tomorrow."

Cushing dropped the note. The abandonment had not then been so heartless as he had supposed. Never had the island seemed so much a prison at this moment, when his means of rescue were receding as fast as four pairs of stalwart arms could propel a ship's yawl boat. The steamer was straining at her anchor, which the crew stood ready to weigh the moment the boat arrived. The blind man was calling frantically.

"Henry! where are you? What is the matter? You won't desert me, Henry!"

Cushing looked back at him in disgust. But for this incumbrance, he would have left the island an hour before. Not only must he be cook and valet to this man he hated, but on his account he must lose the chance of rescue. The note had stated that the steamer would return the next day. This meant at least twenty-four hours of wretched suspense. He would scarcely dare leave this side of the island, nor would he be able to carry Manson back to the camp. Already a curtain of falling rain had shut the ship from view. They would be obliged to pass the night without shelter.

Hitherto the weather had been dry. Cushing had carefully preserved the fire he had made on Manson's arrival upon the island, by banking the embers whenever he did not need to cook. The rain would doubtless extinguish them before he could reach the camp in time to improvise some protection for them against the wet.

He felt vindictive toward Manson. His first impulse was to go back to the camp and leave him there a while in ignorance and suspense; but as he drew near and read the fear in the blind man's face he relented. Manson might suffer any self-inflicted torture that he chose, but Cushing could not give the screw a single turn.

"We are too late," he said. "They've gone and left us."

"Thank God, you are here, Henry! I thought you had abandoned me."

Cushing had an added impulse of anger. He had not cared for Manson's maudlin gratitude; nor on the other hand, did it strengthen his patience to have this man, for whom he had sacrificed so much, deem him capable of going off and leaving a blind man alone to starve and die.

"Listen," he said harshly, "I must go back to the camp and try to save the fire, and bring something for us to eat. I can't carry you back, and there's no shelter here. You'll have to stand the rain."

"Very well, Henry," returned Manson submissively. "You've saved my life again, and I've lost you your chance to get away. If ever I have a chance, Henry, I'll prove my gratitude. Never mind me now; I'll not mind the rain. The wetting will soothe the pain of my sprained ankle."

Cushing had gone several rods toward the camp when he heard Manson's voice calling him.

"Well, what is it?" he asked, turning back impatiently.

"I was thinking, Henry, that there's no reason why you should stay here all night in the rain. I had a very good meal at noon, thanks to you, and I can get along well enough without food until morning. Stay in the hut and keep dry; never mind me until tomorrow."

The proposition seemed reasonable.

"Are you sure you won't mind?" asked Cushing.

"Oh, no, Henry," replied Manson. "*I'll* not mind. I'll know you're over there, and that you'll be here in the morning, and that will be quite enough for me."

"Well," said Cushing, relenting somewhat, "I'll go and look after the food and fire, and if I'm not back tonight, you can expect me soon after daylight."

XVIII.

WHAT MANSON WOULD HAVE DONE

The rain increased momentarily as Cushing made his way along the path, and meanwhile the darkness came on apace. Reaching the camp, he carefully raked out one corner of the covered fire and found the embers still glowing. With a wooden shovel which he had whittled out, he piled earth upon the banked up ashes, and then over this laid broad-leaved branches, torn from the bushes near by, in such a manner as to shed most the rain.

There was some cooked fish in the hut, and of this he made a frugal meal. There was plenty left for Manson's supper, had he been there to eat it. The rain, which had ceased for a moment, began to fall more heavily, and Cushing entered the hut. It was fortunately dry—fortunately, for it had never before been tested by a rain-storm. While Cushing was feeling around the walls to see if the rain had penetrated, his hand came in contact with Manson's oil-skin coat. He had left the poor devil alone. Well, he was alone himself. But there was a difference—he was not so blind. No, but he might as well be, for in half an hour he would not be able to see his hand before his face. The blind man was hungry. Well, he had gone longer without food; to fast one night would do him no great harm. He would have to sit on the sand all night in the rain. If he had only his oil-skin coat—

"I suppose I must," sighed Cushing.

He drew on the oil-skin coat, wrapped the broiled fish in a handful of leaves, and thrust it into one of the coat pockets; gathered up a few articles, including Manson's revolver, still in its waterproof cover, the water-pail and the tin cup, and set out for the other side of the island. It would be too dark to return that night, and the boat would probably be back for them in the morning. The oilskin coat would keep the blind man warm. Cushing would not dare to sleep, and by walking up and down the beach could keep himself from becoming chilled. He would not dare absent himself from that side of the island, for fear of repeating the day's experience.

The darkness came on with tropical suddenness, and for the last half of the journey back to the beach Cushing was compelled almost to feel his way, aided now and then by a flash of lightning. At one time he had well nigh given himself up for lost and resigned himself to spending the night in the woods, when it occurred to him to call Manson. A faint far away response, barely audible above the rising storm, directed him toward the right place.

"And did you come back, Henry? Oh, how I thank you! You cannot know, Henry, what a terrible affliction this blindness is. I was born on a mountain, where I could see vast spaces, stretching as far as the eye could reach. Now, I am shut in by a black wall which keeps out all the light; I cannot see my hand before me. When you are by me, and I know the sun is shining out yonder, I can endure it. But the howling of the storm, the pounding of the waves, the rain, the loneliness, fill my heart with terror! The elements seem like wild animals broken loose, and I among them, and helpless. I would never have told you, I should have kept it to myself, if you had not come back, but you don't know, Henry, how glad I am to hear your voice!"

"I've brought your oil-skin coat," replied Cushing, which will keep you dry. And in the pocket there is food. I'll stay here near you until morning."

"Henry, you are too good to me—always thoughtful, considerate, kind! I was beginning to feel chilled, and hungry; I don't mind telling you, now that I have food and shelter. Oh, but how that ankle hurts!"

"Let me see it," said Cushing.

He knelt beside Manson, and removing the worn fragment of a shoe that remained upon his foot, found the ankle badly swollen. Taking it in his hand he chafed it firmly for five or ten minutes, with long even strokes.

"Ah, thank you, Henry, thank you so much! The pain is all gone. What a doctor you would make, or a nurse, or a husband! Were you ever married? You've never told me."

"No, I was never married. I was engaged once—when I was younger."

"And the lady died before the wedding? Poor Henry! I have often thought I detected a note of sadness in your voice."

"No, she did not die. Another man stole her away, on the eve of the wedding."

Silence for a moment.

"Did you love her?"

"Dearer than my life. She was my first and only love."

Another silence.

"Was he worthy of her?"

"No. He was coarse, uncultured, selfish. He loved her so little that on the first breath of suspicion, without investigation, or a particle of evidence, he believed her guilty of infidelity."

"The infernal scoundrel! And did you not revenge yourself and her?"

Silence on the other side. "What do you mean by revenge?" asked Cushing, when he at length spoke.

"Had you been my father or grandfather, you would have killed him. As it was, you might have horsewhipped him."

"And made myself still more of a laughing-stock? He was bigger than I, and might have turned the tables on me."

"If it had been your *wife*, Henry, that he stole away, you might have killed him, as I mean to kill the destroyer of my home,—if you will help me find him."

"But she was not. She was only my promised wife. But now that your foot is better, I'll walk on the beach, and watch the storm. The exercise will keep me warm."

When Cushing had made several turns up and down the beach, he heard Manson calling him.

"Henry," said the blind man, "I've been sitting here thinking about your disappointment. Your position seems so much like my own! Evelyn—you've heard me mention her name—Evelyn loved me and wished to marry me, and this old reprobate tried to marry her against her will. I was more fortunate than you, Henry, for I saved her, for a while at least, from that loathsome fate. But there my advantage ceases. *You* are not bound to search the world to find a wife's seducer. You could, if you chose, forego your revenge; your honor was not involved. You were wronged, humiliated, but not disgraced. I am all three, and ruined besides. There is not room upon earth for him and me."

"By the way," said Cushing, with a sudden inspiration, "you have asked me if I revenged myself. Suppose yourself in my place. Suppose a year, two years, five years to have elapsed; and that then it had been placed in your power to do your successful rival a deadly injury; or, easier still, suppose that you have been cast away upon a lonely island, as I was, and that he had come to it, blind and helpless, in an open boat, as you did—what would you have done, under the circumstances?"

"I should have considered that the Lord had delivered mine enemy into my hands! It would be as providential as my finding you here. I should have concealed my identify from him. I should have fed and sheltered him, even as my love had been fostered; I should have encouraged him to hope for rescue and cure, as I had hoped for love and happiness. And then I should have dashed the cup from his lips! I should have revealed myself; I should have watched him starve until he had paid back every pang that she and I had suffered, and then I should have let him die the dog's death he deserved!"

"And that would satisfy you?"

"Yes, I suppose it would have to. I don't see what more I could do."

"I had n't thought of your doing anything more; but don't you think that would be a pretty severe punishment?"

"It would be only justice! Ah, Henry, I have n't your magnanimity. For a friend such as you have proved to be, I could do anything—I could give my life for a friend. But I question whether I could have done quite as much for a stranger—even a very grateful stranger—as you have done for me. And I'm sure I should n't have been capable of forgiving my enemy."

The storm was rising rapidly. The rain fell in torrents. The breakers rolled more fiercely inward, like wild beasts seeking their prey, and roaring sullenly when forced to retire. Twice in an hour Cushing was obliged to lead Manson to higher ground.

Cushing kept his eyes anxiously seaward, lest, by the vivid lightning flashes, he might see the ship, their hope of rescue, rushing headlong to destruction. As she was nowhere in sight, he hoped that she had safely reached the open sea.

The darkness, the clamor of the storm, the ceaseless roar of the sea, like the bass of a gigantic orchestra, impressed Cushing with the vastness of nature's forces, and the comparative littleness of mankind. In the profound loneliness of this mood, any companionship was better than none, and he found himself unconsciously drawing nearer Manson, who sat huddled upon the ground, under the shelter of his oil-skin coat. The blind man seemed to divine Cushing's approach; he could not see, and could scarcely have heard.

"Henry," he cried, "are you there?"

"Yes."

"Henry," said the blind man, reflectively, "I've been turning over that matter—the case you put to me, and I am afraid I was a little hard on the fellow. I guess I unconsciously got my real grievance mixed up with my imaginary grievance—*your* real grievance. I could n't have done any more to him if he had stolen my wife, and there ought to be some proportion between the punishment and the crime. Justice ought to be done, but only fair and adequate justice. I doubt whether it would be quite right for me to encourage him with false hopes. It would be enough for me to make my presence and my identity known and then leave him in the hands of Providence. Don't you think that would be better?"

"Oh, undoubtedly," said Cushing, "that would be more humane—by way of comparison."

Cushing did not smile. We think of smiles, tears, laughter, speech, as subjective means of expression; they are, in fact, primarily directed toward others, with whom they furnish our means of communication. Otherwise they are futile—so futile that we suspect the sanity of a man who laughs or talks to himself very much. Cushing was alone—the blind man did not count—and so the cynical thought that came to him went unexpressed by either smile or sneer.

There was a blinding flash of lightning, followed by a crash of thunder that shook the island to its foundation, and then a fantastic play of fire across the heavens, which lit up the sea for miles around. By this illumination Cushing again swept the horizon with swift and eager eye, but saw no sign of the warship. Could she safely ride out the hurricane, or had she already gone to the bottom?

"What a fearful storm!" exclaimed Manson. "I cannot see, but I can almost feel the lightning. By the way, Henry, that was a hard proposition you put to me—a good deal harder than it seemed at first. You see, the man would be blind when he came here, and would have been blind for several days— and I know what that means, to be blind, at sea, in an open boat, alone. He would have been starved—and I have felt starvation. I think, after all, that it would have been better to be merciful, to leave his punishment entirely in the hands of Providence, and not even let him know that there was any one on the island. He could n't last more than a day or two, anyway, even if he recovered consciousness. Then, if I were rescued, and my old feeling toward his widow should revive, there would be nothing to stand between us—my conscience would be clear."

Cushing perceived the humor of the situation. There was no doubt that Manson was in earnest, terribly in earnest. To the average normal American mind, trained in traditions of extravagant humor, such a proposition as Manson's about his conscience would have produced an irresistible impulse to laughter, of a robust and uproarious order. But to Cushing the humorous idea brought no emotional response; his face did not move a muscle. He even wondered, in a purely speculative way, how long a man would have to live alone upon such an island, to lose all sense of proportion, which is the essence of humor. Manson, poor devil, seemed to have lost it already, along with the rest of what had made his life worth living; and himself, while perceiving the situation, had lost the faculty of enjoying it.

They spent the long wet, dreary night together. The morning dawned cool, cloudy and cheerless. They were both wet, tired and hungry. The storm had subsided, but the restless, sullenly muttering sea still rolled great waves against the little island, as though angry at the resistance of so puny an obstacle. At daybreak Cushing bestirred himself and set out for the camp, leaving Manson, whose swollen ankle permitted him to move only with difficulty, to await his return.

His first care was to see if the fire was still alive. Fortunately, the shelter of branches and the coating of earth had preserved it; but there being no dry fuel at hand, he covered it up again until he could have opportunity to gather some.

Suddenly the clouds lightened, the sun shone through, and in an hour the sky was clear. Cushing climbed to his lookout and swept the sea with anxious eye. The air was delightfully fresh and clear, but nowhere was there any sign of a ship.

He climbed down with a sigh. The tropical sun was rapidly drying the sandy soil. He gathered some fuel, made a fire, prepared some food, and having satisfied his own hunger, carried the remainder to Manson, who still sat upon the beach where he had left him.

The blind man devoured the food ravenously. Cushing rubbed the swollen ankle again, and found that the swelling had gone down considerably. He noticed, however, that Manson's cheek was flushed, and, seizing his wrist, felt his pulse and found that he was suffering from a slight fever, doubtless the result of the long night of exposure, acting upon a body not yet fully restored to vigorous health.

All day long, except for the short absences necessary to procure and prepare food, he watched the sea for some sign of the expected ship. But it did not return and his anxiety increased as the day wore on. If Manson should become seriously ill, his own sacrifices in the blind man's behalf would have been in vain. Speculating upon the outcome, he did not know whether he would be glad or sorry. He would have done his duty—for his own sake, and not for Manson's. Manson was young, and entitled to live out his days—if he could. He possessed a wonderful talent, which, properly applied, might benefit the world. Again, it was possible that Evelyn loved him, and in all the bitterness of humiliation and defeat, Cushing had never wished harm to Evelyn. But if fate should resent his intervention, and take matters into its own hands, he would be able to feel that he had done his duty.

All day long he watched and waited in vain for the ship, responding now and then to Manson's now patient, now querulous inquiries. He helped his companion back to the camp, where he could be more comfortable. The next day his watch was equally fruitless, and at the end of a week, there was still no sign of the returning vessel. In the meantime

Manson had grown worse, and was apparently on the verge of a serious illness.

Cushing did not learn until long afterwards that the storm had driven the *Oklahoma* several hundred miles to the north-westward, where she had grounded upon a submerged coral reef, from which she was extricated only after many days and at great expense. In the confusion attending the accident, and in the excitement of the subsequent court-martial, it was not surprising that two seamen, upon an island which might any day be visited by a passing vessel, had been forgotten. The urgency of their case might not have appeared great. They had maintained themselves for some time upon the island, and were in no great apparent need.

XIX.

THE REPENTANCE OF EVELYN

The letter which, hastily misconstrued in the light of Leonie's distorted and malicious statements, had sent Manson on a wild-goose chase to the other side of the world—the deliberately ambiguous letter written by Evelyn, in a moment of unthinking anger, and afterwards bitterly atoned for, would have been perfectly clear to any one who could have overheard the conversation between Evelyn and Cushing while he was accompanying her home from her mother's the evening before.

It had related to her brother. Wentworth's conduct had been irreproachable during the year since Evelyn's marriage. He had graduated from the University at the beginning of Summer, and was waiting until Fall to enter the law school. A month or two of idleness had proved disastrous to his good intentions, which had yielded to a sudden and strong temptation. He had disappeared from home for several weeks, and now, at the end of a prolonged debauch, had been located at one of his old haunts in New York, where, Mrs. Thayer had just ascertained, he lay ill,—so ill, indeed, that serious consequences were not improbable.

Having seen Evelyn home, Cushing had returned and accompanied Mrs. Thayer to the station, where she took a night train for New York. A telegram to Cushing upon her arrival informed him that Wentworth's condition was still dangerous. His note, written immediately upon receipt of the telegram, and mailed promptly, had reached Evelyn at the breakfast table, had caused her unusual agitation, and had called forth the request for money, so lightly denied by Manson.

The one secret which Evelyn had kept from her husband since their marriage, was that Wentworth was addicted to these escapades. Fondly believing that he had reformed, the family were more than willing to forget something which reflected no credit upon them. A sudden access of pure feminine pique, of which even the best women are at times capable, had made Evelyn the easy mark of an impulse to give her husband a bad quarter of an hour in return for her humiliation at his refusal to give her the sum which she had asked. If at this moment she made any involuntary mental comparison between her husband and her former guardian, it was not to Manson's advantage. Cushing was wealthy; she knew his generous nature,—even now he was exerting himself in behalf of a family, one of whom had treated him so unjustly—and she had no doubt, had she married him, that he would have anticipated all her wants and satisfied her slightest caprice. On the other hand, she knew that her husband earned large sums of money, and not being informed—because of Manson's pleasant secret and a good-natured contempt of woman's business capacity—as to how he had been spending his money, she attributed his refusal of her request to a parsimony which, in her eyes, savored of the mean and narrow.

Scarcely, however, had the train left Boston, before she began to reflect upon the possible consequences of her letter. She loved her husband, and as the minutes flew by, found less and less pleasure in the prospect of giving him pain. She knew, too, his simple, direct and somewhat primitive cast of mind, and, while they had never had, during their year of married life, a serious disagreement, she had once or twice felt that he could be capable, under favorable circumstances, of stubborn anger and bitter resentment.

The hours that elapsed between Boston and New Haven strengthened this feeling, which seemed to increase with the square of the distance from Boston. In a little while, too, she began to feel some of the constraint of a long tête-à-tête with the man whom she had jilted, and, at the same time to foresee, dimly, how her departure from Boston in his company might appear in the eyes of others, if it were known.

Cushing perceived her growing restlessness and exerted himself to put her at ease. When there was nothing more to be said of Wentworth, he spoke of his travels during the year. He had been in Egypt, had ascended the Nile, as far as the great dam, then in process of construction at Assouan. He was eloquent of men he had met and places he had seen. But somehow, every now and then the specter of their broken engagement rose between them. Cushing at length hit upon a simple expedient to relieve their embarrassment.

"Will you excuse me, Evelyn, if I leave you a little while? I have n't smoked since luncheon, and feel uncomfortable without my weed. The buffet of this car is crowded, but there's plenty of room in the smoking-car ahead."

"Certainly; go, by all means. But will you first please find me a telegraph blank?"

Cushing looked up the "train butcher," who had not yet been abolished on that line, bought several newspapers and magazines, procured a couple of telegraph blanks, and, laden with his purchases, returned to Evelyn.

"Here are your forms, and here is something for you to read. Make yourself comfortable, and when we approach the next station, I'll see that your telegram is sent."

Evelyn was feeling in her chatelaine bag for a silver pencil-case, which she was not able to find.

"Will you lend me a lead pencil?" she asked.

Cushing gave her his own and then retired to the smoking car. Evelyn wrote a long message to her husband, in which she stated that she feared her hasty note might not be clear, and that she had been suddenly summoned by her mother, to attend the bedside of her brother Wentworth, who was sick in New York and lying at the point of death, and that her former guardian and Wentworth's, had been good enough to inform her of the situation and was accompanying her to New York upon the same errand. She would return, the telegram concluded, as soon as the uncertainty as to her brother's fate was ended. She gave the address of the private sanatorium to which Wentworth had been taken, where any message might be sent to her.

When the train was nearing New Haven, Cushing came into the car and took the telegram.

"It is to my husband," she said, handing him the message open. He folded it without looking at it.

"It explains why I left home so suddenly," she said. "He was not at home, and I came away without telling him."

"Willie Rice is in the smoker," said Cushing. "I have n't told him that you are on the car. Would you like to have him come in and talk to you?"

Evelyn pondered the question for a moment. A conversation with Mr. Rice would involve explanations. She did not wish to tell him of her brother's condition, and some plausible explanation would have to be given for her journey to New York in company with her rejected suitor. She respected

Cushing's delicacy in not having mentioned her name to Rice, but at the same time felt humiliated that the same thought which occupied her mind had probably come into his. She had played fast and loose with his affections. This was part of the penalty.

"No, please," she said, at length, "I'd rather you would n't. I—I don't think I care to talk to any one just now."

Cushing jumped down from the car, and left the telegram at the window of the telegraph office. It was, of course, never delivered to Manson, who was following them on the second section of the train a few miles away, with murder in his heart. Since he had left no address at home, it was impossible to forward it to him from there, though the message was addressed to the office and would in ordinary course have been sent immediately after the person to whom it was directed.

They reached New York at six o'clock. Cushing called a cab, and they were driven immediately to the sanatorium where Wentworth was being cared for. They were shown into the reception room, and Mrs. Thayer joined them in a moment.

"Wentworth is much better," she said. "He awoke this morning with his mind clear, and has been improving ever since. But the poor boy is nervous and unstrung, and so ashamed! He says that he cannot face his friends again for a long time. He wants to go away for a while, until he feels fit to make a fresh start."

Evelyn was relieved to hear of her brother's recovery, but could not prevent the secret regret that she had taken this bootless journey. She had worried herself, during their passage from the station, with various speculations concerning her husband—the misconstruction which he might place upon her note, coupled with the fact that she had come away with Cushing—the possibility that he might not receive her telegram, or that, knowing the facts he might disapprove of her leaving home without first informing him of them. She kissed her mother somewhat mechanically. Her pleasure at Wentworth's rapid recovery was enhanced by the fact that it would permit her to return home so much the sooner.

"I know the very thing for Wentworth," exclaimed Cushing with a sudden inspiration. "I had made all my arrangements for a trip to South America, upon the steamer leaving here tomorrow, before I learned of this affair. I meant to cancel my passage if Wentworth grew worse; but this turn for the better will enable me to carry out my plans, give him the change he needs, and enable me to exercise a closer supervision over him than I could do at home. I've taken a whole state-room, and there's room enough for both of us. If he is willing, and you are, I shall be glad to take him with me."

Thus the matter was arranged. Wentworth was not only willing but penitently grateful for the opportunity. Evelyn was anxious to return home at once, but since there was no convenient train until morning, was persuaded to send a telegram to her husband, announcing her return by the early train. This message, of course, shared the fate of the other, except that it was delivered at the house, to Leonie, who receipted for it, and debated for several months whether she should open it nor not. She decided in the negative—which she subsequently regretted—and left the unopened envelope lying on the table in the hall.

Evelyn and her mother were accommodated with a room at the sanatorium, and Cushing, wishing to be near them, contented himself with a bed at a second-class hotel in the neighborhood. Not wishing to grace with his aristocratic signature the register of so humble a hostelry, and perhaps be published among the hotel arrivals in the morning newspapers, he did not write his name in the book, but, having no luggage, paid for his room in advance.

Evelyn left by the early morning train. Mrs. Thayer remained with her son during the morning. Cushing busied himself in the completion of his preparations for the contemplated journey, totally unaware that a dozen trained seekers of information, with carte blanche as to expense, were watching the steamboat wharves and hotel lobbies for him. Once at least during the morning he passed a sharp-eyed individual poring over the register of his own hotel, but no intuition suggested that the one was seeker or the other sought.

We often speak of coincidences as strange; but the narrow margins by which related events sometimes fail to coincide are quite as remarkable, the difference being that we know of the one and seldom of the other. The material world is only of orderly development; left to itself, it works steadily towards its predestined end. The moral world, whose laws are less well known, and which involves the uncertain element of free will, seems often a world of chance. It was indeed wonderful that Cushing and Manson should have come together on a lonely island in the Atlantic ocean; but it was no less strange that they should not have met in New York. The chances were a thousand to one in favor of the latter contingency. Had chance put Cushing in touch with his pursuer, instead of keeping them apart, this story could never have been written.

A part of the preparations for their southern journey consisted in procuring an outfit for Wentworth. Mrs. Thayer had brought with her from Boston some of his things, and Cushing went with her to buy such others as the boy would need. Cushing's own baggage had been telephoned for the night before, and came from Boston by the noon train.

Mrs. Thayer found an opportunity to thank Cushing in private, before they parted.

"Edward," she said, "you have been kind, so good, to me, and I have been able to offer you nothing in return."

"It's all right, Alice. I want no return."

"My hope that I might, indirectly, contribute to your happiness was—a ghastly failure."

"Don't speak of it, Alice; it was no fault of yours. You were always a true and loyal friend."

"A true and grateful friend I always meant to be, Edward; I should have been worthy only of contempt had I been less. But the sins of the children sometimes react upon the parents, and I could not have complained if you had embraced us all in your displeasure."

"It would not have been just, Alice, for you were not to blame, nor Wentworth."

"It would have been natural enough, and I could not have complained of the injustice. But instead of visiting your displeasure upon us, you have not withdrawn your friendship, and you are willing to burden yourself with my unfortunate boy, who has so poorly requited your kindness."

"Alice, your husband was my friend; to him I owed my prosperity. I could do no less than befriend his wife and children. I have never forgotten that deathbed promise."

Alice sighed. She had loved her husband and cherished his memory, but it was human for her to wish that her friendship might be valued for its own sake. She would have liked her husband's memory to be a tie between them, without being at the same time a barrier.

"There are few who have your exalted ideal of friendship, Edward. But it has meant much to me and mine, and you can believe me always grateful;—it is the only return I can make you now."

"I know, Alice—you did what you could. Your friendship, your regard, is an adequate return for the little I have done. I have led a somewhat purposeless existence. Wentworth gives me, for the present, an additional object in life. I shall take care of him, for your sake."

"Thank you, my friend," replied Alice. That he should care for her son, for her sake, without mentioning his father gave her a feeling of elation. She had long ago resigned the hope that there could ever be any other relation between them than that of friendship, but the extinguishment of its clear flame would have left the altar of her life cold and cheerless indeed; and in spite of her hopelessness of anything more, her heart sometimes spoke involuntarily. Evelyn's defection had wounded her deeply. Instinctively she had taken Cushing's part, and had found it difficult to forgive her daughter. In this trouble with her son, it was a blessed relief to feel that a strong and kind and capable arm, to which she was accustomed, was still offered for her to lean upon.

She accompanied Cushing and her son to the steamer. It was a long drive from uptown to the Brooklyn bridge, and across it, to the wharf from which the Brazilian steamer sailed. She went on board with them, inspected their quarters, kissed her son, wept a little over him, as she listened to his earnest promises of amendment, shook hands with Cushing, and went ashore, where she stood upon the wharf and watched them on the deck as the steamer receded, until their faces were indistinct and their waving handkerchiefs a mere blur of white.

Soon after leaving the wharf her carriage passed another, driving rapidly in the direction from which her own had come. As the windows of the two cabs came opposite each other, Alice caught sight of a white, strained face, leaning forward eagerly. Though she had the merest fleeting glimpse of it, the face reminded Alice strongly of her daughter's husband. But Manson was in Boston, and her eyes were still damp with tears—it was of course a mere passing resemblance, and she thought no more of it.

Had Alice learned, an hour or two later, that by remaining a few minutes longer upon the wharf, she would have saved several of those dearest to her a world of suffering, she would have regretted poignantly that she had not stayed, and would very unreasonably have blamed herself for any harm that followed. But she was spared this knowledge. Whether, when it came to her a year later, her opinion was the same, remains to be seen.

XX.

LEONIE'S AMBITION

Evelyn had left New York at seven in the morning, and reached Boston at noon. She had hoped that after her telegram Manson might meet her at the station, but he was not there. Perhaps he had remained away because displeased with her—or business had detained him. She moved toward the telephone booth in the station, but, on second thoughts, turned away, and preceded by a porter with her bag, moved toward the carriage entrance, took a seat in the nearest cab, and was driven rapidly homeward.

She alighted, paid the cabman, and ran up the steps. She had put out her hand to ring the bell, when a sudden impulse restrained her, and feeling in her chatelaine bag for her latchkey, she opened the door softly. Closing it with as little noise, she set her bag down, laid off her hat and traveling coat, and then looked through the lower part of the house. There was no one there.

She next went softly upstairs, glancing into the different rooms as she passed them, but finding them all empty until she reached her own chamber, from which sounds proceeded, as of some one moving about. The door stood ajar; Evelyn approached it noiselessly and looked in.

Leonie was standing before the mirror, dressed in her mistress's finest gown. Upon the dressing table were piled all of Evelyn's ribbons and laces, while across the bed, which had been slept in, and upon the chairs around, were scattered her choicest articles of *lingerie*. Leonie was just putting the finishing touches to an elaborate coiffure with the aid of Evelyn's own particular private silver-backed, monogramed hair brush.

While Evelyn, stiff with indignant astonishment, stood viewing this spectacle, Leonie's aspiring soul found expression in song—a music-hall ditty, in cockney dialect, which she had heard at a matinee a few days before—she had a good, untrained contralto voice, and an ear for music:

"I wants to be a lydy,
And with the lydies dwell,
To wear the finest garments,
And everything that's swell.
"I——"

Leonie had opened her mouth to voice her further wants, when, in the mirror behind her own reflection, she caught sight of a slowly widening door, in the opening of which appeared an indignant and familiar face.

The words died on her lips, from which the color receded. Her dark cheek turned pale, and the brush, released by her relaxing fingers, fell clattering upon the dressing-table and smashed a much-prized, hand-painted porcelain pin-tray, the birthday gift of a dear school friend.

"What does this—masquerade mean?" demanded Evelyn, when she was able to find her speech.

"Why, I—I—"

Evelyn's accusing eye arrested the lie, for a lie it probably would have been. Leonie would lie on slight provocation, and often merely for dramatic effect. In this emergency it was hardly likely that she would tell the truth. Discouraged from speech, she stood mute.

"When you are through with my things," said Evelyn, slowly and distinctly, in cold, incisive tones, her lips white with anger, "when you are quite through with my things, and have aired them thoroughly, perhaps you'll be good enough to put them back where they belong—all of them—and then I shall have something more to say to you."

Evelyn went downstairs to the telephone and called up her husband's office.

"Hello. Is this Mr. Manson's office?"

"Yes."

"Please call him to the 'phone."

"He's not in just now."

"Where is he? This is Mrs. Manson."

"Oh, yes, ma'am! Excuse me, Mrs. Manson, but we don't know where he is."

"When do you expect him back?"

"We don't know. Mr. Manson has n't been at the office this morning, and we have n't had any word from him, since yesterday noon, when he started home for luncheon. His mail has n't been opened, and there are important matters demanding his immediate attention. We called up the house, but you were not there, and your servant could give us no clear information."

Evelyn was filled with the greatest alarm. Something had happened, probably along the line that she had feared. She must at once interrogate Leonie. Whatever it was that had taken place, would probably account for the girl's unusual conduct. It was imperative that she learn immediately all that Leonie knew.

"Mr. Manson was called out of town suddenly," she said over the phone. "I have been absent myself and have only just returned; I shall be down at the office shortly and explain."

"Very well, ma'am, we're awfully glad to know that everything is all right. We were beginning to fear that something had happened to Mr. Manson."

Evelyn had hardly hung up the receiver when Leonie appeared. In a surprisingly short time she had laid off her silken robe and donned her own attire, including cap and apron. Meanwhile she had debated, in some perturbation of mind, the attitude which she should take, and had reached the conclusion that she would boldly declare her independence and throw up her situation before she could be discharged. Her courage sank, however, while she descended the stairs, at the sudden recollection of numerous small articles in her trunk,—articles to which she had no claim except that of possession, and to which she had meant to add many more, had her mistress not returned so soon. She need not have troubled herself greatly, however, for Evelyn, engrossed with thoughts of her husband, apparently paid no attention to her maid's cringing manner, and said nothing further about her masquerade, going immediately to the subject agitating her own mind.

"Leonie," she asked, "when was Mr. Manson last at home?"

"At noon yesterday, ma'am. But he didn't stay to luncheon. He read your letter, asked me some questions, told me to take care of the house until he came back, and then went away. He has n't been home since."

"Did you see him read my note?"

"Yes'm."

"What did he say, or do?"

"He asked me when you went away, and who went with you, and I—I told him. And then he swore, and went away in a cab, the driver whipping up his horses."

"Is that all he asked you?"

"Yes,'m."

That she was lying Evelyn could read in her face; but no cross-examination could make her admit having told Manson anything further.

"Did he say where he was going?" demanded Evelyn, still seeking light in her bewilderment.

"No ma'am."

"Or how long he'd be gone?"

"He said he might be away several days."

This statement increased Evelyn's alarm. She bitterly regretted the childish petulance which had dictated her conduct of yesterday. She was young, and, though naturally capable, had never before had to rely upon her own judgment in any important matter—not even the matter of her own marriage. Even now, her first thought was of her mother, and what she would advise. But Alice was in New York and would not be home until evening. Evelyn realized that by her own foolish act she had greatly disturbed her husband's peace of mind and interfered with his business. If he had learned her destination the day before and had followed them to New York, he might do some rash thing that would involve him in trouble or disgrace, which she must share, and for which she must suffer a lifetime of repentance and remorse. She had no means of knowing that the steamer had sailed. Perhaps her husband had already met Cushing in New York. He was capable, in anger, she vaguely realized, of acting first and thinking afterwards—as she had done. He might have met Cushing and done him an injury before there was time for explanation.

Her husband's disappearance for even a day had caused embarrassment at the office. She realized that unless some plausible reason for his absence should emanate from his own home, his disappearance would become the subject of remark, perhaps of newspaper comment. Should the real reason transpire, Evelyn herself might become the subject of a scandal, and her name be bandied about in the sensational columns of afternoon newspapers. Or, Manson's conduct might be ascribed to some moral or mental idiosyncracy that would impair his standing with the public, which demands that those who seek its confidence should avoid the appearance of evil. The line between sanity and insanity has been said to be not strictly drawn in Boston. The charge may have seemed truer in the good old reforming days than now, but even then it was insisted that one at least have method in his madness. Evelyn felt that she must protect her husband's name until she could consult her mother, or until Manson's return, which of course might take place at any moment.

So Evelyn put on her hat and went immediately down to Sterling & Manson's office, where she explained to the chief clerk that her husband had been suddenly called out of town on an urgent, personal matter, and would probably be back during the day. The clerk called her attention to several equally urgent matters which concerned her husband's fortunes and demanded immediate attention. Some of them, of which she had not known before, gave her deep concern. After a hasty luncheon down town, she drove to the railroad station, where she waited nearly two hours for the train which brought her mother back to Boston.

XXI.
RESCUE

Manson grew steadily worse. His disorder developed into an intermittent fever, which Cushing had no medicine to combat. The active member of this strangely assorted and involuntary partnership attended to the commissary department, and watched and tended his companion when not vainly watching the sea for a sail.

One morning at daybreak he saw a faint trail of smoke, low down upon the horizon. He watched it eagerly, hopefully, but instead of coming toward the island it drew steadily away, and soon disappeared. The steamer from which it came had not come in sight of the island, or, if so, had passed it at night, and doubtless had not seen their signal.

This incident threw Cushing into gloom, and Manson into a despondency that threatened his health still further. Once at least Cushing, in involuntary sympathy for Manson's sufferings, had begun to consider seriously whether he ought not to tell Manson the facts about himself and Evelyn, in the hope that by restoring his spirits he might encourage nature to shake off the fever which was slowly consuming him. But with his usual fatuity, Manson made this impossible.

"Henry," he chattered one day when the chill was upon him, "I d-d-d-on't believe I could stand this much longer but for one thing, and that is the hope of revenge upon that scoundrel. If my mind was p-p-perfectly free and calm, I believe I should d-d-die. It may seem a f-f-faint hope, but it's meat and drink and m-m-medicine to me. And I feel, in the very marrow of my bones, along with this cursed malaria, that I shall get away from this island prison, and recover my sight, and meet my enemy, and work j-j-justice upon him. Stay by me until then, Henry, and help me in this righteous task, and I'll be your friend, your slave—your tool—your anything, so long as we both shall live. I solemnly swear it, so help me God."

Of course, after such a statement, even the larger humanity to which Cushing had been momentarily impelled, forbade him to enlighten Manson, who, by his own statement, was kept alive merely by the hope of revenge. To tell him the truth would expose him to an agony of self-reproach which might lower his vitality and his already none too great resistance to disease.

Side by side, however, with Manson's passion for revenge, had grown up and was increasing in strength from day to day, a love and devotion for Singleton, as Manson knew him, which rivalled in intensity and resembled in quality the typical friendships of history and romance. It gave Cushing a curious thrill to hear this man whom he had every reason to hate and dislike, profess for him a love more devoted than that of Jonathan for David, or Damon for Pythias; and his mind reverted now and then to the question which had long before suggested itself: Which was the stronger passion, friendship or revenge? The man who was sworn to kill him, protested, in the same breath, that he would die for him. Perhaps never before in the history of mankind had quite the same situation existed. Men had been misled before, of course, as to the true character of those whom they had deemed their friends, and they had afterwards learned the truth. But here the two opposing emotions, each grown to the height of an absorbing passion, were simultaneously directed toward the same object. Singleton had as truly befriended Manson, as Manson supposed Cushing to have injured him.

"It would be a curious experiment," mused Cushing, "to try this question to a finish; to keep the facts from his knowledge until we are rescued—if we ever are—and he recovers his sight—if he ever does—and then put the proposition to him squarely. Here is your enemy—here is your friend; they are one and the same. What will you do about it?"

The more Cushing considered the question, the more interesting it seemed. He was not naturally introspective or analytical—his philosophy was objective in its nature, directed outwardly, rather than inwardly, but the problem developed a sort of fascination for him. It was fully as absorbing as a game of chess, at which he was an expert. He knew very well what he himself would do in such a case—Manson's frank exposition of Cushing's character, as Manson conceived it, had compelled the elder man to a certain amount of self-analysis, the result of which was not entirely satisfactory, but he was reasonably sure what course he would have taken under similar circumstances. On the other hand, Manson's character, unconventional to begin with, and profoundly modified by his misfortunes real and imaginary, was an unknown quantity. What he would do under the given circumstances was entirely problematical—was indeed so interesting a problem that Cushing determined to push it, if opportunity offered, to the test.

The days crept by with aggravating slowness. Cushing became desperate. Life on the island during the rainy season was decidedly unpleasant. All around, a monotonous stretch of gray sea, overhead a leaden pall; half the time, the two coalescing into something like primaeval chaos, before the waters which were under the firmament were divided from those above it. If the rain ceased by day, an oppressive, humid heat; by night, a chill breeze that brought discomfort. They might remain on the island for months ere it was visited again. To provide food for two was no small task. Cushing's mind was not inventive; he was the spoiled child of civilization, and helpless without his mother. To wrest a living from earth and sea by such expedients as were within his reach was for Cushing a harder task than it would have been for an unschooled peasant, bred to toil, or a savage inured to privation. His patient grew steadily worse. His interest in Manson increased as the latter lost ground. He had been company. His helplessness had furnished Cushing with a *raison d'être*, even as Manson's anticipated revenge had served him as a hold on existence. Again, he felt a sort of proprietary interest in Manson, as though he had a sort of lien upon his life. He had nursed and nourished him. To lose him now would seem like so much labor wasted. Cushing wanted to see the outcome of the psychological comedy, or tragi-comedy in which he and Manson were the chief participants.

He was tired of the island—deadly tired—so tired that the perils of the sea, with any chance whatever to escape them, seemed preferable to the weariness of the land.

Day by day he watched the sea, but ever in vain. The young lieutenant from the *Oklahoma* had given the location of the island as several hundred miles eastward of the Windward Islands. Cushing knew that the sailing course to Pernambuco lay still further to the eastward,—probably not more than a hundred miles at the farthest—varying say from fifty to a hundred. On two occasions since the first, he had seen the smoke of a passing steamer—it could have been nothing else—and there were a dozen reasons which might cause a ship to keep to the westerly limit of a purely arbitrary course. The boat in which Manson had reached the island was still there. After the recent storm it had been missing, but was found, after a day or two, where it had been driven up among the bushes by the force of the waves, fortunately without injury. There was but one oar, which he had kept at the camp, but with the hatchet he could easily fashion another from the trunk of a small tree.

If he could gain Manson's consent, two courses lay open to them. They might row westward until they reached the Barbadoes, perhaps; or failing that, they were bound to strike some one of the chain of close-lying islands some fifty or seventy-five miles still farther westward. On the other hand, they could set out boldly toward the east, with a possibility, of course, of drifting far out into the ocean, to certain destruction, but with the far greater chance of being picked up by some vessel, of which, in all probability, many were passing just beyond the limit of his vision. He could at least put out in that direction for a day or two, and if this hope proved futile, they could return to the island.

Any suggestion of either plan met with violent opposition from Manson, whose antipathy to the sea had grown with the decline of his strength. Not until Manson's fever had so increased that he was only semi-conscious for long periods did Cushing take the control of matters entirely into his own hands. He got the boat down to the water, after some effort, coupled with considerable ingenuity. He cut down a small tree and shaped an oar with the hatchet; the task occupied him for a whole day. The boat was provisioned with food which he had been accumulating for a week, with a view to the possibility of this course, and the cask which had come ashore with Manson's boat was filled with fresh water. He made shift to rig up a sort of mast, to which he attached Manson's oil-skin coat by way of sail—the only thing they had for the purpose; it could be taken down, if needed at any time for shelter for the sick man.

Thus prepared, Cushing lifted his patient into the boat, and laid him down upon a bed of dry leaves which he had spread in the bow. There was a light wind setting outwards, and directing his course to the eastward, he made the opening in the breakers, and was soon in the open sea.

Cushing had been impelled to this step more for Manson's sake than for his own. Unless proper medicines could be procured within a few days, Manson would probably die. A westerly course might bring them to some place no better for the invalid than their own island; whereas almost any vessel would be likely to carry a medicine chest.

No sooner had they left the island than fortune relented toward these victims of her caprice. Their boat had been launched early in the morning. The day had turned out clear, and the tip of the tall dead palm which Cushing had used for a lookout, was still discernible against the setting sun, low down upon the horizon, when they were discovered and picked up by a steamer southern bound from New York.

Ere the vessel reached them Cushing asked himself the question whether he should give to their rescuers the true names of his unconscious companion and himself. He decided that he would not. His reasons for concealing his own identity from Manson, were still in force. This he could do no longer if he gave his real name to others with whom Manson would be in daily intercourse. The experiment which had furnished him with mental interest during their island sojourn, had taken strong hold on his imagination. Was gratitude a stronger feeling than revenge? Was hate a more powerful passion than love? Thrown back upon Manson for human intercourse, he had learned a great deal about his character. He had not learned all, for he had lacked sympathy, the only plummet with which to sound another's heart. The blind man, measuring Cushing's feelings by his conduct, had opened up to him the secret places of his soul, but Cushing's heart had not been correspondingly receptive. He learned only so much of Manson's character as the unaided intellect could grasp. Of Manson's shortcomings he missed nothing—his lack of refinement, his narrowness of view, the wall which a low origin and a contracted outlook had built around him in early life. Cushing knew that education had in part broken down this wall, and that through the breach had escaped the wonderful talent which had bidden fair to make Manson famous. The finer side of his nature, which was even now being tried in the furnace of misfortune, Cushing had not yet perceived. He knew very well, however, that even a finer, a more cultivated intelligence, might hesitate between two powerful and conflicting emotions; and he was curious to see the outcome in this man of primitive passions. It would be his return for weeks of wretchedness.

XXII.
ON TO RIO

The steamer proved to be the *Pan-America*, of the opposition line to that by which Cushing had originally taken passage for South America. Most of the crew and passengers were gathered on the deck when the castaways were lifted overboard, but the keen glance which Cushing threw around him discovered no one whom he recognized as an acquaintance. He had traveled so widely that it would not have been surprising had there been among the crew some officer, or even some seaman, whom he had met before.

To their rescuers he gave his name as Henry Singleton, and Manson's as John Martin, passengers on board the brig *Puritan*, bound from Boston to the Mediterranean, and blown wide of her course by the great storm of several months before, and wrecked upon the island from which they had just come. There was some apprehension on board the ship, on account of Manson's illness, because of the constant danger of yellow fever in the tropics; but these fears were relieved as soon as the ship's surgeon, after a brief examination, had declared Manson's fever not contagious and Cushing in perfect health. Cushing's speech and manners being those of a gentleman—his appearance would have been no index— was supplied with clothing contributed by the ship's officers, and admitted to their mess; while Manson was immediately placed under the care of the surgeon, a canny Scotsman by the name of Campbell.

For the same reason, however, which had prompted him to conceal his name, Cushing retained the full and somewhat uneven beard which he had grown during his forced exile; this, taken with the deep bronze tint acquired by exposure to the sun and air, he hoped might prove an effective disguise. He insisted upon remaining constantly beside his sick friend, and was with Manson when the latter became conscious of his surroundings and demanded information.

"Where are we, Henry?" he asked, "and how did we come here?"

"You are on the steamer *Pan-America*, which is at present steaming through the Atlantic, about two-thirds of the way between New York and Pernambuco. I left the island with you yesterday in your boat, while you were unconscious and unable to protest; it seemed our best chance to get away. Toward evening we were picked up by this steamer. I have given your name as 'John Martin.'"

"Why not Hugh Manson?"

"Remember your purpose! You are now John Martin, a shipwrecked passenger of the brig *Puritan*, wrecked on Turtle Island six weeks ago. The disappearance of Hugh Manson, the distinguished architect, has already been commented upon, and you are doubtless regarded as dead. Those whom you seek are therefore off their guard. If you find and punish them, the world would never connect the dead Hugh Manson with the event. It would do you no good to be known as your enemy's slayer. If at a later time you re-appear with your story of shipwreck, a slight change of dates will entirely disarm suspicion."

Manson did not seem satisfied. "You see, Henry," he insisted, "I *want* them to know who's punishing them! That will be the best part of it. When I kill him, I want to meet him face to face and tell him why. It would be a good riddance, so far as the world is concerned, if I poisoned him, or stabbed him in the back; but it would be un-American, don't you see, and what good would it do *me*?

"I understand, of course," returned Cushing, "but since you make it a personal matter, there's no need to take the whole world into your confidence. Even if you killed him, your own life might be ruined, and he would take the odd trick, after all, in the game."

"My life is already ruined," replied Manson gloomily.

"Nonsense!" said Cushing. "You are young, strong, capable, and have proved your powers. No faithless woman is worth a strong man's life. Remember my own story. Of course you want your enemy to know, but why notify him in advance? He believes you dead? Why warn him that you are alive and on his track? He might escape you."

"True, he might try; and while he can't escape—I know it, as surely as I knew I should escape drowning and murder and starvation and blindness!—he might give me a good deal more trouble. Have it your own way, Henry, until I get my eyes back. You can't imagine what it means to have this black curtain drawn over them! I owe you my life already, but I shall owe you more before I can look again upon the green earth and the blue sky. I'll be Tom, Dick, or Harry— whatever you wish; and when I've finished *him*, I'll belong to you. What do you say my name is?"

"John Martin."

So it was understood. The fictitious Martin mended rapidly under the care of Dr. Campbell, whose opinion coincided with Cushing's that Martin's blindness was due primarily to the blow upon the head,—though exposure and starvation may have aggravated the injury,—and that a simple operation by a competent specialist would probably restore his sight unimpaired.

"The best place in this quarter of the globe for such an operation," declared the doctor, "is the hospital at Rio de Janeiro—one of the best hospitals in the world, and I've seen most of them and studied in several. On our last trip one of the doctors there sewed up a seaman's heart which had been almost severed with a knife during a fo'c'sle argument. The fellow, a big Swede, who weighed two hundred pounds, was living when we came away and showed every sign of recovery. Dr. Silva is the eye man; he's a little off color, like a lot of the Brazilians, but he's all right. The color'll all come out in the wash, and you'll find him all white underneath."

In a few days Manson was able to sit up and walk the deck, supported by Cushing, to whose arm he attached himself with a childlike dependence. He developed a great appetite, and soon began to gain strength.

"The fact is, Henry," he said in confidence, "I never once had enough to eat while we were on that confounded island; but I knew you were dividing fairly with me, and I never said a word. I'm simply making up for lost time."

Cushing continued to fill his various roles with grim philosophy. He had a point to make, and was willing to pay the price. But the humor of the situation sometimes overcame him. Sitting alone one evening upon the extreme point of the ship's bow, he burst into laughter. Never would the wildest stretch of his imagination have made him nurse, valet, blind-man's-dog, guide, philosopher and friend, of the man above all others whom he had most occasion to hate.

"And I'm even conspiring murder with him—my own murder—I, who even as a boy would n't kick a dog or kill the cat!"

He laughed so long and so heartily that the lookout on duty glanced over toward him suspiciously, and continued to keep his eye upon him. The poor fellow had suffered a good deal during his shipwreck, and might not be quite right in his mind. They sometimes jumped overboard when they were that way; they saw their wives or sweethearts beckoning them from the water, or their enemies pursuing them from behind.

One day Cushing was in the purser's office, and to pass the time asked permission to look at the passenger lists for the last few voyages.

"We have n't had a great many North Americans for several trips," said the officer while Cushing was running over the names. "We had a number booked for this voyage, but one of our engines got out of order and delayed us a few days. Of course we could n't tell just when we would sail. The other line steamer did n't sail for a week, so two of our passengers took the *Lucania* for Liverpool, expecting to make close connection there with a British steamer for Rio. We got away sooner than we expected, so we'll beat them by several days after all. They came on the ship the day before schedule sailing time—a Miss Hanson or Manson, a stunning brunette, and her mother, a fine-looking blonde, who looked more like her sister. They were both in mourning—which was very becoming, I assure you."

Cushing displayed no sign of special interest in this information, but carelessly flicked the ash from his cigar.

"What was their errand in South America?" he asked, after a pause long enough to mark only the mild curiosity which in the narrow life of a ship at sea finds interest in the veriest trifles.

"Victims of the sea! It seems the husband had taken passage on the *Bolivar*, of our line, a couple of months ago, for this same trip, accompanied by a son, who was all broken up as the result of a long spree, and was taking the voyage for his health. The boy fell or jumped overboard one day—love or liquor, I suppose—more likely liquor—and his father went overboard after him. It was several minutes before they were missed. They picked up the boy but never found the man, though they cruised around for several hours looking for him, and were half a day late in getting to port. I fell in love with both the ladies. I foresee, if they come back on our boat, that I'll have trouble—I won't know which one to propose to."

Cushing restrained a momentary impulse to punch the purser's head. He had found him a very companionable fellow, with a large fund of reminiscence, but for the moment he seemed entirely too free with his remarks. His information, however, was interesting, if not accurate. Evelyn, of course, mourned her husband, of whose existence and loss the purser had not known. But why should Alice wear black? For her son-in-law? He scarcely thought so; she had not cared enough for him. Cushing felt a secret pleasure in imagining that Alice had put on black for the friend who had given up his life to save her son. The purser had made a very amusing mistake in supposing him to be her husband; but the idea was not unpleasing. Manson had first suggested it, during one of his frank denunciations, to his friend Singleton, of his absent enemy Cushing. It seemed strange, in view of

Alice's manifold perfections, that he had never thought of her in this light. The weeks upon the island had left him abundant time for reflection. Alice was still beautiful; she would have brought him a wealth of affection; she would have graced his table, and would never have disgraced his name. His loyalty to his dead friend's memory had blinded him to the fact that his friend's widow was a young and wholesome woman, entitled to a larger measure of happiness than her brief married life had yielded her, or than she could find in the sad luxury of grief. He could now only regret that his eyes had not been opened before he had given his heart to Evelyn, the thought of whose fresh beauty still thrilled him. He had been robbed of her; the robber still gloried in his deed. He had not proved worthy of such a treasure; he had not yet been sufficiently punished.

During the few remaining days of the voyage, Cushing carefully guarded Manson from contact with the purser. If that officer perchance came near them, Cushing turned the conversation upon the weather, an ever ready topic at sea, and hurried Manson away. Manson must soon learn the truth, but not, if Cushing should have his way, until his experiment had been tried. Manson was on his way, no doubt, to recovery and happiness—happiness which would be all the deeper and more lasting when his misunderstanding was once cleared up. There was no special hurry about it—let him wait. Cushing would have to suffer all his life for want of the happiness toward which Manson was rushing as fast as steam and skill and fine weather could carry him.

XXIII.

LA MISERICORDIA

The *Pan-America* steamed into the beautiful harbor of Rio de Janeiro toward the close of an October day. Viewed from the steamer's deck, the city seemed like a city of Southern Italy, or a scene from fairyland; a cluster of alabaster palaces in different tints, against a background of deepest green, the whole bathed in the ruddy glow of the declining sun. It was the Southern Spring, and already the air was tremulous with tropical heat.

After the tedious preliminaries attending debarkation, Cushing went ashore with Manson—the blind man holding the other's arm. They took a carriage for a hotel in the Southern or more modern portion of the city. The purser called out to them as they were taking their seats.

"By the way, Mr. Singleton, those ladies would have done better to wait for us. They'll not get here until Wednesday."

"Thank you, Mr. Powers; I hope I'll run across them."

He gave the coachman the word to go, lest Powers should mention any name that would inform Manson. There would be until Wednesday, five days, in which to have Manson's eyes attended to and prepare for the test to which he meant to put him. By then Evelyn would have arrived, and once in the city, it would not be easy to keep the husband and wife apart. The story of their shipwreck and their rescue would be public property, and Evelyn would be sure to hear of it, and to seek them out in the hope of learning something of her lost husband's fate.

Something of the city's beauty disappeared when they saw it at closer range. Even the friendly softness of the advancing twilight could not hide the fact that many of the streets through which they passed were narrow, ill-paved, damp, dirty, reeking with repulsive odors, and infested with wolfish-looking dogs. The population was typically South American; the people were of all shades, from the occasional German or English white, through the olive Latin of pure race to the stolid Indian or full-blood Negro, mixed breeds predominating, as though nature had selected this hot land as a laboratory for fusing again into one race the various types into which primeval man had in remote ages become differentiated. There was no great novelty in the scene to Cushing, to whom there were few strange scenes or peoples; and Manson's eyes were sealed.

By and by they advanced into a more pleasing neighborhood. Here the houses were of yellow, brown and pink, with tiled roofs and variegated trimmings. Everywhere were signs of the Latin race and the Catholic religion. Curious spires and domes of churches pierced the sky.

By the time the carriage reached its destination the sun had set with tropical suddenness, and the broad front of the hotel at which they drew up was in a blaze of light. They drove through a wide arch into a court, in the center of which a fountain was playing. Two sides of the court were lined with broad piazzas, upon one of which a band of mulatto boys in white uniforms were playing, with rare taste and skill, a selection from *Les Huguenots*. Waiters were darting hither and thither, and gaily dressed men and women came and went. The back of the quadrangle opened upon a tropical garden, redolent with strange, sleepy, aromatic odors. Lights twinkled in the shrubbery, in various detached cottages which supplemented the main building of the hotel.

The two Americans were assigned an apartment in one of these cottages. Their quarters consisted of two sleeping chambers and a sitting-room, all connected. The varnished floors were bare and cool, the furniture was of bent wood; the beds had cane bottoms and thin mattresses. The windows were screened, and there were hammocks for day lounging. The accommodation was simple, comfortable, adapted to the climate, and conforming to the Latin ideal of luxury. There was no lodging place for dirt, no lurking place for insect life, against both of which in tropical lands life is a constant struggle, in which civilization does not always maintain the upper hand.

They dined shortly after their arrival. The meats were poor, the bread all that could be wished, the fruits excellent and the wine good. Cushing had ordered the dinner *à la carte*, and for curiosity asked to see the bill.

"How much do you suppose it is?" he asked of Manson.

"It was n't at all a bad dinner," returned the blind man. "I suppose at least three or four dollars."

"Fifteen thousand milreis!"

"I am blind, Henry," returned Manson reproachfully, "but you should n't make sport of me. Remember the fate of Samson, and think of the roof of the house falling upon your devoted head! I don't know what milreis are, but if they have any value at all, we have fallen into a den of thieves."

"It sounds larger than it really it; it equals just exactly four dollars and twenty-five cents, at the current rate of exchange."

"A millionaire in this country would have to be worth all of five hundred dollars, and thirty cents would sound like a comfortable fortune. But you can't afford to keep me, or yourself, at such a place. We are flying too high! Remember that I have nothing, and no way of getting anything. I am as helpless as an infant, but for your friendship."

"I have several acquaintances here," replied Cushing, "and will establish a credit at a bank to-morrow. I am not entirely without resources."

"You are always thoughtful, and resourceful and kind; while I, as usual, think only of myself. You've been my physician, my nurse, my guard, my guide, and now my banker. My debt to you keeps piling up. I can never pay it; a lifetime would be all too short to make it good."

"It is nothing," said Cushing. "Try another glass of this excellent amontillado. I have drunk no better outside of Spain."

They smoked a couple of fragrant cigars; they were astonishingly cheap. The evening air throbbed with the music of the band. They listened for a while in silence.

Manson spoke. "Henry, you know why I started for South America. In spite of all delays, I am here—thanks to you, and to God—which proves that my business is a just one. You will find out from me if they are here? They might be at this very hotel."

"I'll ascertain and let you know. If they're not in the house, and have n't been here, I'll search the town. But your eyes must be our first care. It will do you no good to meet your enemy if you cannot see him. Meantime you should avoid excitement."

"You are right, Henry, as you always are! It was good for me that I went blind; I was too stubborn—too self-satisfied—too sure of my own opinions. Had I never been blind, I should never have known you, and should never have learned the meaning of friendship. Closing my eyes in one way has opened them in another. But look them up, Henry, and tell me they cannot escape, and then I'll be as calm as—a glass of jelly!"

Cushing left him after a while and crossed the court to the hotel office. He inquired at the desk, examined the register, and returning to Manson reported that neither Mrs. Manson nor Mr. Cushing had registered at the *Ingleterra* during the Winter.

"They may have registered under assumed names," suggested Manson.

"I thought of that too. No couple of their description has put up here. But there are other hotels; they would be likely to select one less conspicuous, if they apprehended pursuit. I'll inquire further in the morning. You had better go to bed now. You'll need all your nerve for the examination of your eyes tomorrow."

Manson obeyed submissively. Cushing went back to the piazza and sat listening to the music. There was dancing in the adjoining *salon*. He remained until nearly midnight, smoking and watching the dancers.

After breakfast next morning Cushing looked up the specialist recommended to him by Dr. Campbell of the *Pan-America*. Dr. Silva was attached to to the staff of the Eye Institute, as well as to that of *La Misericordia*, the finest hospital in South America, but could be consulted at home during certain hours.

Cushing soon found the place. It proved to be on First of March Street, a wide and pleasant thoroughfare, approached by way of Immaculate Conception Street, which was far from immaculately clean, St. John the Baptist Street, and the Street of the Good Jesus. The doctor was in and momentarily disengaged. He spoke no English, but was thoroughly conversant with French, which Cushing spoke with equal fluency. Cushing formed a good opinion of the doctor, who impressed him as a grave and scholarly gentleman, who had traveled much and understood his profession thoroughly. Cushing stated the case in terms of the profession, of which his own training gave him perfect command.

"Your friend," said Dr. Silva, "has doubtless suffered an injury to the optic nerve, the result of the blow upon the head. There may be a splinter, or an abnormal growth, pressing upon the nerve, or it may be permanently atrophied. If it is either of the first two, an operation may restore his sight. An examination will of course be necessary in order to determine."

He fixed an hour for the interview. Cushing returned to the hotel. Manson, assisted by a servant of the establishment, had bathed and shaved, and was awaiting his friend's return.

"Henry," he exclaimed, "I am myself again—except for this cursed blindness. Have you found them?"

His voice was tense with eagerness. It seemed to vibrate with the pent-up anger of all his weeks of suffering.

"No, they are not here."

Manson's face revealed his bitter disappointment.

"I am on their track, however. They will be here within a week."

Manson's face became transfigured with a joy that was not holy.

"Ah! Did you find the surgeon?"

"Yes, he will examine your eyes at four o'clock this afternoon."

"The hour cannot arrive too soon. It will seem like a week till then. Where are they?"

"You must take my word that they will be here. You are under the surgeon's orders to avoid all excitement until he has seen you."

At four o'clock a *calèche* driven by a colossal black driver conveyed them to Dr. Silva's office. The examination was brief. The doctor first demanded a history of the case somewhat more in detail than Cushing had been able to give him. Manson's French was impossible, in spite of the doctor's polite attempt to understand it, and Cushing acted as interpreter. The doctor asked many questions, carefully palpated the skull in the region of the injury, and applied several tests to discover the reaction of the nerve.

"I think," he announced as his conclusion, "that the case will not prove difficult. A delicate operation will be necessary, and several days of careful nursing. The operation can be best done, and the best care obtained, at *La Misericordia*. You in the United States know of our great hospital, messieurs?"

"We could not well be ignorant of it," replied Cushing diplomatically. "Its fame is world-wide."

He did not deem it prudent or polite to admit that the people of the United States, even the best informed of them, generally speaking, knew less about the Southern half of their own continent than about Turkey, or the Congo Free State—politely so called.

"Your friend will be carefully tended by the good sisters. I will give you a note of introduction to the director, and you can go now, if you wish, and make the necessary arrangements. I can perform the operation most conveniently at ten o'clock to-morrow morning."

"The sooner the better," said Manson, when the doctor's statement was turned into English.

They drove to *La Misericordia*. Dr. Silva was justly proud of this splendid institution, one of the finest hospitals in the world, and one of the crowning glories of the capital. Built of granite and brick, two stories in height, and covering an area of ten thousand square meters, it stood close to the shore of the harbor, where refreshing breezes blew through its windows and wards to the beautiful gardens of the interior quadrangle. Here all that skill and kindness could do to combat disease and death may be commanded by the humblest; none are turned away.

Leaving Manson in the carriage to await his return, Cushing entered the hospital. Arrangements were quickly made for Manson's—or Martin's—reception.

"There are 1,200 beds in the hospital," said the director, not without pride. "The general wards are free; but special accommodation and privacy can be provided, if your friend is able to contribute toward the expenses of the establishment."

Mr. Martin was able to contribute, Cushing replied, and a fixed sum was mentioned. It was a delicate way of stating a charge for special privileges, but why not be delicate, when it was just as easy? A little more delicacy would soften many of the roughnesses of our over strenuous national life.

"Our nurses are sisters of charity. Sister Laurentine is our only available English-speaking nurse at present. She has one American patient, but can attend another."

"What is the name of the American patient?" asked Cushing. Ties of race and country are always stronger in a foreign land. An American abroad will welcome a yellow dog from his native town.

"A Monsieur Thayer."

He pronounced the word in such a manner that even Cushing did not understand it, though he was vaguely conscious of something familiar about the sound.

"He was nearly drowned at sea," continued the director, "and has been sick of a fever, but is much better."

It was evidently Wentworth Thayer. Cushing made some general inquiries about the American patient's condition, but did not ask to see him.

"He is a compatriot, Monsieur le Directeur; I am interested to know that he is doing well in your excellent institution."

"*Merci, monsieur!* You are interested in the welfare of your compatriot, *bien entendu*—of course!"

Manson was taken to *La Misericordia* in the morning, and at ten o'clock the operation was performed. An anesthetic was first administered, the skull trepanned over the seat of the injury, and a splinter removed, releasing the pressure upon the nerve, which was found to be uninjured.

"*C'était facile—étonnamment facile*—I did not think it would prove so easy," declared Dr. Silva, when he had finished dressing the wound. "Your friend has a fine constitution. In two days he can see as well as ever, but he must be careful of his eyes for a week or two."

A cool and spacious room had been secured for the patient, and under the watchful care of Sister Laurentine, varied by visits from Singleton, the time passed swiftly and the wound healed apace. By some connivance with the nurse, re-enforced by the doctor's orders, Cushing arranged that Manson's eyes should be kept bandaged for a day or two, and that when they were uncovered the room should be darkened, until the wounded nerve should have time to recover. The success of Cushing's experiment, which grew in interest from day to day, required that Manson suspect nothing until the final revelation; and while it was unlikely that Manson would recognize him—they had seen each other only once or twice in Boston, and had never been introduced—Cushing wished to take no chances.

For two days Manson had not spoken of his revenge.

"Henry," he said on the third day, no longer able to contain himself, "I've been training myself, in preparation for the meeting. I must be perfect master of myself, in order to carry out my purpose in the right way. I feel that it is my right to kill this man, and my duty; and I wish to do it in the right way. But I can't wait much longer."

"'Vengeance is mine,' saith the Lord," quoted Cushing.

"The Lord works through his chosen instruments, and he has selected me to rid the world of this scoundrel. Have you heard anything more about them?"

"They ought to be in Rio to-morrow."

"Where have they been?"

"In various places; I do not know them all. But they will be here."

"Ah! He has been in hiding! It is quite consistent that a coward, a weakling, who had stolen another man's wife, should seek to hide himself. But there's no place where he could escape me; I would follow him to the end of the world—on my hands and knees, if need be. To-morrow, may it come quickly! I should like him to be the first man upon whom my eyes shall rest, if it can be so; it is for him that I have been given back my sight. But forgive me, my friend! To be blind is to be selfish—it narrows the world to what one can touch. One is not only the center of one's universe, but the circumference as well. What I should wish to see first of all is your face, the face of the friend who has succored and maintained me. But you are strong, and I am still weak, and you will consider my infirmity."

"Do not apologize, Manson; I understand. I will see that you have your wish—both your wishes," he added under his breath.

"Give me your hand, Henry. I love you, my friend. I thought the fountain of my heart was dried up, but you have restored its flow: for you it has naught but tenderness, for him, nothing but hate—black, bitter hate. The world is not large enough to contain us both. Bring me face to face with him, and I shall be content."

"You have never fought a duel or seen one fought? You know nothing about the code?"

Cushing was not without a certain curiosity as to the course Manson intended to pursue. The question was meant to draw him out.

"Duel? Who said anything about a duel? A duel always seemed to me rank foolishness. *I* haven't done *him* any harm; *he* has no right to shoot *me*. On the contrary he has done me a deadly injury, and now it's my turn!"

"But," exclaimed Cushing, "you don't mean to assassinate the man, to murder him?"

"Assassinate him? Well, I should n't call it that, nor murder. When my people in the mountains killed an enemy, they didn't call it murder: it was no more than self-defence—it was either shoot or be shot—they did no more than the other fellow would have done if the chance had been his; or it was revenge—no, not revenge, punishment, and crime should be punished. This fellow deserves no consideration whatever; he is a criminal, taken in the act, and it is my right to kill him."

"But the law does n't recognize your right, and you are not taking him in the act."

"Not taking him in the act? Why not? Did n't he take her away? Has n't she been with him for weeks? Is n't she with him here? I don't mean to shoot him in the back; I want to come face to face with him, and let him know why he is to meet his end. If he has a weapon, and is the quicker of the two, let him use it—I'll take the chances. But I'm quick as lightning with a gun, and a dead shot—I was n't brought up in the woods for nothing. I *know* I shall kill him; I'm as certain of it as I am of your friendship. I'm ready for him. In the drawer of the bureau yonder is the revolver I bought in New York, loaded with ball cartridge—for him. I can hit the head of a nail at sixty paces—I don't think I could miss his wicked heart a mile away."

"And she—your Evelyn?"

"Ah, Henry, spare me—yet a while! I cannot speak of her. When he is out of the way, then I can take up her case, but not now. He is the most to blame, and must be the first to suffer."

XXIV.

THE MYSTERIOUS LETTER

The English steamer came in at ten o'clock next morning. It was twelve before the passengers were landed. Cushing was at the landing-place. He had taken his station near a pile of bales of merchandise, from which he could see without being seen. In two ladies in deep mourning who came ashore, attended solicitously by the captain and the purser, he recognized Evelyn and Alice. Evelyn had lost some of her bloom; grief and anxiety had left their mark. Remorse too, he could imagine, had contributed its effect. Without her roses, and with her expression of chastened sorrow, Evelyn had lost much; she was beautiful, but it was not the radiant beauty of a year before; nor did the sight of her quite revive the old thrill. Alice, on the other hand, had changed but little. That her face showed signs of past grief gave him pleasure; for it was for him that she had mourned; and the mother-love that now transfigured her countenance at the prospect of meeting her wayward son was a feeling that bordered on the divine.

The purser called a carriage, and Cushing heard the order given to drive to *La Misericordia*. He followed in a second carriage, giving the coachman orders to keep at a certain distance behind the other. When he had seen the ladies dismount, and enter the hospital, he in turn left his carriage and, by a side entrance, sought Manson's room, to remain on guard against any premature revelation.

The room was vacant, but looking out of the window upon the quadrangle, he saw Manson, with bandaged eyes, leaning on the arm of a male attendant whose services had supplemented those of Sister Laurentine. Young Thayer's room looked out upon another quadrangle, and there was therefore, little danger of recognition from that quarter.

Keeping his eye upon them, Cushing swiftly drew out the drawer in Manson's bureau, and took out the revolver and unloaded it, refilling the chambers with cartridges which he had so prepared over night as to render them harmless. He had no sooner replaced the weapon than Manson, still holding the attendant's arm, came in.

Cushing had drawn the shades, so that the room was in semi-darkness. Manson suddenly pulled the bandage from his eyes.

"I can see as well as ever, Henry," he exclaimed; "and the sight of you will complete the cure."

He threw up the shade and let the daylight play upon Cushing's features. Manson's eyes lit up with curiosity and pleasure, but gave no sign of recognition. Cushing's incognito was still safe; but he was asking himself whether he could restrain Manson's impatience, now that he could use his sight, when Manson drew down the blind.

"It's a little too much for me yet. I must let in the light gradually. I'll be all right by tomorrow. And now, have they come? Are they here?"

"They are here."

"Thank God! Find out where I can meet him, Henry, and bring me face to face with him, and I'll tax your friendship no further. I owe you so much already that I shall never be able to repay you. But you'll find me not ungrateful, my friend."

"I will arrange a meeting," said Cushing, "for tomorrow morning. I have a plan which will bring you face to face, alone—the wronged and the wronger."

The two ladies, upon entering the hospital and making their errand known, had been placed in charge of Sister Laurentine, who conducted them to Wentworth's bedside.

"My poor boy!"

"Mother, dear mother!"

There was a long embrace, after which Evelyn in turn greeted her brother.

"We have come to take you home, Wentworth," said Alice.

"You are too good to me, mother. I have grieved you, disappointed you; I have cost you the life of your best friend. I am no more worthy to be called your son—and you cross half the world to come to me."

"Wentworth, you are my son, and I shall not lose faith in you. My love will yet make a man of you."

They talked with him long and lovingly, of his voyage; of his mad act, and of Cushing's heroic but fatal attempt at rescue.

"It was noble of him," said Alice, proudly, through the tears which moistened her eyes. "But, oh, Wentworth, how could you do so desperate a thing as to try to take your own life?"

"I was despondent, mother," he said, "and hoped to end it all. To think that he should be taken and I left! It does n't seem right."

"God's purposes are beyond mortal ken," returned his mother devoutly. "I have lost my friend, but the memory of his friendship and of his heroic death, will console me for his loss. To have lost my son by his own act, would have been unspeakably cruel. Remember, Wentworth, my son, what his effort to help you has cost us all, and has cost the world, and try to make good the loss."

"I will mother. Evelyn, can you ever forgive me? But for me your husband would never have left home, and you would not have lost him."

"It was my fault, Wentworth. I do not reproach you, but I can never forgive myself."

Sweet-faced Sister Laurentine conducted them to the door, when at length they went away. Wentworth was not quite ready for discharge from the hospital. His mother and Evelyn would put up at the *Hotel Ingleterra*, and come in the morning to visit him.

"Ah, mesdames," said Sister Laurentine, as they were passing through the hall, "tomorrow perhaps you may meet the other American patient and his friend. Perhaps you have already his acquaintance?"

"What is his name, Sister?" asked Alice.

"Monsieur Martin. His friend is Monsieur Singleton. Monsieur Martin has lost his sight according to an accident.

Our great Dr. Silva—you have heard of the great Dr. Silva, who cures the eyes?"

"He is a great physician, is he not?" answered Evelyn.

"Oh, the most great! Yes, mesdames, the distinguished Dr. Silva, who has medals from all the crowned heads of Europe, performed an operation and restored the sight of Monsieur Martin. His friend, Monsieur Singleton, is very devoted. He is a kind gentleman and very rich."

The devotion of one's life to good works does not necessarily dull the intellect, and good Sister Laurentine knew that Cushing paid liberally. The monastics of the Roman Catholic Church may vow themselves to poverty, but they are keen for the interests of the Church, and the charities under its management.

"I do not think we know him," returned Evelyn.

"Ah, well, he is well worth knowing. You may meet him at the hotel. He stops at the same place as you."

The ladies had registered at the hotel, had dined, and were comfortably installed in their apartment, when a servant brought in a note addressed to Mrs. Manson.

"It is from some one of the ship's officers," said Mrs. Thayer.

"No," said Evelyn, "it is addressed in French—

"A Mme.
   "Mme. Manson,
       "Hotel Ingleterra,
           "En Ville."

"From some tradesman," returned her mother.

They played with the letter thus for several moments, after the manner of their sex, and then Evelyn opened it.

"Oh, mama!" she screamed, turning white to the lips and dropping the paper from her nerveless grasp.

Mrs. Thayer picked it up.

"'If Mrs. Manson'—it ran when translated 'would have news of her husband, and will follow the guide who will present himself at the hotel and inquire for her at eight o'clock in the morning, she will learn what she most of all things desires to know.'"

"Evelyn, Evelyn!" she cried, "it is a voice from the grave!"

"No, mamma, my husband is alive; it is a summons to meet him. What I most desire to know is that my husband is not dead."

"It is in Edward Cushing's handwriting," returned her mother solemnly, raising the paper unconsciously to her lips.

"It could not be, mother; he was lost at sea."

"So was your husband! Poor Evelyn!"

"But, mamma, Hugh was alive when last seen."

"No one has ever seen Edward dead, Evelyn, and the note is in his handwriting. I have seen it too often—I know it too well to be mistaken."

"It is improbable that either should be alive."

"All things are possible with God, Evelyn; I have seen too many of his mercies not to believe it. We will cherish the hope until it is blasted."

They sent for the servant who had brought the note, but strangely enough, he could not be found in the hotel. There were a hundred people employed there, and Alice and Evelyn had not looked closely enough at the messenger to identify him.

They examined the hotel register. A week back they found the names of "Henry Singleton" and "John Martin," both written in the same hand that had penned the note. Alice stared at the writing with wonder and with joy. "It is his!" she whispered. "Oh, my heart, it is his! He is here!"

Evelyn was comparing the letter with the signature.

"They look alike," she said. "They were written by the same hand. They are the names mentioned by Wentworth's nurse, the sister of charity,—Mr. Martin and Mr. Singleton,— and Mr. Singleton wrote this note."

They inquired of the clerk and received a description of Singleton—not a very clear one—which only mystified them. The gentleman had been at the hotel for a week. He would send a card to his room.

"Whoever he may be," said Evelyn, "whatever he may mean by this eccentric proceeding, we can safely follow his messenger—since he is an American, and rich, and good— as Sister Laurentine has assured us."

Alice said no more, but nursed a lively hope. She had been familiar with Edward Cushing's handwriting for many years,—as familiar as she had been with his face—and no disguise could long have hidden from her either the one or the other.

They waited in the parlor until the servant brought back the card, stating that the gentleman was not in. They waited until midnight, hoping he might come in. But he did not, and at length they went to bed, Evelyn to lie awake all night, Alice to sleep with a light heart.

They were up at six, and ready an hour before the messenger came. He was a neat-looking mulatto, in white linen, and brought a note identifying him, and stating that he could speak neither English nor French.

XXV.

ENEMY OR FRIEND?

"I will manage a meeting," Cushing had said the night before, "for tomorrow morning. That is, I shall decoy him to a secluded spot and then bring you face to face."

"And the Lord have mercy on his soul," said Manson solemnly.

He was up early in the morning and out of an abundance of caution, drew all the chambers of his revolver and loaded them with fresh cartridges. Cushing called for him at half-past seven. Manson had removed the bandage from his eyes, and merely wore a green-lined shade, which, supplemented by a broad-brimmed Panama, guarded his eyes sufficiently from the glare of the sunlight.

"Are you ready?" Cushing asked.

"I am ready."

"Let us walk. The distance is not great."

Cushing purposely avoided offering Manson his arm; there was no occasion for it, since Manson could see and Cushing had never felt less inclined to intimacy with his enemy-friend. Manson came over and took his arm with the unconscious ease of custom.

They walked down the broad street upon which stood the hotel. The street led upward toward Corcovado Peak, and in the near distance the blue mountains reared their heads in splendid majesty. They reached the environs of the city, and turning aside from the street, followed a well-beaten path through a forest of splendid trees, shrubs of pleasing odor, gigantic ferns and marvellous orchids. The air was of crystalline brightness, the sky without a speck of cloud. In a normal state of mind, Manson would have reveled in this tropical beauty of nature; but at present his thoughts were all of the impended meeting.

"Are we nearly there, Henry?"

"A few rods. It is an old duelling ground, where gentlemen of Rio used to meet to settle their disputes."

"An appropriate place in which to kill a scoundrel. But suppose he does not come? I know he is a coward. Are you sure he suspects nothing?"

"I'm sure he will come. I've seen to that—I've awakened his curiosity; he'll be here to gratify it."

They had reached the end of their walk; a forest glade, surrounded by a wealth of tropical verdure, and dominated by four tall palms, placed, like sentinels, on either side.

"This is the place," said Cushing. "In five minutes he will be due, and I shall leave you to meet him alone. It is an affair in which it were better, perhaps, to have no witnesses."

"Very good, Henry; you are always thoughtful. If he should attack me, and I should kill him in self-defence, there will be no one to question my story. And now, Henry, before I meet this seducer of wives, this destroyer of homes, this damned, double-dyed, villain,—before, in killing him, I subject myself to the remotest chance of losing my own life, I want you to understand,—to try to understand, Henry, how much I feel that I owe you, how much I love you for your goodness, how hopeless I am of ever repaying it. You have been eyes to me, tongue to me—for I can speak nothing but my own language—you have been my banker, my physician, my more than friend, my more than brother. Henry, when I have done the duty nearest me, ask me my life! I would give it to you cheerfully."

"Would you?" asked Cushing, moved in spite of himself by this display of devotion. "I may put you to the test, and that soon."

"It cannot be too soon. And now," he said with changing voice, "send him to me!"

There was a fierce eagerness in his glance, a tenseness of passion in his accents, that impressed Cushing more strongly than even his recent fervency of friendship. Until this morning he had no pronounced view as to which—love or hatred—gratitude or revenge—would prevail in the curious test to which he was about to put his friend—or his enemy;—he hardly knew at this moment how to regard him. The long weeks of enforced companionship had given strength to ties of which he had hardly been conscious. A few moments would bring his experiment to an end. To what end? To what end had he woven this tissue of lies—lies in fact, if not in terms? Had the game been worth the candle? With a word he could terminate this tragic farce, and bring it to a happy ending.

And yet his curiosity persisted. What would Manson do? The happy outcome was assured; even should revenge prove the stronger passion, Manson could do no injury for his weapon had been rendered harmless; and before his destructive impulse could find other means of expression, Evelyn, the *dea ex machina*, would appear and bring the performance to a happy climax.

He turned away and took the path along which they had come. Manson waited with eyes fixed upon the point where Cushing had disappeared. The lust of blood reddened his eyes and flushed his cheek. So had his forbears waited, beside mountain paths, behind concealing rocks, for those who had crossed them in love, or in trade, or in ambition.

There was a rustling of the shrubbery, a sound of soft footsteps. His hand grasped his revolver. A figure appeared.

"Hold up your hands!"

A pair of hands went up; and at the same moment Manson let fall his own hand which held the uplifted weapon.

"Ah-h!" he exclaimed with a strange intonation, like that of a wild beast balked of his prey. "It is you—I thought it was he. He has not come, the coward, the cur? It is what I feared—until you assured me he would be here."

"No," returned Cushing, "he is no coward."

"But he has not come! He has been warned!"

"He has learned all."

"He has fled—the coward!"

"He has not fled; he is here, prepared to meet you."

"Well, then, Henry, why this mystery, this delay? Why does he not appear, and meet me face to face? I had not expected him to be prepared, but I am ready for him."

"He has appeared; he is facing you now."

Manson's face expressed sheer bewilderment.

"But—I—I—don't understand. Can I be blind again, or do my poor eyes deceive me? I see no one but you, Henry—my friend, you only!"

"I am your enemy. I am not Henry Singleton, except to you; I am Edward Cushing, whose promised bride you stole almost from the altar."

Manson seemed dazed for a moment, as though vainly struggling to shake off a mental incubus.

"Ah," he muttered, dully, slowly, like a man in a dream, who would speak but finds his organs paralyzed. "I see! She had thrown herself overboard, and you had tried to save her, and had failed, and had been cast upon the island, before I came there. You had injured me, and I had sworn to kill you, and you knew me; I was blind, and could not see; and you repented of your crime and by way of expiation you succored me, and fed me, and sheltered me; you grappled my heart to yours with hooks of steel, until I loved you with a love surpassing that of woman. Ah, Henry, I had meant to kill you, but you have conquered me. I could not take your life, you know it, for you come unarmed—I owe my life to you! And since I cannot kill you, because you have befriended me; and since I cannot forgive the injury you have done me, there is but one thing left. I have nothing to live for; I have promised you my life. Take it by way of sacrifice!"

With a quick movement he raised the revolver and turned it toward his own heart. But quicker still a piercing shriek rang out upon the morning air, and a woman's form burst through the shrubbery and a woman's hand grasped Manson's arm.

"Hugh!" she exclaimed, "my husband!"

Evelyn's hand diverted the bullet from her husband's heart, but did not prevent the explosion. The flying missile found a lodging place in Cushing's breast.

Manson stood looking at his wife with coldly hostile eyes. Cushing tottered and would have fallen, had not Mrs. Thayer, who had followed close upon Evelyn's feels, caught him in her arms, and let him sink gently to the ground, upon which she knelt by his side, supporting his head in her arms.

Cushing with a groan had closed his eyes.

"Edward, dear Edward! Edward, my darling, speak to me," she cried in endearing tones. "Oh, my friend, my love, do not leave me now that I have found you, after mourning you for dead. Speak to me, Edward, speak to me!"

Manson had dropped the weapon from his hand, and still stood facing Evelyn, oblivious to all else. She was the first to find her voice.

"Hugh," she cried, "it was all a ghastly mistake! I have never left New York, except upon the voyage which brought us here yesterday, and I have been with mother all the time. Until last night, we thought that you were drowned, and only now—this minute—did we know that you were alive. Oh, Hugh, how could you mistrust me so?"

Manson passed his hand slowly over his eyes, as though brushing aside a film. His mercurial temperament responded immediately to the removal of a great weight.

"But the letter," he demanded, "and the journey to New York—with him."

"It was my fault," she confessed. "My brother was dangerously ill in New York. I was ashamed to let you know. You refused me the money; I wrote the letter to spite you, and you did not get the telegram that followed."

While Manson's eyes wandered, in sympathy with his bewilderment, they rested upon the group on the other side of the glade. Shaking off Evelyn's hand a single bound placed him on his knees beside Cushing.

"Ah, Henry, my friend, you saved my life and I have killed you. Live, live, my friend, for my sake; or I shall never forgive myself."

"Yes, dear Edward, live for—for—our sake," sobbed Alice.

Cushing opened his eyes. They fell upon those of Alice, his friend Alice, bending over him—blue eyes, as yet unfaded, eyes suffused with tears, for him, lit up with love, for him, lips not yet withered, tremulous with apprehension for his fate.

Behind her, beside her husband, stood Evelyn. To Cushing she seemed at this moment no more than the child whose guardian he had been for so many years; while his head was resting upon a true heart, which had always beat for him. Though faint with the pain of the wound, even at this moment, which for aught he knew might be his last, the thought gave him a new pleasure.

"Alice," he murmured, with a smile, "dear Alice!"

And then a paroxysm of pain seized him, and he fainted dead away.

XXVI.

EXPLANATIONS AND THE END

Evelyn had her explanation with her husband that afternoon.

Where both loved, and both had suffered, and both were young, and the long years lay before them, explanations were not difficult.

"It was all my fault, Hugh. I should have explained, in my note, where I was going, and why."

"It was my fault, Evelyn, and the fault of that she-devil Leonie. She helped me to you, Evelyn; but she has cancelled the debt. It was monstrous in me to doubt you."

"And wicked in me to tempt you. Such a beautiful house you were building me, too, as a pleasant surprise, while I was acting like a spoiled child!"

"Poor house!" he murmured. "It was to be, of its sort, my masterpiece. Now it is only a heap of gray ashes."

Evelyn smiled. She had a pleasant secret, too, relating to the same subject.

"Secretiveness with those we love is a dangerous game, Evelyn. Had I told you my plans, there would have been no surprise, but it would have saved us a world of suffering."

"Had I been less selfish and less exacting, and trusted your love," replied Evelyn, "I should never have doubted your love, or left you one moment in doubt of mine. And now, Hugh, I meant to surprise you upon our return home; but your solemn denunciation of secretiveness serves me as a warning, and I will tell you now. Your house, *our* house has gone up exactly as you planned it."

"But it was burned down—I saw it in the newspaper!"

"It was not totally destroyed. The newspapers were no more accurate than usual. The bulk of the damage was done before noon, and there was no trouble about the insurance. You forget that an architect's friendship and patronage is valuable to an insurance agent; he is not likely to let such a one's policy expire without good grounds. When I thought you were dead, my dear, for love of me, I built the house again, brick for brick, line for line as your dear heart had planned it. It would have been my monument to you, as it was to have been your love-gift to me. Now we will enjoy it together, in mutual love and mutual ownership."

"But shall we be able to keep it, Evelyn? My credit is ruined. I saw the last shred of it vanishing as I left New York."

"Your credit is better than ever."

"But my note—"

"Did not go to protest. The bank protected it. Your business is worth much to the bank; and I was there next day to attend to it."

"But how? When I left Boston I was insolvent; and, now to Boston I am dead."

"You were not reported dead for several weeks, and even now you are not legally dead. There was your B. & E. stock."

"It went to smash the day I left Boston. I read it in the New York papers. That alone was enough to ruin me—all my ready money wiped out."

"Not so. Your broker could not sell it that day, and, like a prudent man, held it at your risk, and so notified you in writing. You see your credit was very good. Next day the stock went soaring. I presented the broker with his letter, and ordered him to sell the stock, and deposit the money to your account. It paid your note and left a balance. You did not know your wife was such a good business woman."

Manson gazed at her with growing respect.

"You're a wonder!" he exclaimed. "If you could only have saved my contract for the public buildings, I should be even with the world, and ahead of it. Whose plans were accepted?"

"Whose would you suppose?"

"God knows!—Howell and Baker's, I suppose; they were next in favor to our own. I lost interest when ours were rejected."

"You are wrong," she said, with a smile so bright, so tantalizing, so full of pleasant mystery, that a great hope sprang up in his heart.

"Evelyn," he said, extending his arms to her, "Evelyn, you do not mean—"

"Yes, my dear, I do. Sterling & Manson's plans were chosen. Why not? They were easily the best! When you did not appear at the meeting that day, the matter was adjourned until the next, and Mr. Sterling came back in time to sign the contract, and the commencement of the work was postponed for six months. You will be there to superintend it."

Manson clasped her tightly.

"You are my good angel," he said. "You bring me not only love and life, but are the messenger of all good tidings. Now that I have you in my arms, Evelyn, I find it hard to believe that we were ever separated. The past seems like a bad dream. We will never doubt one another or leave one another again—"

"Until death do us part!"

Evelyn and her husband dined together at the hotel. Manson had a tremendous appetite, and nothing was too good for them. The bill was 40,000 milreis. He gave the waiter a banknote for 50,000 and told him to keep the change. Alice was at *La Misericordia*, where she had remained to nurse Cushing. After dinner, in the cool of the evening, Evelyn and her husband drove over to see them. Cushing's wound was doing well; it had been painful, but not serious. He would be confined to the hospital for several days, but could see visitors, if they did not remain too long. He was lying on a cot, pale but smiling, Alice seated by his side, and gray-clad Sister Laurentine fading into the background as the young people came in. Cushing held out his hand to Manson, who took it in a cordial clasp.

"Manson," he said, "I was wrong. I played an ignoble part, and I am justly punished."

"Henry,—I shall always call you Henry—you saved my life, and I shall always love you for it. I had misjudged you from the beginning. When I think of all the horrible things I said to you on that hideous island,—you know I never saw it, though I lived there six weeks,—I am surprised that you did n't let me starve."

"But I let you suffer worse torments; I let you believe Evelyn false."

"It was my own fault, and only my just punishment. I was too quick to believe evil. I've no one but myself to blame for my sufferings. And I wronged you, Henry. You had loved Evelyn, and I had taken her from you; and only now, after this ordeal, do I realize what that meant. My conduct was not honorable. The field was not open; I suborned a servant; I persuaded Evelyn to break her promise. And I'm in a hard place—I can't even say I'm sorry. I can only plead our love, and beg your forgiveness; for we must be friends henceforth."

"My dear fellow, all but my pride has forgiven you long ago. Your instincts were right—youth should mate youth. Your young blood made ducks and drakes of my rights;

I cheerfully renounce my wrongs. I hope for other rights to take their place."

Alice had sat beside him with swimming eyes. As the others turned away, absorbed in their own renewed love, he reached out his hand for hers.

"Alice," he said, "I must have one of the family. Evelyn has gone to a better man. There remains only you. May I hope?"

She could not resist the feminine impulse. "You will take me as a *pis aller*; since you cannot pluck the rose, you will break off the stem?"

"I will take you, Alice, if I may, as the dearest, noblest and most loyal of women, who will bring me happiness, and whom I shall do my best to make happy in turn."

Sister Laurentine appeared like a gray ghost.

"I fear," she said in her soft accents, "that you will tire monsieur. Too much of conversation is not good for him."

"Never fear, *ma belle et bonne soeur*, the wound does not touch any vital organ, and happiness can do me no harm. It will prove the best of medicines."

The remainder of the story is briefly told. Evelyn and her husband left for home on the next steamer, Manson being eager to take up the dropped threads of his life. Alice remained with her son and Cushing, sharing her time and care between them. Both of the invalids were ready for discharge within less than a month.

As they were leaving *La Misericordia* good Sister Laurentine stood looking at them wistfully. They had been kind and liberal, and appreciative, and her gentle heart was grieved to see them go. They were Protestants, but had spoken kindly of her faith and her vocation, and they had praised her English, of which, before they came, she had not been entirely certain.

"You are going home," she said softly, "and monsieur will marry madame—she has told me."

"Yes," said Cushing, "we are old friends; new ties will simply strengthen our friendship."

"You will be happy," she sighed. "May *le bon Dieu* grant that it may be so!"

Alice turned and kissed her impulsively. "You are His bride, dear sister, He will be good to you."

"*Merci*, madame, and—*adieu!*"

The good sister turned away, with tears in her eyes, and began to tell her beads remorsefully. For a moment she had come near to forgetting her vows, by which she had renounced not only worldly love, but worldly memories and regrets.

"Poor girl!" said Cushing, as he turned and watched the gray-clad figure slowly retreating. "She is not happy—but may she never know it!"

"Amen," returned Alice with less fervor. For while she had learned to love the gentle-voiced young nurse, she knew that sorrow and longing and renunciation were the lot of women; and yet she knew that even these were not without compensation, and that Sister Laurentine would find in her life of service the surest solace for whatever else she may have given up.

Wentworth, too, was fully recovered from his illness.

"My boy," said Cushing to the lad, now clothed in his right mind, but pale and slim from his long confinement, "henceforth, I shall occupy a father's place to you. Between us, God helping, we can put the devil to flight and make a man of you."

"We can try, sir," returned the boy, humbly but firmly.

To the credit of human nature be it said that they did; and that Wentworth Thayer, still a young man, bids fair to be a credit to his family and his country.

A year brought some changes to the little group of related lives whose fortunes we have followed, and these all for the better. Manson's return home, and the thrilling story of his shipwreck and subsequent sojourn with Cushing on the island, had made a three days' sensation—a long time for this rapid age—had given them both much gratuitous advertising and had added to Manson's popularity. The public buildings were under construction, and Sterling & Manson's office was overwhelmed with commissions.

Cushing's marriage, which took place shortly after his return with Alice and her son from Brazil, gave him the needed stimulus to effort, perhaps Manson's merciless dissection of Cushing's character, during their island masquerade, had not been without a contributing effect. His book on South American Capitals attracted much attention, and an active interest in a presidential campaign, to the success of which he was held to have contributed, brought him an appointment from the administration as minister to Chile.

One evening, after Cushing, accompanied by his wife, had left for his post of duty, Evelyn and her husband went to Keith's, for an hour or two of recreation. One of the numbers announced in the program was a "Song and dance by Mademoiselle Leonie St. Clair, the popular young French vocalist, fresh from the London and Paris music halls."

When Mademoiselle St. Clair tripped lightly forth upon the boards with a smile, Evelyn thought her face seemed familiar, even as her name had; and when the singer burst into song—

"I want to be a la-ady
An' wiz ze the la-a-dies doo-well
To wear ze fines' ga-r-r-e-ments,
An' everything zat's swell"—

"Why, it's our Leonie!" exclaimed Evelyn. "When did she go on the stage, and where did she get that accent?"

Mr. Willie Rice was seated in the next chair. He was not yet married. He had proposed, that afternoon, to a charming young debutante, after having had the matter under consideration for a whole season, only to find himself an hour too late. He had gone to the Mansons' for consolation and they had brought him with them to the show. He had shown little interest for a while, but was beginning to wake up, albeit a little cynical.

"You recognize the girl?" he said. "You know she married old Solomon Valdez, the Portuguese pawnbroker. He used to beat her at regular intervals. She took the beatings philosophically, because she knew, as Valdez did n't, that she deserved still more. When he became enlightened, and they parted, she went into vaudeville. The accent is part of the act—the *act-sent*, you know."

This atrocious pun completely restored Mr. Rice's good-humor.

"Thus again," said Manson, oracularly, "has the stage robbed the kitchen, to make of a good servant a poor player."

"Oh, but don't you know," said Rice, "I think that's rather clevah; I've seen it done much worse."

Evelyn surveyed them both disapprovingly.

"A good servant, indeed!" she exclaimed with asperity. "A good-for-nothing! She ought not to be at large! Think of all the trouble she caused us!"

Manson smiled into her eyes, but discreetly said nothing. While he could never be proud of the manner in which he had won Evelyn, he could never forget, although she had tried to balance the obligation, that Leonie had contributed to their happiness. The web of life is woven of many threads, of many colors; and the practical test of its quality is whether it wears well. Measured by this rule, he figured that he had not done at all badly. Had Evelyn married Cushing, four lives might have been spoiled. Her elopement with himself, brought about by Leonie's connivance, had, after a little righteous chastisement, brought happiness to four lives, to which, he had lately been given ground to hope, there might soon be added a fifth.

When Mademoiselle St. Clair had finished her act, Rice and he joined in the applause. The singer bowed her acknowledgments, and pulling the rose from her hair, threw it daringly into their box.

"Well, of all the impudence!" gasped Evelyn.

After this utterance neither gentleman dared to pick up the flower; and when they left the box as the curtain went down, Evelyn, accidentally, of course—crushed it beneath her heel.

The critique of white male society that Charles W. Chesnutt (1858–1932) launched in *A Marrow of Tradition* continues in *Evelyn's Husband*, one of six manuscripts left unpublished when this highly regarded African American innovator died.

Set in Boston society, on a deserted Caribbean island, and in Brazil, *Evelyn's Husband* is the story of two men, one old, one young, in love with the same young woman. Late in his career Chesnutt embarked on a period of experimentation with eccentric forms, finishing this hybrid of a romance and adventure story just before publishing his last work, *The Colonel's Dream*.

In *Evelyn's Husband*, Chesnutt crafts a parody examining white male roles in the early 1900s, a time when there was rampant anxiety over the subject. In Boston, the older man is left at the altar when his bride-to-be flees and marries a young architect. Later, trapped on an island together, the jilted lover and the young husband find a productive middle ground between the dilettante and the primitive.

Along with *A Business Career*, this novel marks Chesnutt's achievement in being among the first African American authors to defy the color barrier and write fiction with a white cast of main characters.

Charles W. Chesnutt (1858–1932) was an innovative and influential African American writer of the late nineteenth and early twentieth centuries. His novels include *The House Behind the Cedars, The Marrow of Tradition, The Colonel's Dream*, as well as the posthumously published novel *Paul Marchand, F.M.C.* from University Press of Mississippi.

MATTHEW WILSON has written introductions to *A Business Career, Evelyn's Husband*, and *Paul Marchand, F.M.C.*, and is the author of *Whiteness in the Novels of Charles W. Chesnutt*, all from University Press of Mississippi. He is associate professor of humanities and writing at Penn State University, Harrisburg. MARJAN A. VAN SCHAIK edited both *A Business Career* and *Evelyn's Husband* along with Wilson and is a part-time instructor at Millersville University.